The Crossword Solver

Andrew Dutton

GW00496591

LEAF BY LEAF

Published by Leaf by Leaf
an imprint of Cinnamon Press
www.cinnamonpress.com

The right of Andrew Dutton to be identified as author of this work
has been asserted by him in accordance with the Copyright, Designs
and Patent Act, 1988. © 2021, Andrew Dutton
ISBN 978-1-78864-929-2

Designed and typeset in Adobe Jensen by Cinnamon Press.
Cover design by Adam Craig © Adam Craig.
Cinnamon Press is represented by Inpress

Acknowledgements

To Neil for 'Bowkism' and sharing memories.

To Jo, Tarka and forever Otter

The Crossword Solver

Pilot Ken Gets His Morning Paper

Pilot Ken strolled into the pub with his morning paper tucked under his arm. The paper was folded at the crossword page and several clues were already scribbled, jotted in as Ken made his way across the playing fields after visiting the supermarket. Ken's morning paper, or rather his visits to the supermarket, caused his friends a small, cold shudder. He would emerge from his flat at the bottom of town, wander past a small row of shops, ignoring the newsagents, and make his unhurried way towards the supermarket, the playing-fields and then the pub.

The supermarket was a shortcut; passing the metal hoppers filled with newspapers, he would browse, pick up his favoured broadsheet, turn to the crossword and tuck the folded paper under his arm before walking away, steadily, slowly, through the side-door and down a set of broad concrete steps to the field, looking like an opener coming in to bat. By this time his pen was already in his hand.

'Ken, mate, one of these days some security guard will stir from his slumbers and spot you, is it worth it?' pleaded Ken's great friend Jim, uncharacteristically fussy and clucking in his concern.

'It's been five years and nothing's ever happened,' sniffed Pilot Ken, 'besides, I was walking through that patch of land long before there was any building there; they plonked that thing directly in my way. The papers are a sort of... restitution.'

This sort of talk would always cause Jim to fuss and cluck again, but it never lasted long and that was the end of the discussion—until the next day.

At The Bat And Ball

Pilot Ken would usually arrive at the Bat And Ball early-doors and sit at the largest of the circular tables, spreading his newspaper, reading for a while with his hand pressed to his chin and then turn to the back page, slowly uncapping his pen, putting on his glasses (at this moment and never before) and concentrating with a friendly frown on the day's cryptic crossword, confirming his sketched, tentative answers, working at the tougher clues. Casual observers must have wondered why one man would want to sit alone at that big round table. They failed to realise how that table would fill up as Ken's friends and acquaintances, who will come to this story soon enough, drifted in for a drink, to relax and chat with Ken.

Ken was not a large man, but he was stocky and carried himself with confidence; no swagger, surefooted except when his path zigzagged not due to drink but because his gaze was on the paper.

'Why Pilot?'

Ken's mate Jim, the fully-qualified giant, was always on hand to explain. 'He's got this battered old leather jacket with like woolly lapels, only the wool has gone thin, if you look; it's like the sort of thing you see in those old RAF movies. Emily here named him Biggles, but I preferred my name; Emily's was a name to mock an idiot and I knew from the start, this was no idiot.'

'He was the newcomer, but only for a short while,' added Emily, 'dribs and drabs of us had started to meet for lunch every now and then, this became our place, but when Ken came along it wasn't too long until the usual table of friends became Ken's table, we became his visitors, looking forward to meeting at Ken's pub.'

'I never saw him drunk, what's more he never got people drunk.' Gina toyed with her own drink, sunlight catching the glass and the ice, issuing cold sparks. 'He loved the pub but he was no toper, and wasn't fond of the company of drunks. He liked people, he liked to talk. I often thought he was like a chat show host, encouraging everyone to have their say, but never humiliating them, always making them welcome. Though sometimes it was as if he was writing a book, just listening, letting us write it for him.'

Up close Ken exuded easy cheerfulness, a warm, open friendliness that took determined, hard-faced effort to wear down; some managed the feat and proceeded to regret it. His eyes had a focussed intensity even after Guinness, his face crinkled attractively and a little knowingly when he smiled, and he smiled a great deal; his aspect was of a small boy who had always known how to charm his way out of trouble. He managed to look boyish even though his next major birthday would take him into his seventh decade and he was bald, with only a little whiteish hair dusting the back of his head in a narrow, almost invisible strip. 'We experimented with "Egg Head",' Jim would explain, 'Cos of his cleverness. But it sounded like another insult or some kind of naff super-villain so it never caught on. "Pilot" it was, for good.'

The Bat and Ball was Ken's favourite pub; it wasn't the only one where his face was known, but if you wanted to find him, you looked there first: it was known to the cognoscenti as 'Ken's living room'. Pilot Ken worked at home, from the top-floor 'studio' flat he had occupied for about ten years. He lived alone and had no family locally; his periodic absences were explained, should anyone trouble to ask, as visits to his mother in London. Nobody knew Ken's work; it was generally thought that he 'designed', but beyond that there was little explanation. 'I dunno,' replied Jim when pressed, 'he designs things. Computers maybe, or furniture or clothes or space rockets or atom bombs, dunno. He never discusses his work when he comes here, there always seems to be something more interesting to talk about,' Ken claimed—and it was generally believed—that he rose well before dawn, did much of his work before breakfast, and was consequently a free man by lunchtime. People reckoned that this whateveritis-work must pay well. 'After all, he's here from the forenoon onwards day in day out,' observed Frank Speke, shaking his head.

'There's only one way you can know that, Frank,' Jim jabbed with a cold slice of a smile, and Frank shut up. It was true Ken arrived not long after opening and could be there past teatime, Guinness and the crossword every day, long chats with friends, discussions, disputes, but often he began with coffee and didn't pick up a pint-glass for hours—on rare occasions, not at all.

Although the Bat and Ball served real ales, it was scarcely a traditionalists' pub: it was a modernist curio, far from the venerable model of dark wood and frosted panes, it admitted too much light through far too much fenestration, allowing no shadowy corners or nooks. If you stood outside you could see clean through the place, a decided advantage from the point of view of some (it attracted women there, especially when it came under the matriarchy of the still-regnant Evil Mand), but it was an outrage according to a noisy minority. One devoted real-ale bibber once walked out, not in protest at the beer but because he 'can't stand drinking inside a fucking paperweight.'

The pub had a large lounge bar, which some years back had been made even bigger by its gulping up the old, rather small public one; the bar itself was generously sized, running three quarters the length of the room—handy for getting served on a busy night—and the floor was populated with tables of different shapes and sizes; little squares two people could barely get their elbows on; two or three-tiered tables on tall columns with scaling-ladder stools set at thin-air heights; conference-style circular tables set on a raised platform under the widest of the windows; and finally a twelve-foot unvarnished wooden table paralleled by plain

10

wooden benches that lent its part of the pub a monkish, refectory look. (The only other monkish thing about The Bat And Ball was that it sold a brooding dark beer called Tonsure.)

A pool table occupied the space that used to be the public bar and here and there fruit machines chattered and burbled to themselves in an alien electronic gibberish, their obscure challenges increasingly easy to translate as the night went on and the booze flowed. On one wall, close to a tall archway that led on to the steps up to the biggest tables, was the juke box, which had for some years stubbornly retained its vinyl 45s, resisting heroically the changeover to compact discs until a visiting brewery manager muttered the words 'collector's item' and it was gone within a week. Ken, amongst others, wouldn't have minded if it had never been replaced, but the new one duly arrived—louder and more powerful, with no embarrassing sticking or slipping or occasional refusal to operate, slick and soulless just like the music it pumped out.

Like any other pub it had walls full of pictures that nobody was expected to look at; there was nothing amongst the occasionally-changed display that was especially memorable, but regular drinkers could point the curious to where the very first Bat and Ball sign, retired after decades in the wind and rain, hung, and where a poster featuring the local team's fixtures for 1950-51 was kept in pride of place behind cool glass. Other than that there were only bland portraits picked by the brewery with the intent of offending nobody; old photographs, sports-related to fit the name of the pub, but snapped when the ground it stood on was still occupied by cattle; and superannuated advertisements for beer, shampoo, crisps, nuts and cigarettes nobody made any more, which looked like a job-lot from a junk yard. Fortunately, because it had so many windows, the Bat and Ball wasn't overstuffed with these trophies and the eyes of most drinkers, if not drifting purposefully towards the pumps and optics, would usually settle on the flat green of the sports field outside. Yes, if you wanted to mess with the real thing you could take a bat and ball outside and play on the grass as long as you didn't stray on to the cricket pitch proper; some yards over and you could kick a football about and use real goals (no nets, except on local match days) or run in endless stretched circles around the athletics track. It was a fine place to put a pub; those who had done their stint on the green fields could come in for their reward, and everyone else could wear themselves out watching.

The place had borne several names before the owning pubco settled back on its original cricketing title, most cashing in on passing crazes, but which lasted perhaps a few months, a year at most. And so, the sign of bat, ball and stumps was dusted off to swing again in the breeze, inviting drinkers and reassuring everyone that the little universe within it hadn't really ever changed.

Landlords came and landlords went; good, bad, indifferent, competent, incompetent, middling. The Bat and Ball was a tenancy, the owning company a body of notorious rapacity (Pilot Ken dubbed them GodzillaCorp) and each landlord struggled to make even a scoopful of cash as the pubco squeezed ever harder on the beer prices. It enjoyed an Augustan age of happiness and stability under Jeff and Julie, whose names were frequently muttered by the regulars in later times, always preceded by, 'It was better when…' They departed to run a touristy pub in Wales, and Ken and some of his friends made occasional weekend visits, surprising the couple by keeping promises that they had considered offered in a spirit of rather sozzled and transient amity.

Some of Jeff and Julie's successors tried to make the place more attractive with fancy food, cocktail evenings, entertainments, quiz nights, imaginative (i.e. crazy and tasteless) refurbishments, even witty chalkboards importuning fresh custom.

'THE PUB IS THE HUB,' said one cheerily, aspiring to make the Bat and Ball a 'family-friendly centre of the community'. This was the work of an enterprising clever-dick pub manager who wanted to make a 'feature' of everything; he dubbed Pilot Ken and his gathering 'The Cabinet', making fun of their frequent, earnest and vocal discussions. The clever-dick only succeeded in embarrassing his regulars with a big chalkboard half-blocking the pavement outside the pub, inviting would-be drinkers to:

JOIN THE DELIBERATIONS OF THE CABINET
HERE AT THE BAT AND BALL!
Hear PM Kenny pronounce!
Watch Chancellor Jim count up the Treasury
of the next round!
Order, order with Frank the Speaker!
Beer, lager, Guinness, wine, spirits!
Don't be a Stranger to the bar!
YES, LET US MINISTER TO YOUR NEEDS!

The council ordered the board to be moved, but it had already been hurled in a skip by an irritated Jim, a shy man who didn't appreciate 'being treated as a fucking freak in a peepshow'. The 'feature' idea fizzled out, not long after, the tenure of the clever-dick reached its end.

Then came Fun Day. A good idea, albeit a legacy of the clever dick. Some significance lurked in the name of the new landlord; he was known as Danny DeeBee; a nickname, one he was irritated to find had followed him across county boundaries, if relieved its origins had not. The usual crew had a few guesses at the meaning, but only perfunctorily; Frank Speke's 'Danny Dole-Bound' was prescient but lacked his customary bite. A little closer investigation would have helped to explain the Fun Day debacle.

Danny—known on his former patch as Danny The Double-Booker—was well-meaning. Too well-meaning. He had a chronic inability to say no. He was also incapable of remembering what he had failed to say no to, and his diary went forever unused. He had approved thoroughly of the Fun Day, but he had also approved and forgotten two other afternoon events that day, allowing the Bat and Ball to be the second or third major stop-off for a rolling hen-party and the venue for a 'jolly up' by a rugby club for a nearby village. The two booze-fuelled waves collided in an unhappy happenstance just as the Fun got swinging.

The Fun Day began thinly, a few families threading their way to the pub, parents ushering nervous children who were wary and watchful on unfamiliar ground. Cheerful music struck up on the pub patio and the French doors were open wide, inviting all to inspect the small number of tiny stalls—cakes, toys, balloons and what have you, set up in the beer garden. Pomo the Clown was in full costume and makeup; he had already taken friendly flak from Pilot Ken's table where all were duly assembled, and he began to juggle nimbly and chatter in his friendliest manner to attract the shy eyes of his young audience. There was an air of building enjoyment. Perhaps this was to be a fun day after all, and everyone was very happy that the weather was holding off. But the rain came, at first in spots—which could be ignored—then blobs—which proved harder to wish away—then rods, which drove everyone indoors as water fell, bounced, rattled without mercy, drowning the beer garden and its fragile stalls. Pilot Ken and his crew found their fun stretching thin as their space was invaded by families seeking shelter and Pomo the Clown attempted to restart his act in the middle of the pub.

All of this would have been inconvenient but bearable, except for the fact that the two large and noisy drunken parties now surged into the pub, clashing at once. As Jim later put it, unoriginally but effectively, hell broke loose. It was a photo-finish as to which of the groups was the more whammed—each had already drunk well and arrived expecting nearly exclusive possession of the Bat and Ball. Danny Deebee's helpless what-have-I-done embarrassment was plain as he attempted to cope with the influx, a problem made worse by the fact that the one thing he had failed to double up was the staffing on the bar. Pomo the Clown was swept, almost dashed aside, and he gave up attempts to entertain, sitting dejectedly in full costume and at the one spare seat at Pilot Ken's table. Ken, having just been served before the invasion, ordered a consolatory pint for poor Pomo who, as ever, was potless and the recipient of disapproving stares from Frank Speke.

The hen party crashed into the Bat and Ball, close on the heels of the rugby boys; their wild, sky-high cries overtopped the bass boom that had already killed conversation there. The rugby crowd was soberly dressed; white shirts, grey trousers, sensible shoes and blazers; whereas the hen party wore abbreviated white shorts, shocking-pink pumps and t-shirts bearing what Ken called 'interesting' slogans, but also tinsel haloes or devil-horns, and, just to ensure nobody was confounded by mixed messages, all waved shocking-pink plastic penises, some obscenely bendy, others even more obscenely stiff.

This boy-meets-girl scene was scarcely replete with romance. In truth, they met as invading armies battling over the fragile forage of an innocent city in their unyielding paths. Danny Deebee sweated and struggled to meet their oncoming rapacity, but the queues grew, supplies ran out, tempers frayed. Gentlemen did not buy drinks for ladies, they used their height and weight, elbowing their 'inferiors' out of their way so that resentment escalated to a pitch battle-mood. Pink plastic penises, bendy and stiff, were deployed, and more than one grey-trousered crotch assailed with lusty violence.

A three-quarter, full of lager, attempted to rally his troops by climbing on a chair, probably on someone sitting in it, waving his glass and crying over the growing hubbub, 'Here's to rugby! Here's to beer! Here's to women!'

'Here's to bigmouths!' yelled a tinsel-devil, who shoved him hard, his form vanishing over the heads of his comrades.

An initial gust of laughter was swallowed by silence, but then the two armies remembered what armies were for, and battle was joined, in the bar, in the doorways, on to the still-soaking patio and beer garden as parents attempted to shield shrieking charges, some of whom shrieked not from fear but from a raw appreciation of the marvellous melee.

Pilot Ken's table was sufficiently removed from the engagement for its occupants to be spared anything but a few flying glasses, which hit nobody, and the approach of the odd staggering figure, easily fielded and returned to the ruck by the big hands of giant Jim. Ken put himself at risk once, as he rushed to the main door to protect Emily who had just arrived for a quiet lunch to walk straight into the battle-ground. A rugby-player stalked toward them, vengeance in his eyes, but he was pulled back by a comrade, whose mouth moved violently but whose voice was lost in the din.

Emily read the restrainer's lips. 'Not him mate—look, he's bald; he's hard!'

Once the police had removed the combatants and guided shell-shocked parents and thrilled children home, Danny Deebee surveyed the wreckage and contemplated a bleak future. Pilot Ken, Jim and Emily surveyed the wretched figure of Danny and pondered his future too. Frank Speke was uncharacteristically silent; like any good commentator, he knew one should only comment when there was something to add. Pomo the Clown, a sad Pierrot at the table, was unable to comprehend the chaos that had swallowed his precious Fun Day gig and fretted about his fee. The stalls in the beer garden stood sodden and forgotten, cakes now a rain-pounded mush, a tea urn lidless and slopping over with cold brown water.

So it didn't work, but perhaps in 'The Pub Is The Hub' the departed clever dick had hit on something, after a fashion. It was not long before Danny Deebee also took the long road to obscurity; what followed was a brief dark age during which The Cabinet, against its wishes and in the face of hostile action, was forced to adjourn to other meeting-places. More of that tale anon.

Evil Mand (so dubbed by Ken, but in a spirit of deep admiration) came along and put right a great deal of the grotesquery of the recent past, winning respect by dint of simple accomplishments such as actually bothering to keep the beer properly and the lines clean, making sure people were served at the bar in the order of arrival and not through the twisted forms of favouritism that existed in previous regimes, but also by engaging in determined battle with GodzillaCorp over its latest accounting trick. The pretence in their profit and loss forecasts was that every drop of a firkin of cask-conditioned ale could be pulled and sold without there being any sign of undrinkable sediment. Mand fought hard, arguing that she would lose thousands a year because her forecast profits were too high and the pubco charged rent on the basis of this fantasy.

Evil Mand, having won back the regulars, celebrated her accession with an impressive new fascia for the pub, a costly work of art from a local signwriter.

'Nice piece of work that, Mand,' said Ken, his eyes crinkling attractively. 'May I have one of these "cast ales" you're advertising?'

Mand reached for a glass, reached for a pump, hesitated, turned back to Pilot Ken, was about to say 'Wha?' when Jim chipped in with, 'I'll pay for this round. I gather that all major cards are 'excepted'. So actually, I don't know how I'm going to pay after all…' He did some comic business with his wallet as Mand mouthed another, 'Wha…?' and her eyes sprang wide open with nascent rage. She banged up the flap of the bar, stalked through, slammed it back down as if to prevent any self-service, and shot outside; Ken and Jim could follow the progress of her inspection of the fascia through the modulation and inflection of her impressive and inventive swearing.

'No cast ales then, mate. Just the usuals,' Ken mummed disappointment.

'My god, there's a signwriter round here who's gonna find out soon why she's called Evil Mand,' whispered Jim, awed.

On a forlorn, failed summer day, low, hazy clouds extended ghostly, bone-white fingers to tickle at the sodden surfaces of track and field and casually brush scatterings of cold rain over the generous windows of The Bat And Ball. Pilot Ken took a long sip of Guinness and surveyed the semi-dark-at-noon, drizzle-soaked outdoors sombrely.

'The light here... defies physics...' he mused aloud.

'Oh bloody hell—Theory Alert!' Jim laughed, quick on the uptake that one of Ken's regular parlour-games was imminent, performed to the amusement of all but Frank Speke.

'Yes, indeed.' Ken settled back in his chair to talk in a slightly distracted way; Jim felt that what was needed to complete the ambience was a log fire and a sleeping dog. And Ken should be wearing slippers. 'In the rest of the world, light comes in thin white beams which, if put through a prism, spread into bright branch-lines of constituent colours; put through another prism they close up, tight, and are a thin white beam once more. Round here, however, the beam is grey. Through a prism it's... greyer. And the bloody prism gets wet.'

'Pah,' spat Frank, unaware of having made the gesture.

Theory Alert began accidentally, but became an irregular feature of their days; some of its popularity may have been to do with annoying Frank. Its origins were in a newspaper article at which Ken, crossword done, was half-mooning with amusement.

'Listen to this.' He waved his glasses in one hand and the paper in the other. 'There's an academic to-do about whether Napoleon was murdered.'

'Who cares?' grumbled Frank Speke.

'These lot do.' Ken tapped his glasses on the paper. 'They've found traces of arsenic in his body, and reckon his jailers poisoned him.'

'Bit late to file a case, I won't call Nev,' said Emily.

'Another lot say the arsenic wasn't in his food, but the wallpaper. And if you ask how on Earth the Emperor got it from the wallpaper—I know. It's all to do with booze.'

'Oh God,' muttered Frank.

'Remember a few weeks ago Jim—you had a bourbon and cola?'

'I *like* bourbon and col...'

'Not the point. If you recall, I tried it. And what did I say it tasted like?'

'Something stupid... wallpaper paste.'

'Precisely! Case proven!'

'Eh?'

'It's like this—I've realised that history is not made by "great men" at all, it's made by drunk people!'

Frank Speke stirred in his chair and Emily slapped his arm to warn him off.

'Old Boney was on St Helena having lost at Waterloo. The reason he lost? He was drunk! What else could have impaired his peerless skills of generalship? Remember the brandy!

'Anyway, there's our exile, far away from civilisation, and supplies get low, the booze runs out and he's *pegging* for a drink. Desperate, he remembers that wallpaper paste tastes just like bourbon and cola, he starts licking the walls, only to fall accidental victim to the use of arsenic in the manufacture of wallpaper!'

'Have you quite finished?' Frank Speke tried to douse the laughter.

'So there you are—history is nothing but the mis-steps and mishaps of people under the influence. Fire was discovered by someone so pissed that, for a laugh, they thought up the pointless activity of banging stones together; gods were invented so libations could be poured; cities only founded so pubs could be built: Julius Caesar was so blotto he didn't know he'd crossed the bloody Rubicon; Columbus was trying to get to India and went the wrong way, the

19

reason for which must now be clear; Isaac Newton and the apple? Cider, more like. See? It all fits!'

A querulous tone pierced the fun again. 'Don't you ever look at yourselves and wonder if you are in fact wasting your entire lives?'

'Oh shut up, Frank.'

The Reign of Evil Mand

AMANDA P.K. ETHERIDGE
Licensed to sell intoxicating liquors
ON or OFF the premises

'You are in love with two women,' said Jim to Ken, evenly, without spite, 'the first we all know about. The second is Evil Mand.'

Ken grunted meaninglessly, but he also smiled.

It is perfectly understandable that when a pub reopens after a fallow period, drinkers pop in to take a look at the place and size up the new regime; perfectly understandable but not especially desirable, in the view of Pilot Ken. Not when it came to Scamp and Gizmo, the two disreputable-looking gutter-scrapings who slithered in to the Bat and Ball, still trailing the shadows of the dingiest corners of the PH Bar, obviously looking to see if they could drip some of their darkness in this peaceful oasis now that a lone woman was known to be in charge. Ken kept a suspicious, disdainful eye on them, but thought little more about the matter until they approached the bar, making their way through the first-night crowd and getting their first view of the new landlady.

The eyes of Amanda P.K. Etheridge lit on them, her welcoming look becoming quizzical, troubled even. She leaned, peering over the pumps at the new visitors. They returned her gaze for no more than half a second; both men physically quailed, one grabbed the upper arm of the other and steered him out of the bar, their feet moving like clumsy tyro dancers heading for a sprawling, limb-tangling fall. The landlady looked minded to follow—perhaps 'pursue' was a better word. She placed her hand on the flap of the bar but was called back by the commercial realities of new drinkers pressing for her attention.

'You from round here, or jus visitin?' the landlord of the Hidden Garden asked Mand, but headed off any response with, 'You're not visitin are you? Who'd visit round here?'

'I used to live not far—Maxton. I've moved here now, though.'

'Brave woman.' He smiled, displaying variegated teeth: off-white to ochre.

'I've taken the tenancy at the Bat and Ball. I've come to say hello.'

'Even braver woman. I thought the Bat was a goner this time, thought the last parcel o'clowns had put the steel shutters on it for good. Good luck, and yer drink's on the house. In my eyes yer not a competitor, more a fellow sufferer.'

'I've been popping into the pubs I knew; not as many as there were.'

Mand's words caused the landlord to shudder. 'Steel shutters and wooden boards, girl. You've chose ell of a time to run a pub. Or anything, round here. Others'll tell you the same.'

'Yeah; they have.'

'They said there'd be a cold wind. They didn't mention it wouldn't stop.'

Mand nodded as she stepped towards the door.

There was a cold wind; darkness had oozed into the streets too, like oil in to a network of vials, filling them up and stifling the feeble streetlights. From the Garden, Mand told herself, I go down this side-street here, and then right, and then I'll be in the town centre, taxi to the Bat And Ball. Big day tomorrow. Got to be ready. You know, any other town would be showing some signs of life even at this time of night, but this one is dead as dead, no sound and no lights. And with the wind making mournful experimental music, plucking at the stark steel street furniture, moaning hungrily outside locked doors and testing shutters and bars with cold fingers. Looking for the turning to the underpass that led down to the Bat and Ball, Mand found herself lost, going in rough squares—it was impossible to go in circles in that sharp-edged town—with every route looking the same, street-signs terse and uninformative, except to those who already knew their way.

'You Are Here,' said Mand to herself. 'How did I get lost on a crossword grid?' An instinct thrilled through her head; she had seen nothing other than cloying, gaining darkness, heard nothing apart from the musician wind, but she was instantly sure that she was being followed. Yes, there were two of them, she could hear their steps now, carried unevenly by the wind's mocking song. She couldn't shake them, she was lost after all, and a foolish move might deliver her to them as easy meat. What did they want? Don't... think about that. She stopped and turned, yes, two shifty shadows melted just out of vision, they were coming but they weren't ready yet. There may still be time to find light and a little life. Whatever had happened to that damn café culture that was supposed to have swept the country? She had seen a café but it was dipped in stale streetlight, closed up like a fortress. Mand herself tried to make use of the darkness, scuttling away from the middle of the street and under jutting shop frontages where the dim light didn't penetrate, letting her eyes grow accustomed to the thick gloom. If she spotted an escape route, she could make a dash, maybe a turn of speed would leave them huffing; they were probably awash with ale and not in good shape.

It was not time to run, she just needed to maintain her distance. The problem was, they hadn't lost their local knowledge; they had chosen their ground and were driving her to it.

There was still no sign of people or light. Mand was getting worried. The jackals were closing, cautiously. That her next step was vitally important made her reluctant to take it, made her lose pace and time. Advantage was accumulating to the jackals. The stalking was over; they broke cover, lumps of darkness shaped as men, soon they would rush her, what to do? One took a bold step, his oppo slithered as if to cover any escape, slow-step, slow-step they came, but they would rush soon and the only question was how bad this was going to be. Mand was walking backwards, and her erratic path inevitably got her into even more trouble as she backed into a circle of flickering light and then bashed the breath out of herself as she stepped straight against the cold metal of the poorly-maintained street lamp. She heard one of the men laugh. She could hear a whirring from inside the lamp, the sound of the faulty mechanism. There was no hope, but one thing to try. Sucking in her breath, Mand stepped toward the edge of the light, looking into the dangerous shadows, hoping fear would not make her voice a puny dream-squeak, she bellowed

'BANNER OFF!'

Her suddenly-huge voice echoed across the town, rattling windows, even coaxing a shrill counterpoint out of the mournfully singing street furniture. The jackals, just as their confidence had reached its peak, stuttered in their tracks, shooting one another uncertain looks. An engine coughed and then roared, brilliant light bathed the little alleyway, a loud howl broke the silence and the would-be attackers rat-scampered back to the protective darkness. Blind and backwards, Mand had found the taxi rank and her stentorian yell had found her a lift to the Bat and Ball. And in that blaze of light, she had seen their faces; faces she recognised on her first night in charge at the Bat and Ball. It was a while before Mand told Pilot Ken the reason why she had so frightened the wretched Scamp and Gizmo.

We all cultivate an image, it's useless to deny it. Most of the time it's an exercise in deception, usually mild, to manage and shape the opinions of others, to head off harsh words—minimise them at least. Many people project an idealised self, those with some self-knowledge highlight the better aspects of their character, swathing the remainder in shadow. Others just flat-out fib, as a defensive shell.

Precisely what Evil Mand was intending image-wise was difficult to make out: she was small, slim, of indeterminate age, her favoured hairstyle pinned-back with an unostentatious bun, there were no signs of grey and yet this and her round-framed tortoiseshell glasses aged her, the impression being deepened by her sober colours of dress, her woollen shawl, dun, unpretentious, always draped over her shoulders. When Mand took over at the Bat And Ball, certain wags referred to going for 'a drink at granny's'. The first of said wags to use that name to Mand's face received a dousing in slops, and was frog-marched to the door; this incident laid the foundations of Mand's enduring soubriquet, and forced out of Frank Speke the half-admiring statement, 'She's not the granny, she's the wolf.'

Nobody knew if Mand was a granny, or even a mother; she never spoke of family and although she was occasionally visited by friends, showed few signs of loving anyone, which raised occasional *sotto voce* comparisons to Pilot Ken. Frank Speke grew curious and tried to persuade first Emily and then Gina to wheedle information out of Mand on a female-sympathy basis, but came away muttering obscurely about the 'bloody sisterhood'. Pilot Ken told him to stop being so damn nosy; when Frank asked if he didn't want to know just a little about Mand, to lift the veil a smidge, Ken refused, smiling. 'Perfect as she is.'

'I reckon she's buried three husbands already—at least one of them alive. You watch yourself, Kenny.'

Evil Mand sometimes relaxed her rules of the bar, but only occasionally and only in a manner imperceptible to all but those who were there a great deal and watched closely. Pilot Ken spotted them: a curious collection of mendicants, always men, never young, who appeared infrequently and one by one, bearing little resemblance to one another in appearance or demeanour, apart from their solitude and the fact that, apart from Evil Mand, they spoke to nobody and did not stay long. These men rarely returned. Ken was also sure that not one of these individuals was ever asked to pay

25

for his drinks, no matter how much he put away, and these were the only drinkers ever to be served by Mand as soon as they arrived, ahead of those already waiting. To preserve laboratory conditions, Ken did not mention his observations to anyone, not even Jim, and he waited many, many months before testing his hypothesis.

A spindly-tall middle-aged man with all the hallmarks of a classic consumptive had not long sidled from the bar when Ken took advantage of a quiet spell to beard Evil Mand.

'A relative, Mand?'

'Just someone I know. Knew. Used to know years back. He worked for my father; he drove for him.'

'Did all the others?'

'Yeah; how did you know…'

'Your dad was in business?'

'You could say that.'

'Drivers—cabmen?'

'Nope.'

'A bus company?'

'No.'

'What sort of drivers, then? Ambulances, funeral cars…'

Mand said nothing.

'Good god—getaway… get away!'

Mand nodded and poured Ken a pint, refusing payment.

'For being a clever boy. And so you can be one of an elite crew.'

Back at the table Jim was astonished, cackling when he heard the tale.

'Her dad…'

'…dy was a *la-la-la…*' hummed Ken.

'Great Scott. No wonder there's never any trouble at this pub. The local scumbags must know they'll end up set in concrete or something.'

'I think he was a bank-jobber, not Don Corleone.'

'You love her even more, now, don't you?' said Jim, grinning.

Pilot Ken said nothing; he did not need to.

The Cabinet Discusses Policy

Very, Very Back in the Day

'A custom loathsome to the eye, hateful to the nose, harmful to the brain, dangerous to the lungs, and in the black, stinking fume thereof, nearest resembling the horrible Stygian smoke of the pit that is bottomless.' (King James I, 1604)

Rather less Back in the Day

'I had to catch a bus yesterday, business up the road. I was a shade too early at the bus station, but there wasn't enough time to have a coffee and, as you'll recall, it was lashing it down all day, so I was stuck in the bus shelter, that ultra-modern glass lozenge. And at that point remembered why I always avoid the place. I stood at the 94 stand and prayed the bus would pull up early and the driver show mercy; no such luck. It wasn't long before the woman standing right by me lit up, blew the smoke in my face and then sucked her cheeks in to do it again, so I retreated to the 98 stand, where of course it happened again, then the 102 stand, ditto at the 105 and so on down every last one, it was like the progress of the Olympic bloody Flame!'

'There's a no-smoking section, Ken,' came the reasonable objection from Little Mal, the power-broker of the local council and Golf Club.

'Ah yes, a prison cell with an automatic door, and you know what happens when I'm in that lifer's space? One of them lights up and then comes and stands close by— *shhhhhhh* goes the door, opening obediently: I ask her to stand away but it's too late, *shhhhhhhh*, but the condemned cell is now a fume-cupboard then *shhhhhhhh*, she steps close again and gives me a refill!'

'Aww, life is hard innit Ken?' Frank Speke sneered, unable to contain himself.

Even less back in the day, but some time prior to 1/7/2007

'Voovoom, voovoom, woovoom, voovoom, voovoom!'

Ken was clenching and unclenching his hands, palms outwards, staring across the room, crooning.

'Voovoom, voovoom, woovoom, voovoom, voovoom!'

'Ken? You quite alright mate?'

'I'm exercising my power.'

'Eh?'

'My power over ciggie-lighters, look!'

Flick-flick-flick in the far corner of the pub, a tall man was leaning over his lighter as if to shield it from a high wind, but all that emerged from the little gas-bottle was feeble and transitory sparks as the wheel ground fruitlessly. The man's expression of concentration deepened into furrow-browed frustration and he flicked harder, harder, but still no flame came.

'Voovoom, voovoom!'

'Ken...'

'Don't break my concentration! While the spell lasts, that fag will never get lit!'

'You're weird.'

'Voovoom, voovoom, voovoom! See my powers, he hasn't got a chance!'

The frustrated smoker abandoned his failing flint and borrowed a match, which struck first time.

'Bloody cheat,' moaned Ken. 'Voovoom' he intoned, trying out his power on another lighter-upper not far away.

'Never mind mate, it'll all be banned soon.' A white puff of smoke departed Jim's mouth as if a piece of his greying beard was detaching: the plume defied physics to make a hairpin-turn, setting off with grim determination for Ken's face. Jim flapped his hand in the air in a comically ineffectual gesture, the malign cloud dispersed but then visibly regrouped and the dirty airstream formed a beach-head for its renewed attack.

'Don't bet on it.' Ken tried in vain to dodge the worst of the assault. 'The smokers will make us pay for it somehow.'

'I love the way you say "the smokers" as if no one round this table was amongst that number. It's as if they were an alien menace or a bogeyman to you, or maybe cardboard cut-out villains from some daft adventure film.'

'I hate the smoke, not the smoker, Jim,' said Ken. 'But why do smokers assume their smoke *won't* affect others? Don't they know that smoke is not only intelligent, it's *maliciously* so, and hunts down the vulnerable. And there's no point in pubs trying to have smoking areas and no-smoking areas, first of all they never separate them properly and even if they did, the poison-cloud *knows* where it's not supposed to go, and so—that's where it heads!'

'For someone who spends so much of his time in pubs Ken, it's a bit queer that you object so strongly to two of the greatest pub occupations—smoking and swearing.' Jim raised an eyebrow.

'That's more or less what a mate said to me once, not long after I'd tasted my first Guinness. We were in our local and they were all fag-on, the windows were shut, the doors tight-sealed as if it were a lock-in, the extractor fans still and dead. All was as if it were some experimental attempt to reproduce the atmosphere of Neptune. I couldn't catch my next breath, I couldn't even take a step to get myself outside, my lungs were full of smoke and it seemed to be filling my head, through the nose and eyes but also creeping up through the roof of my mouth. I felt sick, even the beer tasted of smoke, it couldn't wash it either down or away. And, well, I turned dizzy, next thing I was on the floor, being dragged outside.

'Everyone was very sympathetic—except my dear pal. He waited until I felt better, you can say that much for him, but that was it. "Coming back in?" he asked, knowing the answer. Then, "Maybe you shouldn't bother coming back at all. You're not cut out for pub life." It was a friendship that didn't last.'

'But your love-affair with the pub…'

'In spite of smoke getting in my eyes on many an occasion, yes.'

Back in the day—closer to 1/7/2007

Ken's pen flicked and swiped energetically, but for once he was not filling in crossword clues or jotting formations of broken-up letters to forge a new word from the splinters of an anagram. He had stripped the front from a beer mat and on the bare white space had sketched a sort of upside-down fishbowl with curious sci-fi attachments, a little grille mouth, a screen, buttons, sliding switches, what looked like small flashing bulbs; it was The Helmet.

'It's based upon NASA technology, you see. It solves the vexed age-old problem of setting out smoking and no-smoking areas in public places. It means the poor smokers won't have to go outside, like so: they fancy a fag, they slot said fag into the little holder just inside, behind the face-plate here, then they pop The Helmet on, press the "Light Up" button on the control panel on the right cheek, so to speak, a little flame sparks inside, the fag catches, and they can smoke away in peace without bothering anybody else.'

'How do they see out?'

'Visor—here. It'll need quite a lot of cleaning…'

'How can they speak or hear?'

'Transmitter mike inside—speaker mounted here, external mike here, receiver box inside, just by the mike and fag-lighter.'

'What's that shaded bit underneath?'

'A neck-seal—total, impermeable. Keeps the smoker and his smoke in the most intimate of contact, and only releases once the ciggie has burned out and all smoke has been inhaled.'

'But there'd be no *oxygen*!'

'Since when have smokers valued oxygen?'

'You bloody non-smokers are the ones who should wear a helmet, leave the rest of us free to do as we wish,' declaimed Frank Speke, lighting up with a defiant flourish.

'Can't you settle for something more reasonable?' gasped Ken, 'Can't you chew the stuff, or take it in liquid form—a pint of nico-tar-and-catarrh perhaps—or how about as suppositories? Or a pneumonia jab, one that causes it, just to get it over with? An injection of the deadly poison of your choice?'

'Fine talk for someone who's so fond of holding forth about human rights!'

'The right to die horribly? And to take your mates and kids with you for good measure?'

'You're caught by your own pontifications about freedom, Ken; you've got to let people have a choice.'

'Well, my choice is to punch smokers up the nose. I demand my freedom to do this. You may suffer but I get my pleasure; you can't control me, health fascist!'

Everyone laughed at that last sally, Ken later recalled, laughed as he had intended. You could talk like that, back-in, lob in an absurd, over-inflated insult and it would explode like a party-popper, harmless, no shrapnel. Ken considered himself a word connoisseur (a dilettante, Frank Speke would say), but it was not the words that had changed—it was the tone.

Discussion, disagreement, argument, they were as much a part of pub life as beer, wine, crisps and, if you must, smoke. The prevailing tone was always bantering, companionable, even in opposition. People could adopt grotesque balloon-debate stances, defend an alien viewpoint vigorously and yet playfully, and only occasionally would they overdo it, method-acting their way towards an uncharacteristic excess, more devil than advocate; a delayed, sobered-up apology was the usual outcome. There were outliers who revelled in excess—Frank Speke in his right-to-offend crusade, for instance—but now it was

31

everywhere. If someone gainsaid you, they were not just wrong but idiotic, callow, vicious dupes.

Sometime after 1/7/2007

Frank Speke didn't mind battling alone, but he was happy to have the support of a table newcomer, a fellow controversialist quickly known as FMC. He was first noticed as a voice, a grating sound from another corner of the pub, lecturing unseen others on the history of Afghanistan, more specifically how despicable was foreign interference and invasion, with the exception of that of the Soviets, who were there to save lives and civilise the benighted land—they had been invited, it was no invasion, unlike the criminal actions of the so-called coalition... There was more, but it was lost in the pub-noise.

'Gatemouth,' said Ken, having lent an ear. 'Just another gatemouth.'

No more was thought about the harsh-voiced stranger until one afternoon controversy was in abeyance and Ken was treating the table to one of their favourite strains of reminiscence, which always began, 'That reminds me of my old girlfriend, who...' He was describing his unclear relationship with a wildflower beauty who bore a passing resemblance to the late Sharon Tate.

Without ceremony, a tall figure unfolded from a nearby chair and landed next to Ken, wafting a smell of drink that was simultaneously fresh and stale, stomach-turning. The voice was familiar, the man would become so; he was studiedly scruffy, black drainpipe-ish jeans, never-clean white t-shirts, never bearing slogans, black denim jacket, often an ancient beanie hat which he wore indoors and out.

'Instant rebel. Too old for the look,' grumbled Frank Speke, who rapidly found his personal brand of apolitical libertarianism attracted the bitter scorn of FMC, who regarded anyone 'apolitical' as a moral coward and a Tory to boot. On this first occasion, however, FMC didn't wish to preach politics, but law. 'Charles Manson was innocent of that killing,' he decreed, leaning uncomfortably close to Ken, 'innocent of them all. He never took part in any of those killings, all he ever did was to tell his people to kill. They didn't have to do it, and he didn't make them. So Manson is innocent, shouldn't be in prison.'

There was a long, appalled silence that appeared to afford FMC a great deal of satisfaction. Gina broke through it, holding her phone to her ear and then setting it down after a series of 'uh-huhs'. 'That was the legal team for Stalin, Hitler and Pol Pot. They say thanks for getting their boys off the hook. Now—see you later.' FMC took the hint and left, glaring hatred at Gina; his subsequent regular appearances were scarcely more comfortable or comforting.

FMC and Frank were to clash bitterly and regularly, but regarding the smoking ban, the cause of liberty united them in arguing alongside one another. 'Are you not satisfied Ken? You've got us going outside, exiled in cold and wind and rain and god knows what else, you're protected from our horrid smoke. Why isn't it enough for you?' Frank loved fighting for the underdog, and in this way part of him almost welcomed the smoking ban.

'Has this added suffering never made you think of giving up?' Ken teased.

Frank Speke glowered; the ban had hardened him, made him more determined, if anything he smoked more. He hated smug winners and would fight back with all the bitter obstinacy at his disposal. FMC merely boggled; the idea of giving up had never occurred to him.

Frank and FMC loved to argue, whether with one another or not; FMC tended to rise to political provocation, sticking within the rigid lines of his set beliefs, but Frank would argue the toss long and hard over anything, even switching sides if one faction began to flag, lending it the spark of his stubborn fury if only to extend the lifespan of the dialectic.

'Air flows,' said Ken flatly.

'Non-sequitur that again?' Frank spoke with irritated puzzlement.

'Airflows. You clever exiles are attempting to take your revenge by going outside to smoke, yes, you do that, but where do you stand? As close to the door as possible, where the air flow will carry your smoke into the pub and make the place stink of your pleasure almost as much as it did before.'

'God, you're trying to dictate where we fuckin stand now!'

'And you're taking petty, spiteful vengeance like the sore losers you are!'

'You're the mouthpiece of an elite, smug liberal do-this-do-that fuckin middle class snobs...'

'Is that what the Party says about it all, FMC? I thought Lenin hated people smoking?'

'Stalin was a pipeman though,' Frank Speke chipped in, as if this decided a vital point.

'You're in pretty "interesting" company gentlemen—marching in freedom-loving lockstep with Big Tobacco, lots of right-wing Tory MPs...'

FMC flinched, but Frank Speke was unmoved.

'You talk democracy, but this is just petty dictatorship, the nanny smugocracy!'

'Oh come on Frank...'

Hardly back in the day at all, in fact it seems like yesterday

The arguments swirled again, the perennial cloud-of-smoke controversy, the points in a different order but otherwise identical, with all participants claiming to be leaping to the defence of freedom. Ken and Jim were lightly teasing, Jim having performed a neat reverse-ferret, irritating FMC and Frank Speke with his newfound purity as reformed smokers (or 'traitors' as FMC termed them) tend to. Frank Speke was weary, making Ken wonder if the years were finally dissipating his elan for the game. FMC, however, remained inexhaustibly combative, albeit three sheets to the wind, louder and more effin sweary, having laid effective siege to the Bat And Ball's stock of Irish whiskey.

Enraged by Ken and Jim's illiberal-liberal elitism, FMC snatched a packet of fags from his pocket and roared, 'So if you take this fuckin ban so seriously, will you stop me smoking here and now, will anyone report me and get me fuckin fined? Are you that *up* yourselves?'. His lighter appeared in his hand, the cigarette bounced on his lips as he roared, 'So—who's gonna fuckin do anything if I light up?'

'I will.' The voice in his ear was sweet and light. 'I will break your head, shove your fags up your arse, set fire to you with your own stupid lighter, kill you and then bar you for life just to make sure. Because you wouldn't be fined, *I* would. The price of your freedom is too great for me—got it?'

Evil Mand had crept up on FMC without anyone in the group spotting her.

FMC, his ciggie, his lighter and his now very muted defiance slunk toward the door. Relieved, the Cabinet ordered another round and changed the subject.

A Quizzical Night

Wayne was setting up his gear for the quiz night: it wouldn't take long as there wasn't much: question sheet, answer sheets, spare pens for the people who forget, a cordless headset to plug into the pub's speakers, and a bottomless tankard—that was it. The need for the mike was questionable; Wayne never allowed talking while he asked questions, he was apt to half-kill incorrigible chatterers, who then became very, very corrigible. Besides, Emily declared that his fine, rounded, burring voice would resound in her theatre as well as that of the finest pro who ever trod the boards. The Bat and Ball was always full for quiz nights, which was useful for Evil Mand. Pilot Ken watched Wayne's preparations and waited for his usual team-mates—those who had not been present all day.

Question One—How long will it take for Wayne to get so plastered he can't read out the questions? He used to make it to the final round, but these days he starts to slur about mid-round three, and the questions become a little... free-form. Strangely, people love it, it's one of the reasons they come. Wouldn't be surprised if there was some private betting going on, about where he starts to lose control, where Mand needs to ease him off the chair and take over.

Question Two—There's a rumour scuttling round on spider legs that the drink isn't just making Wayne a bit wayward and amusing as he gets sozzled on a quiz night, but that he's within a few gulps of the end of his days—and he knows it, and doesn't give a toss. True or false? I don't know, I daren't ask that.

Jim gave off a guard-dog growl, and Pilot Ken knew without looking who had come through the door.

'*Oh shit*, here comes the eminence grease of the council chamber and Golf Club. Stand by to repel bores.' Frank Speke looked peeved, as it was Jim who delivered the attack.

It took a great deal of personal toxicity to provoke friendly, generous Jim, but whatever was required, Little Mal exuded it. Still, thought Frank, it is my right to take people down, and I do a far better job of it than that nancy niceboy.

When Pilot Ken insisted on quiz nights that Mal Stokely should always be on his team, a suspicion formed that he was being uncharacteristically competitive and mean-spirited; he was jealously guarding a key asset, a sure-fire quiz winner. Heads shook, disapproval was voiced. It took Jim, laughing at the accusation, to explain to an opponent who challenged him openly.

'You know how the quiz works,' said Jim, 'at the end you've got five minutes to ask for repeats of questions, and to sort out among yourselves about answers you're unsure about, then one of you takes the answer sheet to the bar—yeah?'

'Course, but what's that got to do…'

'Who goes up to the bar from our team?'

'Ken, usually.'

'Hmh. And who never gets to go up to the bar from our team?'

'Eh?'

'There's one member of the team who is never, ever allowed to take the answer sheet up: Mal. And the reason? The bastard changes answers he thinks are wrong, crosses em out and puts *his* answers. And he is always-always-always bloody wrong! So: far from being a tight git, our Saint Ken is providing one of his many social services, to our team as much as others—we win most weeks cos we stop Mal ballsing it up, and we keep him from playing his little trick on other people's teams, who'd be too polite to stop the little git.'

Mal looked as if he had been sketched, hastily and in rage, in a series of vicious upward strokes; all sight-lines were carried sharply up—a very short distance, the others would inevitably point out—to his face, where the dash-lines became shorter but angrier, making his goatee and tache push out and up, his eyes flare and stretch, the resulting fanatic effect magnified, manic-fied, by round bottle-bottom glasses, his mouth spike in to a rictus sardonicus, and his hair stand as if crackling with energy-perpetual. Mal's overall appearance was as the upflaring of a match or a firework, albeit one that detracted from the light, added to the night. Little Mal was a regular at Ken's table, but he was hardly a friend to all; not that this grieved him; he behaved as if he and Ken were the only ones present, casting the others to the folds of his darkness.

Jim, hackles high, took Pilot Ken aside after his debut exposure to Mal and demanded angrily, 'Who's that calculating little weasel? I've not had a conversation just then, I have been bluddy well interviewed, processed! I was quizzed and probed about this and that, then he clearly decided he had no use for me, and that was that, not even a glance thereafter.'

'Oh,' interrupted Frank Speke, 'I thought you'd get on. Isn't he one of yours?'

'Frank, just because we're both queer, doesn't mean we're part of a bloody hive mind. I'm allowed to dislike a fellow poof, y'know.'

'A devious little rat,' pronounced Gina, whose own 'interview' had been monosyllabic.

'But how can he be such a *successful* devious little rat, when his true nature is written all over his devious, ratty little face?' Emily spat; Mal had never even spoken to her, but she had felt the side-swipe of his power. 'He even looks like a shifty little rodent, not to mention a fanatic, he looks like…'

'Trotsky,' said Jim, holding his pint up to the light and then setting it down again in apparent satisfaction. Ken, though, was not satisfied, he wore his hard-clue frown and shook his head.

'No, no, it's nearly… nearly but not quite. Trotsky, yes, he's got the beard, the tache, the glasses even, but there's something about the eyes, something even more manic than

38

old Leon, something as if he's permanently surprised, pained...' he mused further, as if on the last brush-stroke that would complete a masterpiece.

'Trotsky... with a hedgehog shoved up his arse.'

'Yes, that's it... yes!' Ken's puzzle-solver's cry of triumph disturbed a few lunchtime chatters, but they soon looked away—the bald guy in the corner was probably mad.

Ken was apt to believe that Mal possessed super powers; well, one anyway. In the presence of everyone he could create a conversational bubble, an exclusion zone that recognised only his chosen interlocutor, reducing the pubbub to a nothing and transforming everyone around to a faceless, miming shadow. Mal was all that could be seen or heard: release came only when he deemed, and you could guarantee that nothing had escaped the bubble, no word, no gesture, no twitch or tic of facial muscle.

'I know what the others say about me.' Enfolding Pilot Ken in the bubble, Emily was within touching distance and yet beyond reach; Little Mal allowed no emotion to leak either into his voice or from his deep-bottled eyes. 'They call me a fixer—it means nothing nice.' He throat-clicked contempt. 'Well, I am a fixer, an influencer, but the proper sort—I see problems, I see what needs doing before anyone else has an inkling, I find the person who needs to know, I have a quiet word, and... problems fixed.'

A town councillor, never its leader, not even the deputy, Mal was never seen to wield power or boast municipal regalia, yet whispered ideas to those with smaller minds and louder voices, seeking no credit for successes and slithering out of sight and occasionally removing himself from the council in tactical retreat, waiting for the fuss to die when particularly controversial plans went awry and resignations were in the air. 'We're in trouble, Ken; the town, the Ring O'Villages, it's all... well, you know perfectly well what's going on. There's no stopping it but we can buy time. I know how. It just won't be pretty. Even I want to turn my head from some of it, but it's better than anything else. I'm not hearing any alternatives.'

This must be what he tells his proteges of his latest schemes, mused Ken from the invisible bounds, feeding his fledglings with whispers in the ear made of swirls of swarf and scoops of slime, stepping back as someone else puts the pieces together and comes up with Mal's scheme, after which, as politicians are wont to do, they can redecorate reality and convince themselves that the concept came to them whole and unmediated. Should disaster occur, Little Mal's hands were stainless and in extremis he would stand down for a bit.

A while back, Mal had hissed in the ear of the cash-strapped council that it could cut its staff in what he dubbed 'Operation Deadwood'. The idea was to shake the tree—offer generous terms to leave and leave quickly—and the dead wood, the time-servers, the uninspired and superannuated, would take the bait and fall gladly. Predictably, the deadwood, not quite so dead after all and unwilling to hazard the exigencies of the outside world, clung tight to the life-giving trunk, while the fresh limbs, the talented, the inspired and the effective, took the hint and the money, and headed for something better.

The latest imbroglio was Democratic Retrenchment—again, this was the bubble-coining of Mal the influencer—'a natural expansion of people-power', it was the proposed absorption of the too-parochial powers of the Ring O' Villages into the authority of the town. A few sops had to be offered to the existing leaders to make them feel mighty even as they were shorn of their petty powers. The selling-point was 'efficiency', by which was meant more cuts, with a spinning, silvery lure of lower local taxes. Mal had, not for the first time, encountered another species of influencer; he had bent his ear to one Petronella Veber, who had recently joined the authority as a 'director', for a high salary which would be justified over and over again by the miracles she promised. Slick, persuasive, hard-shelled, she had wowed everyone at her interview, Mal especially, perhaps as it appeared to him that he was gazing at a mirror.

Pilot Ken cavilled that 'retrenchment' was entirely the wrong word, it didn't mean expansion at all, far from it; not to mention that the concept of democracy didn't belong anywhere beside it. Mal shrugged off the criticism, he liked the words, he was determined to use them; nothing else mattered. But however well Democratic Retrenchment played with Mal and his colleagues, it was received in the Ring O' Villages as would have been news of the return of the Plague: the very-parochial councillors ceased their customary on-off feuding and united against what they noisily labelled the Land Grab. It was more of a power-grab, but they needed a label that would stir up their villagers and make them feel personally at risk. To a goodly extent they were; the savings promised by Veber would need to be wrung from the Ring, bringing among other blessings the termination of their few remaining local services. The town's beleaguered staff had also made their calculations and decided that the bulk or the balance of the savings would be extracted from their collective hide, and a total strike, supported even by those who usually scabbed like a grazed knee, brought the town council shuddering to a halt. The ramrod-resistance of the councillors lasted three days, at which point Democratic Retrenchment became a non-phrase, but its skinflint spirit lived on, and the search was on for scapegoats. Just like her promises, Petronella Veber became evanescent; she was signed off sick until the arrival of her resignation. Not long after, she was heard of in a far-flung municipality, cutting an impressive figure at interview and outlining a scheme of cuts and renewed power that bedazzled her captive audience.

'A potentially delightful human being...' Ken weighed the evidence, '...eclipsed by a twat.'

'I just see the twat,' said Emily firmly. Gina nodded vigorously, as did Jim.

'Ooooh now, see how the all the girls hate him!' Frank Speke moued.

Question Three—So: this time will Little Mal brazen it out or bail out?

'Ken, will you concentrate on the quiz please? You're on the drift! Stop it! Ooaryer are looking smug; they know we're flagging,' Gina pleaded. 'By those smiles, they know they're about ten points ahead!' Ooaryer were a rival team, the rival team, a cluster of amiable but dangerously knowledgeable sages from the Ring O'Villages who enjoyed coming to the Bat and Ball Quiz to trounce Ken's team. It was a point of honour to defeat Ooaryer.

'Sorry... sorry...' Ken gasped like a man opening his eyes to a harsh dawn hangover. He realised Gina was rallying the team in his near-absence. He didn't know what was wrong with him tonight, inner thoughts were swimming up and blurring his concentration, taking over... Wayne was asking another question. He sounded sloshed, so it must be late on... ish. Ken looked across the table: Gina and Jim engaged in whispered consultation or disputation, Gina covering Jim's mouth with her hand when he became loud enough to be overheard at other tables; Little Mal was listening keenly, ready to disagree with them and slot in his own—wrong— answer; Frank Speke was silent, looking wistfully at the opposition's table, as if contemplating defection.

Gina took the quiz a little too seriously; she was competitive, but then, she wouldn't have been in business otherwise. She never bragged about her income, but her husband wasn't doing badly either, Ken gathered, and at least in economic terms they were the power-couple of Ken's extended, disparate group. Almost the only ones not on a fixed, falling or threatened income. Now there's a sign of the times, mused Ken... not that the two of them, Gina and Mart, had appeared as a couple at the Bat and Ball very much lately. If he showed up, Mart was always late and always driving. He never drank at all. He was friendly, but inevitably, an outsider. Frank Speke called him a countinghouse water-sipper; Wayne scorned him on the latter count if not the former.

That Mart was rarely seen and that Gina came along regularly and conspicuously without him was noticed in various quarters. And then, as always, the talk followed; no one ever knew who started it, and what's more nobody was ever caught red-handed spreading the talk (except that old fool JC), and yet it spread so that everyone 'knew' the facts.

Question Four—What's going on? Should we worry? What should we do? Is it our business? Do we pull together or keep our noses out? Do we...

'Ken!' This time Gina was shouting: but his reverie was smithereened, anyway, by the coming of a hellish howling worse than Gina's reprimand.

'*Nyerr-yae-ee-arrr, nyerrr-yae-eee-arrr,* gi's yer pots, gi's yer pots, give em up, gi's yer pots, pay yer Poll Tax, pay yer fuckin Poll Tax! *Nyerr-yae-ee-arrr, nyerrr-yae-eee-arrr!*'

A goblin figure flitted from table to table, making a lunge for glasses abandoned, empty, half-full, but also sometimes even still in-hand, if the drinker was suitably incautious. Drinkers in the know would signal one another whenever the little man commenced his erratic rounds, 'JC's coming!' Warned and prepared, they waved JC away and the old man crow-voiced again, '*Nyerr-yae-ee-arrr, nyerrr-yae-eee-arrr!*' causing everyone around to clap their hands over their ears.

'C'mon darlin!' bellowed JC as he swept an unfinished gulp of wine out of the hand of a shrinking young woman; he was surprisingly agile. 'Pay yer Poll Tax darlin!' he advised her cheerily as she half-rose, her courage and indignation nearly but not quite strong enough to make her challenge the strange little intruder and demand her glass back. JC and the glass were gone. As she resumed her seat, Pilot Ken arrived at her table, placing a fresh glass of wine in front of her with a gesture of apology.

'Who... what is he?' asked the stunned newcomer to The Bat And Ball.

'He's JC,' said Ken, unhelpfully, returning to his table.

43

'Nyerr-yae-ee-arrr, nyerrr-yae-eee-arrr!'

JC was small and thin, grizzled, whiskered; he was certainly old, but how old? The parts of his face not covered with stringy grey hair and whiskers were dominated and distorted by his glasses, thick screens in which the entering light seemed to turn corners, turn again, again, and then become lost in shifting mists. Everyone who encountered JC remembered those glasses, the scraggy hair and trampish, disordered appearance, as well as the antique, dirty flat cap that topped the ensemble rain or shine, outdoors or in. But those impressions were overmastered by his near-constant smile, a bare-fang grin that injected a strange, shrinking feeling into nearly everyone. Those teeth were yellow-black, jagged and as daunting as rock-faces. His voice, too, was gargling, grating and angry-sounding even when he was in the grip of bonhomie, his tone and volume rose and fell without correlation to his words, which were often an incomprehensible garble as they crisscrossed in his mouth and fought their way over the broken mountain-range of teeth. He was given to outbursts, lengthy monologues, yells, mumbles, cries and peculiar exhortations, especially his favourite 'Pay yer Poll Tax!' All of this was patched together with laughter, which gurgled and glugged like boiling tar, a deeply joyless, distracted sound. There was a silly rumour that JC could see the future and that his was the laughter of vengeance, of celebration of the cruel fate that awaited all.

'Why's he called JC?'

'He was born on Christmas Day, so they say. God knows what year. And no one knows his real name, unless the initials are the last remnants of a lost identity. It's not that he isn't telling, he's forgotten.'

'Poor man.'

'He's just an old drunk. But he's harmless. Scares people though; specially children.'

'*Pay yer fuckin Poll Tax!*' bellowed JC, striking at a table on the other side of the pub, causing two people to spill their drinks in simultaneous, jerking alarm.

'Why's he say that?'

'Dunno. It may have been the last new thing ever to have penetrated his sozzled skull. The last signal he received from the modern world.'

'*Nyerr-yae-ee-arrr, nyerrr-yae-eee-arrr!*'

'JC, what is that god-awful noise you're making?' demanded Ken querulously as the old man drew near and everyone defended their drinks.

'Noise? It's singin! I works ere. I'm the singin pot-man!'

'You? Work?'

'I c'leckt enuff glasses, I gets a free drink from't bar. *Nyarr-yae-eer-aarrr!*'

'Go and sing somewhere else, will you?'

'I'm makin a joyful noise!'

'A noise, anyway.'

'You finis wi that?'

'Gerroutofit, JC!'

The Cabinet often discussed JC: he was a human puzzle, so what else was he for but solving? Yet he was clueless— and neither did he offer clues. A mystery-man, but mystery-men were supposed to be suave and appealing. The Bat and Ball's own walking enigma was a tatty bargain-basement offering, this shattered, bat-blind odoriferous old gimmer who couldn't—wouldn't?—part with his secrets. Any attempt would lead to the same performance—*woss-yer-name-sarah-jane-where-ja-live-dahn-the-grid-wass-yer-number-cucumber!*—accompanied by cackling gobbets of half-chewed laughter. But where did he live? Down the grid made a sort of sense—the gutter anyway.

But JC, unlike the many stories regarding Wayne, never spent a night in the gutter: he never went without a good meal either, and he always found his way to a hot drink too, or rather it found its way to him. He had no real friends and no family that anyone knew, and yet he was always looked after, looked-out-for. Word was that neighbours near and around the mysterious local-not-locality of *dahnthegrid* brought him foil-covered trays and plastic beakers that he couldn't break, and as the old man reeled home each night, grumbling, bellowing, singing, telling passersby, if there were any, to pay their fuckin Poll Tax, there was always someone who would guide him home or give him a lift, even convey him to hospital as was occasionally required, and this unofficial but highly efficient neighbourhood network not only expected no reward but also put up uncomplainingly with the frequent tantrums and abuse bestowed in return from their peculiar neighbour. Whenever I think, as I too-often do these days, that this town is becoming a cold, closed-off, mean and spiritually shrivelled hole, said Ken to himself, I shall try to remember JC's own little neighbourhood watchers and curb my cynicism.

Inevitably there were rumours that JC was an eccentric millionaire, and that his indefatigable helpers were merely hanging around in the hope of a handout, a tasty legacy, but of all the tales that circulated about JC, hidden riches featured amongst the unlikeliest. Some considered him malevolent and cunning, a cadger as well as a codger, a sponger who well knew what he was doing, living on the cheap by pulling at do-gooder heartstrings, gouging the gullible. While that was impossible, it was true that the old man had a malicious streak.

JC was a notorious gossip. He was ancient but not deaf, his ears keen-tuned to the embarrassments and misfortunes of others, friend or stranger, the excitements of which lured him out of his parallel world at least for a short time. He would muck-spread like a good old-fashioned farmer: when he gossiped he did so childishly, spitefully, cackling in his joy—and then forget, totally, cliff-dropping either to silence or back to his trademark Poll Tax cry. JC was saved from being a serious nuisance by the short goldfish loop of his mind—the information running through erasers. His

46

forgetting was always a mercy, and all you had to do was wait for the forbidden knowledge, along with the intense but passing thrill it afforded him, to tip out of the shallow bowl of his head. He existed in the now, and into an uncertain stretch of future time, but his past was a possession lost.

Question Five—JC's mind is indisputably broken—but who or what broke it?

The most-touted theory was that the old man was a soldier, a survivor of the conflict in the Far East in the 1940s, captured and tortured by the Japanese at the noon-height of their madness before cruel fire consumed their imperial dreams. The stories varied; that the youthful JC had been staked out in the hot sun in a bamboo plantation so that the light-seeking new growth would push against and then penetrate his body; that he had been crucified in sadistic mockery of his name, or had seen all these things done to his comrades, forced to watch as they screamed, groaned and died. The problem, Ken thought, apart from the general tinge of the apocryphal, was the maths: for JC to have fought in the Second World War he would have to be... it was impossible.

Tragedy, heartbreak, riches-to-rags bankruptcy, mad gambling, dispossession at the treacherous hand of someone he loved and trusted, ruin and prison—through that fuckin Poll Tax, perhaps? Did the old man's broken mind bear the indelible impression of the last hammer-blow to fall upon his head—or, if you like, the last boot up his backside? Other variants were rehearsed on the broad themes of disastrous downfall, or innocent witness of unbearable horror: people tried all explanations and combinations. Some claimed to know, and all were lying, or had believed liars.

'Nyerr-yae-ee-arrr, nyerrr-yae-eee-arrr! Nyerr-yae-ee-arrr, nyerrr-yae-eee-arrr!'

May I never become like him: please, never, please. To be talked about, guessed about, burdened with stories, laughed

47

at. He joins with the laughter but never understands its cruelty. A human ruin, a man who should be long-dead, but here every live-long day and showing every sign of outlasting us all. I could bear being forgotten, but not, please, not alive and self-forgotten, vanished but present, stripped of recall, unreflective, no life within, sometimes craving company through some vestigial social instinct, but never able to break my extreme, eccentric orbit, contact with others being incidental, tangential. I'm not afraid of JC, the idea is absurd, but I shrink from him, I can feel it within. I'm afraid, then, of being JC, of becoming like him.

It's the forgetting; that's his protection, his power over us, the reason why, when we are gone and this town has been bulldozed, JC will emerge from the ruins enjoining people to pay their Poll Tax, on the lookout for a drink.

If he really is sheltering from some deep, un-faceable shock, we have no right to call him back to it. Least of all to satisfy our pub-table curiosity, or settle an idle bet. But why, in this nosey, your-business-is-mine town, does nobody know the answers?

Question Six—Who let Mal take the bloody answer sheet to the bar?

They lost to Ooaryer: it was a long time before Gina forgave Ken.

Uxorio

A Frank Speke adventure

'Noel, comfortably married—overly? Eight letters. That's a bit of a sod,' muttered Pilot Ken, drumming his pen on his chin.

'Got any letters yet?' Jim leaned over to take a look.

'Ends in an s—not too helpful.'

'What are they after—name? Noel someone? Or is it about Christmas?'

'There's only twenty-five letters of the alphabet at Christmas, cos the angel said no-l,' chipped in Frank Speke.

'Brilliant—you've done it!' Ken cried in triumph, with a florid flourish of the waiting pen.

'What?'

'It's a word that begins with an l, or rather I'm looking for another word, one that appears if you knock off the l, massage the vowel...'

'What's the married bit about? A red herring?'

'No... it's... comfortable... married... overly... god, yes, it's...'

Ken beat his pen in the air like a baton, and then wrote out the word: 'U-x-o-r-i-o-u-s'. Frank Speke tapped the freshly-inked paper.

'Meaning?' he asked; and as the word was explained, Frank Speke's face was filled with light, in the manner of mountain crags in the dawn.

'Brilliant—you've done it!' shouted Frank Speke to Pilot Ken, who gave him the intimidated, humiliated, rising-angry look of someone who has been closely and uncomfortably, mimicked. Frank, with unusual sensitivity, gestured reassurance to Ken, who was comforted that Frank was sharing, not mocking, his ecstatic inspiration.

'That's his name—old *happy*-man—too proud, too fond of his wife—Uxorio!'

Frank Speke did not like to waste time in forming an opinion of someone. He saw no point. He would size and sum up an individual or group swiftly, tagging him or her or them with what could be called a pre-label; he would then offer comment in accordance with that, and reluctantly adapt his view if emerging facts prayed against it. He prided himself on rarely having to stray too far from any pre-label. For instance, his first impression of Pilot Ken had been that the man was a smartarse. Frank Speke had revised this view somewhat, but it was by no means withdrawn, and Frank noted to himself every time Ken's conduct justified his pre-label. For instance, he could be just a bit too smug-triumphant when he hit on an inspired solution to an Across or Down. Frank had Jim for a mincer at first glance, even before Jim's loud self-declarations he was unimpressed by Jim's unconvincing straight-acting and the defensive elisions and evasions of the others. Emily had told Frank that Jim wanted to make sure that he could be trusted with the truth, which Frank found offensive on the grounds not of presumed prejudice, but because it should be clear to all from first principles that Frank Speke knows the truth and does not have to be spoon-fed. As for Emily, nice enough girl but a coddler of causes-lost, forever shying from reality's harsh glare. Little Mal was all too often the reason those causes were lost, Frank disdained his poisonous works. Gina? She and her seldom-seen husband urgently needed either some nice, trendy counselling or a bloody stiff talking-to, and that was flat.

'Frank takes against people right away—it saves time,' Pilot Ken would say lightheartedly; both a justification of his pre-label and unoriginal, though Frank couldn't recall quite from where Ken was borrowing.

Frank's view of his activities was rather different; he was not 'taking against' anyone, he was simply stating truths which, if he did not, would remain imprisoned in silent neglect. Frank had a sense of mission, plus faith in the determinative power of his name: it was his purpose, destiny, to speak out, clearly, boldly. Naturally and annoyingly, Pilot Ken had to weigh in.

'Aren't you just saying what you please no matter how bloody offensive it is? Is that really free speech? What about there being no right to shout fire…'

'Yes, yes, yes, Oliver Wendell Whatsit.' Frank adopted a weary got-the-tee-shirt tone, he had slapped down many a Holmesean objector. 'But I'm not claiming the right to spread false alarms or gossip or slanders or stupid rumours, I'm claiming the right to reveal the truth, and, all right, along the way the right to call a pillock a pillock.'

Frank's dislikes became a conversation-piece at Pilot Ken's table, which Frank didn't mind, providing he could satisfy everyone that he had never subjected *them* to such treatment. He took particular exception to an on-off 5 to 6pm drinker whose pre-label was Too-Happy, the short version of a nickname-in-progress. Sometimes it was 'The Happy Man'; but his full title, as declared by Frank Speke in his ironic crow's tone, was 'The Happiest Man In The World'. 'Too-Happy' was never a part of the regular gathering, none of them knew his name, none had exchanged a word with him. He was a man observed from a distance, discussed and *theorised* about—by Frank Speke alone.

'God Above, there it is again, that pink self-satisfied babyface, it looks like it never needs a shave, you just want to *slap* it: the bloody boy who never grew up and never will! He comes for a weak half-pint after doing too few hours for way too much, to boast to his mates and lord it over them and us and to use his ingratiating, disarming grin so no one minds too much that he's treading them in to the mud. You can just tell no one has ever said "no" to him, luck falls in his lap and money into his pocket, he's happily married and can't stop being smug about it, the woman will be well out of his league, looks and class-wise, though she's bound to have a fat arse—no offence, Emily—and everyone but him will know she's too good for him. They've got kids and

51

they're *just like him*, just horrible new versions, and he boasts about them, how cute they are, how clever they are, how they will dominate the world in some all-too-far-off day when he's too decrepit to do it; they will carry on the line in all possible ways: they get their looks from their mummy, but their brains and their damned cocky attitude from him—of course. He's always had immaculate luck, much as he doesn't deserve it. He was the Good Boy sent round the school by his teacher to show off his perfect work, Employee of the Month Eternal, who fluked into a high-fly job without flapping a wing, who may make mistakes but never gets the blame. He'll pile up money, produce progeny, dominate and then die in bed, surrounded by a loving family who are just as appalling as him and who will go forth and multiply, foisting his icky legacy upon the world. And you *know* he's got pudgy boyscout knees. How I hate people with pudgy knees.'

As the tone of Frank's anti-Uxorio propaganda grew more frenzied, laughter, that of rising hysteria through repetition and expectation, grew around Ken's table; it was like waiting, knife-edge, for a favourite comedian to crack the killer catch-phrase. Frank did not obsess about Uxorio, well, not all the time: when the man was not in the pub, which was most of the time, he went unthought and unmentioned—he ceased to be. But as soon as his pinkish face bobbed into view, off Frank went.

'I bet, I just *bet*, that he used those very words, *the happiest man in the world*, as he stood and made his speech at the overdressed top table at his too-bloody-expensive bloody wedding. And that he's still using it, regularly, when he wants to impress—and turn stomachs.'

'Supposing he says it, what if he means it, what if it's nothing more or less than the truth?' asked Gina.

'Makes it even bloody worse!'

Frank regarded Gina as another star-struck romantic, her and her invisible husband.

'The happiness of others brings you out in a rash, doesn't it Frank?' Gina's eyes crinkled, she intended no cruelty.

'Happy Rash...' mused Jim. Everyone but Frank laughed; he did not appreciate this counterwave of jollity, it threw him sufficiently to allow Pilot Ken to insert another objection.

'Frank, I just don't see what's wrong with the man. Him and his mates, they're... well, just like us, not drunks, not pests, not bloody gatemouths who talk bollocks loudly; they just come in, have a drink, chat, laugh, do no harm and then go off again. What's so wrong? He's completely inoffensive.'

'That is what is so... *offensive.*'

'I'm minded to go over there and just *ask* the man what he's all about. Coming?'

'You'll do no such thing!'

'Against the rules of the game, Frank?'

'Very much. I like to be proved right in the fullness of time, not by shortcuts. It'd be like you using one of those cheat-machines to solve a crossword. Oh, and you're not allowed to find out via Mand, don't try that trick neither.'

Everyone enjoyed Frank's ecumenical spite—male, female, black, white, young, old, none were safe, they were pre-labelled and processed: but Frank never picked soft targets; he never attacked JC, for instance, who offered himself for mockery. In fact Frank was one of the old man's strongest defenders. He never attacked Rob The Writer, who had won a short story competition way back when, but paused his writing career there and then, inspiration draining, next bottle please. Rob looked ex-military— shabby military—can you be chucked out of the army for shabbiness?—if so it was that and drink. Rob spoke with the plum-mouth of an old-fashioned actor, and in The Bat And Ball he sounded posh, his appearance and voice of a man who doesn't belong. He sat apart, not writing, not reading, not watching people or listening, observing the business of life, but after all, a writer can be working hard while apparently doing nothing. Rob had a dogeared, jaundiced copy of that story in the inside pocket of his jacket, next to his heart, and if you asked to see it, he would unfold it and offer it shyly; and it was a good story, possibly based on experience, of soldiers waiting to die in battle who after a cold-sweat build-up are then told, 'Come on boys, we're going home'. It made you wonder at just what promise Rob the Writer had pickled; was there a pile of paper to be found, tales of battling booze, life eking out a puny pension in a tatty flat, the fear of eviction, the letterbox rattling with final demands, the door shuddering under the blows of bailiffs' fists; or would Rob sublimate into alcoholic fumes, leaving nothing? A could-have-been, an internalising, silent, collapsing drunk, a gentle, desperate ghost and his untold tales. There was plenty to attack, but Frank demurred.

As Frank's old man had always insisted, you don't mock the afflicted: it was, however, a different order of things to mock the affected. And when Frank decided he needed to speak, he did—he considered that most of humanity needed telling, and telling hard and quick.

'What demons are you battling, Frank, that you need to be like this about people?' God, Pilot Ken was a smartarse. Never had a pre-label been more apt.

'My only "demon" is the truth. People must be told the truth—about themselves, most of all.'

'For their own good?'

'Yes, Ken. And for the good of us all.' Frank couldn't conceal his irritation, why did the man have to be like this? Ken, for all his crossword-solver guesswork, was wrong; Frank was not struggling with a demon. He contended with The Imp.

Frank's self-belief was absolute. Harsh as he may be, Frank Speke was a benefactor, a public defender. Yet still there was The Imp. He knew that it was there and that its aims were different to his, sometimes complementary, sometimes directly inimical. The Imp wanted to test boundaries, and not just that, it sought to break them; it rose with his gorge, and from a presence in his mind it took physical manifestation as a churning in his stomach, a burning in his chest, a raised heartbeat, a throbbing in the head. It tried to use, abuse, his ability to speak out, to say the unsayable; it attempted to commandeer his voice, force open his mouth, and make him say what should not be said—which was a different thing from the unsayable. He felt its vicious, stinging pleasure whenever it forced him to let himself down, to hit and hurt out of spite only. Had it a voice of its own, The Imp would doubtless have argued that its aims and Frank's were inseparable, they both wished to tell people what they did not wish to hear. The Imp, however, was bereft of any proportion—indeed, for its purposes, the more hurt and argument the merrier. Frank Speke was independent, truthful, careful, measured, sincere, regretful of necessary pain. To all of this, The Imp said 'Sod That', it sought weaknesses to exploit, scorning Frank's ideals, sullying his voice. Frank would feel and act just as did The Imp—were he not, it chided, so appallingly weak. Perhaps, just perhaps, Frank sympathised with The Imp a little, a little too much, and this was why he sometimes struggled to resist it.

Ken's objections to his attacks on Uxorio troubled Frank—to the extent that he worried who was speaking, himself or his malignant other. But each time he thought on it, Frank was satisfied that no line had been crossed, no one but himself was in command of his voice, and that although on this occasion he was not exactly speaking truth to power, he was attacking one of the invisible hegemons who ran the world, the self-confident got-it-alls.

Stifled giggles rippled around Ken's table as Uxorio entered the Bat and Ball once more, and everyone cocked an ear, willingly or otherwise, to await Frank's next outburst. Like a seasoned trouper, he made them wait a while before starting the main performance. He was also testing to ensure the absence of The Imp.

'You will take note that I never look directly at the man,' lectured Frank, 'I never let him notice that he has been noticed. I employ the old astronomer's trick of using averted vision—keep your gaze off-centre and you can pick up detail that would be otherwise concealed. I see all, I see him, through him. And he doesn't know a thing about it.'

'If he doesn't know,' dropped in Jim, 'Why did he come up to me last week and ask me who is that ugly, malevolent old git who keeps giving him dirty looks across the pub?'

'He said nothing of the sort, James.' Frank kept up a bantering tone, but Pilot Ken noticed that Frank, for a tiny moment, *flinched*: the reason would have to wait till later.

'Now—do you see that sloppy bloody cardigan he's wearing? It says "married man, married man, happily bloody married man," dinning it into us loud enough to deafen. It's smugness in its most revolting form. I cannot stand a man who advertises his sodding contentment so blatantly! That bloody cardy-wearing contentment, it makes me *itch*, uncomfortable, restless, filled with the desire to wipe the bloody smiles off the bloody faces of him and all his kind. *This* is a man who indulges in stupid self-conscious romantic rituals; he calls to his wife as he comes through the door, laughs "Kisses, Mrs!" and puckers his lips like a chicken's bloody bum—so does she—and they peck, oh god, it's revolting! He calls her "the wifie" and she simpers, he makes coy noises and uses cutesy-pie euphemisms when he wants a fuck, cooing like a dove, he...'

'Frank...' Pilot Ken was growing a little weary among the music-hall laughter.

'Ahh, shut yer neck yer spoilsport smartarse,' snapped The Imp, who was having too much fun to allow interruptions.

'Suits and ties, no faces, no eyes.' Frank-Imp never wasted any more time or words than these on Uxorio's companions. They all arrived after office hours in smart work clothes to spend an hour chatting in over-loud voices before driving home—having drunk responsibly, of course—to their lookalike families in lookalike suburban estates: the better-paid, Uxorio amongst them, would repair

56

to their expensive des res in the more sought-after of the Ring O'Villages, from which they would pour scorn on the town and its populace, always assuming they gave thought at all to anything outside their four walls and the evening's needs. Frank repaid the scorn of them all, concentrating it, sun-lensing it, to their leader with his perfect life and pudgy knees.

'Have you considered it yourself, Ken?' Jim cast a playful sideways glance. 'Uxoriating I mean? Did you ever consider making an honest—if frankly quite bizarre—woman of those old girlfriends of yours?'

'No; it never occurred. Honestly. Besides, any attractive woman already has a husband called Ian. It's an iron rule of life.'

'Theory alert!' Jim warned.

'Are you saying that a woman isn't attractive unless...' Emily cut in with theatrical huffiness.

'There are exceptions of course...'

'To an iron rule? You charmer you.' She tossed her head magnificently.

'Anyway... I throw the ball to you James.'

'His sort is *not permitted* to marry,' growled Frank Speke gracelessly.

'Yet!' Jim grinned brightly. 'Anyway; me, married? I can never keep up with who I'm with, I forget names, I use serial numbers: "Ah, tonight it's darling 540263/ZX!"'

'You shouldn't despair of wedding bells for yourself Kenny,' Frank interrupted. 'Mand would snap you up, I'm sure of it.'

'Or just snap him,' Jim added.

'Gina—is it to be recommended?'

'She's got the ideal marriage: she never bloody sees him.'

Gina assumed an inscrutable expression and said nothing; Ken was quick to divert attention from her.

'And what about you, Em? Are you and Nev in a Yes-No or No-Yes phase?'

Emily wrinkled her nose and took a gulp of her wine. 'A maybe-maybe phase. I'll get back to you.'

Frank was tactfully left out of the round of questions. But had his own principles been applied to him, thought Ken, the old grouch could scarcely have complained.

Uxorio went unseen, and so unmentioned, for a long period, and even then, it was his friends and not he who appeared at the Bat and Ball. Jim arrived from his own work-related long absence and negotiated his way to Ken's table through a small crowd at the bar.

'Everyone okay for a drink? Hey, what's all the posh duds for over there? They're a bit quiet for a wedding.' It took Jim a moment to register that Pilot Ken was also in what could be described as more-posh-than-his-usual duds, and that the well-dressed woman beside him was not Gina or Emily as it would have been on an ordinary day, but a near-unrecognisable Evil Mand, liberated for once from the bar and her shawl, a neatly turned-out customer in her own pub.

'Correct,' said Pilot Ken quietly, 'it's the other reason for posh-duds wearing.'

'Oh,' whispered Jim, sitting himself down and trying to shrink his huge frame in apology for his misplaced bonhomie.

People often dropped into the pub, which was the nearest to St Matt's Church, for what Ken called a pre-funeral wake. They often returned for a pre-wake wake. Uxorio's friends, never ones to stray beyond their bubble-group, were cleaving closer than ever to their accustomed territory, eyes cast down, smiles tight, fleeting and rare.

'You haven't asked whose funeral it is.' Evil Mand was eyeing Frank Speke, who had arrived not long before Jim, and was looking, Jim thought, shifty.

'What's it to me?' growled Frank, but his voice betrayed a guilty timbre; not that he had done anything to merit the feeling, but...

'There's a story to all of this.' Mand's voice had an edge too.

'I'm not much for stories, never was.' Frank didn't even convince himself. An emptiness within told him The Imp had deserted him—for now, at least.

'Well, here's the story anyway. We only learned it today. It's remarkably like the one you've been spinning here for all this time; you should be pleased; you've been very acute. His name was Lyle. I knew that, from talking to him at the bar, but I never knew the rest. He was as much in love with his wife as you thought, Frank, he talked about her all the time, he'd stop off for a pint with his pals but he couldn't wait to get home. His wife, his kids, his home, they were everything. He loved his wife and trusted her, he was wide-open, everything revolved around them, a whole personal atom-universe.

'Lately, he was only ever here for a quick drink, if he came at all, because he was rushing back home to look after the kids. His wife was taking turns with her sister, going off for a few days at a time looking after their mum, who's ill, fading fast, those friends of his say. He'd keep things running while she was away, and he'd wait for her to come back and for everything to be normal and wonderful again. One night she was due home but she wasn't back when he got there, the kids were at her sister's, and even her sister didn't know where she was. She remained missing, her phone was on but she didn't answer it no matter who called or how often, they were all worried: he'd only just put down the phone to the Police when his wife reappeared. She'd come for her belongings, some ready-packed, hidden. She'd spent some of the time with her mother, but also spent a fortune on paying private carers, all as a cover for her... carryings-on. She'd "met someone", a pure fluke it seems, their eyes encountering across a crowded room, god knows what clichés in the air, but before long those visits away were visits to him, not to poor mother, and the pair used their time to decide what to do with their inconvenient spouses. On the day she disappeared, the man-friend had dumped his wife, so she was ready to get rid of

'Uxorio.' Frank spoke as if the word was forced out of him: impelled.

'Who?'

'Never mind, and let me say how much I respect your delicacy of expression Mand. "Carryings-on"—very fetching. Like your outfit.'

'Sod off, Frank.'

'That's more you.'

'And don't try to distract me again, you're getting the story whether you want it or not, mush. So—she fronts up at home and he, who's suspected nothing, is trying to work out if this is a joke, hoping he's not watching his universe falling apart in fast-forward, but realising, quick as you like, that that's just what is going on. And as he tries to stay calm, fight off the desire to fall to his knees and scream, she drags off her bags to her car and tosses over her shoulder that she loves him but she's never been "in love" with him, whatever that means; she *is* "in love" with this new bloke; she sheds a few tears, packs her car and...

'A week later she comes back for the kids. He calls her, texts her, begs, pleads non-stop; he offers her anything she wants, even to "go to mediation or arbitration" to save their marriage as if that's some form of magic potion: she wants nothing to do with any of it, she's in her new world, got what she wants, and that isn't him. He takes to his bed, shock, he's not fit to look after himself never mind the kids, doesn't lift a finger, can't, and that's it, he's alone. Friends come round one day to see how he is, but he's already done it.'

'Done it?'

'Use your common savvy, Jim.'

'Good grief.'

'So, Frank—did he deserve it? Did he bring it all on himself with his intolerable smugness?'

Frank decided not to comment: if Mand then chose to misinterpret his silence as shame, it was her problem. No doubt they all felt shame in some way, or would when they heard the ending of the tale; all the regulars who'd laughed immoderately at his sallies, even smarty-Ken had cracked a smile occasionally. But Frank would not entertain shame: he had been right in all essentials, spoken the truth to shame a particular sort of devil, and what had happened between Uxorio and his wife was not a part of it, nor was its fall-out of Frank's wishing or doing. He hadn't called for a reckoning, but simply pushed aside a veil. Admittedly he also did not feel satisfied; this was no triumph, he had not remained in charge, had allowed The Imp too great a licence to distract himself and, worse, everyone else, from the seriousness of his purpose. Perhaps that was something to reflect on. Later. Frank, then, had nothing to say, but the story had stirred something in The Imp.

'Mediation! Arbitration! Pah!' it spat, angrily.

'There's only one positive thing we can draw from this sad business,' sighed Jim.

'What the hell might that be?' Ken's tone was querulous, anticipating.

'You should marry Mand, you looked smashing together today. Let's have a happy ending, let love triumph over betrayal.'

'Who says I love Mand?'

'Everyone.'

How Jim became a fully-qualified giant

Jim's face and voice were those of a man declaring war; his other actions, flowery gestures emphasising the rapid wiggling of his little finger, were scarcely consonant with this.

'I,' he boomed grandly, 'am going to buy a pinkie-ring. For that is the one thing that will say, loud and clear: *I Am A Poof!*'

'Must you?' protested Frank Speke in a groan, his hand cradling his forehead.

'Yes,' said Ken decisively, 'he must. Now shush Frank, or we'll all ask why this always upsets you so much. Loudly.'

'I just don't like people making a *spectacle* of…'

'I said shush.'

Frank shushed. Temporarily. Emily, who happened to be there, leaned over and kissed Jim on the cheek. Gina, who happened not to be there, would certainly have done the same. Jim wasn't normally one for making any kind of spectacle of himself. From time to time, however, he felt the need to restate his qualifications as a giant.

Although he had all the appearance of a giant—albeit a wholly benign and non-bone-grinding one, nearer seven feet than six, broad-built, bearded, imposing, basso-voiced, he looked like a man who was ready at any moment to set off to capture grizzlies with his bare hands, it was as if he lacked something yet. 'The big bloke', 'the large feller' was all he tended to be called, 'That stiff youth,' said the friend of a friend, and Jim was not best pleased when he learned what 'stiff' meant in that visitor's part of the world. Emily once fled crimson-faced to the cool protection of the Ladies when she said, without the least smutty intent, that Jim was 'big all over'. The mockery merely paused in her absence, waited with predatory politeness, and revived joyously once she returned to sit opposite Jim, their cheeks a-blush like lovers discovered.

While he gave Emily no quarter at the time, Pilot Ken conceded that, truth be known, she had a point, especially once he had heard a particular tale from Jim, which made it clear that Jim truly was a fully-qualified giant, and had been for a long time. Not only was he a physical giant, but he had long ago achieved gianthood on many other planes also. Once he knew, Ken told Jim that he could tell his tale any time he wished, he could repeat it every day if he desired; some tales are worth telling and retelling, they never tire.

It was many years before Jim had met Ken and the others; not much more than teenage, new to town, alone and tender-green, looking like a juniors rugby player, he had been working some miles out and, too broke to own a car, far from a bus route or train line, had to catch a taxi back to his digs. The driver was friendly and gabblingly garrulous, unable to interpret or uninterested in the signs from a dog-tired and silent Jim. The driver divined straight away that his passenger was a newcomer, and he delighted in delivering a detailed tourist's guide of the highlights and lowlifes of the locale as they passed this spot, or that one loomed ahead: his talk spilled over Jim like radio DJ patter; matey, unrelenting, annoying, but Jim eased somewhat when he realised that the driver's many questions were entirely rhetorical, and that answers would have surprised him and spoiled his flow.

They came to a halt at a junction just outside town, and as he waited impatiently for the lights to change, the driver gestured sharply at an unpromising-looking clump of prefab buildings that looked as if they were the hideouts of dying enterprises, gloomily awaiting bailiffs and liquidators.

'See over there? Look, where I'm pointing.' Jim shook himself and obeyed, surprised that his participation was now required.

'Somewhere over there is the fucking Poof Palace they've just opened. Our goody-twoshoes Council has just given a bunch of willy wooftas thousands of pounds, thousands— to have a queers' club over there. Now come on, queers can be queer all they fuckin like, but why should they do it using *my* money? Why should I subsidise perverts, eh? They say they wanna be equal, but that int "equal" is it? Some people say we oughter go up there with a few baseball bats, show em what we think of their "equality".'

'Turn left here,' said Jim.

'Eh? Thought you said Barnet Field? That's…'

'I know. Turn left. Then next-left next-right.'

Both men lapsed into tense silence.

The cab drew up outside one of the unprepossessing buildings, a shuttered, anonymous semi-wreck that only lacked a 'Condemned' sign. Jim extricated himself from the cab with difficulty, as if he had expanded in height and girth during the ride. He went to the driver's window, fiddled with his wallet, paid in exact money, then laid his hand upon the driver's door, a friendly-looking gesture at first but then with a tightening grip, whitening knuckles, as if refusing to let the driver wind up his window and depart.

'This,' announced Jim in as steady a voice as he could manage, 'is your Poof Palace. The only place where I can get a drink and meet people in perfect peace and never worry about some twat coming at me with a baseball bat or just a mouthful of abuse, someone who hates me and my kind, hates totally and blindly, never knowing why. Oh, and it was a loan. And it was two thousand pounds, bit less actually, business start-up stuff. And it's been repaid, with interest. "Your" money is safe, in fact you're up on the deal, why not go and ask for your cut? Oh, and, just in case you're thinking of it now, you know where we are, we've got baseball bats too, we'll use em, especially if we catch anyone else trying to firebomb the place like some stupid inadequates tried last week. Don't try us. Okay?'

The driver, his patter switched firmly off, said nothing: Jim's question, like most of the driver's, invited no answers. The driver unlocked his gaze from Jim's and there was a too-loud clack as he put the cab into gear.

'Wait a minute. I've got something more to tell you.'

The driver opened his mouth, but Jim cut across his protests.

'I've something to tell you. It won't take long.'

But it did. And the driver remained there, engine purring low, until Jim was ready to dismiss him, held fast by one strong hand.

I was young, sixteen maybe, and doing a holiday job. Mick, who worked at the next bench, gave off a strong, manly smell, a powerful odour that drew me to him. I mentioned it to the others in the workshop, remarking that to me he smelled like a horse. I like horses.

'Like horse-shit, you mean,' Ginner would say, Mick's neighbour.

'Horse shit!' sniggered Scott, next along, always repeating the last thing said.

'Don't take the piss.' The testy interjection came from Arthur: we called him The Gaffer. 'He's a good worker, puts his back into it; that's the smell of work, that is. You should respect it.'

They didn't know what was really on my mind, Mick least of all.

It had only been two weeks and my mind was full of Mick. But I'd learned what's what pretty fast, I could keep my mouth shut and try to give off no signals: couldn't stop myself sneaking glances at Mick, though. I prayed he just thought I was checking his technique at the bench as I learned more about the job, but I was watching the muscles and sinews in his arm as he pushed and strained against his work, thinking of that torso that could earn him a fortune as a model. I'd have loved to see him clad only in tight white undies—*calm down, I thought, I've got to calm down.* Can I really-really fancy a guy who, according to Ginner, 'Buys his B.O. in bottles from Satan himself? Mick hadn't got much to say, and when he did speak up it was generally not worth hearing, but I tried to tune out the actual words and jog along with the sea-deep tone of his voice. Another five weeks and I could relax; no more job, no more Mick, and no fear of someone blowing the gaff on me.

The lads didn't know; some blokes just aren't much good at spotting the signs, and for that, at this time, I was grateful. He wouldn't have let me anywhere near him if he'd known. Tragic but true, I always know how to choose a wrong un. But don't imagine I was pining, touching neither food nor drink for love of Mick; no, it was just a passing lust, I'd got used to them. I slept, ate and drank well and, yes thank you, was getting plenty of the other too. It was just that the best ones always seemed to have this woman-fixation, dammit. When you're covering something up, it's always on your mind, you're afraid you're going to give it away, you examine everything you say and do, everything said and done by everyone else too. And this is where women come in—as a problem. The men were blind, but some of the women know, and, worse, are determined to give me away. Some were fascinated with me, they hung around the factory gates waiting, wanted to chat me up, seemed to want to mother me, others wanted to... oh god. They goosed me as I went by, then they laughed, shrieking, piercing shrapnel-laughter; were they mocking or did they want me to join in the fun? I just didn't know. It was a game to some, but others, I feared, were serious. 'You're a shy one!' they'd shout in the canteen. 'I'll bring im out of imself!' yelled one, and they all shrieked again. I'm not shy, but in front of them I hadn't a frigging clue. I confess part of me adored the attention, but I was afraid of what they might call attention *to*. Superficially, I seemed to have my pick of the girls, yet didn't go out with any of them. What would that say to the lads in the workshop?

I'd already encountered trouble and misunderstanding. One girl, a genuinely quiet and shy individual, had a crush on me; I could feel her eyes (as Mick might mine) and knew in my heart that she was dreaming romantic, half-desperate little dreams. I knew it because I'd dreamed them too, almost like for like. I felt for her, but what could I do? And worse—bloody love triangle, wasn't it?—she'd got her own admirer, one who was not at all pleased with me. I found this out when Mick beckoned me aside and ushered me to a store room just off the workshop. He sat me down on a stack of boxes. Speaking of romantic, or straightforwardly sexy, dreaming, I smelt his body and imagined making hot, fast love to him in that narrow room—but Mick's mind was firmly elsewhere.

'Look mate,' he said awkwardly, embarrassed and unskilled with words but determined, 'I don't want to interfere or nothing, but I've got for warn you. I hope it don't make you angry.'

'Mick, I don't think I could ever be angry with you.'

I'll come straight to the point. Get your top off! 'Like I said, I need warn yer. I dunno what you think of Sarah Carter, but even I can see she's virtually made her bed up for you. S'up to you what you do, but you need to know that Ginner's got is eye on her: mad for her, he is. Now he's so fuckin thick he thinks all those little glances she shoots at us lot at dinnertime are for him, but I know better, sunbeam. I can read a woman. It's you she's after and if you go for it, good luck to yer. But Ginner won't be appy, and if I've learned one thing workin here it's that you don't piss Ginner off. Ever. That's all mate; I just thought you ought know.'

I nodded and hoped the gesture was manly and understanding, and then slipped out of the room leaving Mick lurking, as if we were covering up for a genuine liaison.

Sarah Carter is a sweetie, I reckoned, *she can do better than this place for both work and a man*, but some of the other girls didn't seem so sweet to me. They couldn't leave me alone, they considered me a challenge. Ain't he pretty?' they'd call, as if talking about a baby, 'Come on give us a smile!' One ran up and gave me a fierce hug and a kiss on the cheek, at which I writhed, trying to escape.

'Oooh, you're a queer one aren't you?' she pealed, and then it was, 'Oohahah, sorry luvvie!'

Was she toying? Was it malice or just playfulness, well-meaning teasing? It kept me permanently on-edge. How much did they know? If Mick could read women so easily, could they read men equally well and spot the misfit? Could they translate my body-language or follow my eyes to a tight crotch, a good arse or pair of pecs, could they see how my erotic x-ray vision went dead at the sight of a woman? *How much did they know?* Five weeks to avert my unmasking, either by catastrophic accident or the action of some clever git. I covered up because… because it wasn't anyone else's business, was it? The one time I did tell, a woman at university I considered a close friend, a confidante, she listened in icy silence and then said, 'That's your problem!' We're not friends any more, though she remains distantly polite, and at least she won't split on me. About that I don't know whether to be grateful or murderously angry. And so, if I can't tell a friend, why would I tell strangers?

The lads in the shop were always on about girls—what they did with them, or would do, and they were always helpfully pointing out 'nice pieces' for my delectation, especially the ones with big tits. Luckily, I like big tits too, lots of gay boys do, so I could play along using this as cover; I know I shouldn't have, but it gave me time to think, at least.

I was considering deepening my cover by inventing a girlfriend, a sort of Frankenstein-woman made up of discarded fragments of the others' conversations, but I was unsure whether or not this tactic would blow up in my face. What if they wanted to meet her? What if they tried to follow me on one of my alleged dates? Christ, that'd wake em up. They were always on about women, always putting their dirtiest thoughts into the crudest, most infantile language. Mick liked Sarah Carter too, and he said, not in front of Ginner, 'Fuckin ell I'd love to do her. I'd grease her dirt-box for her alright!' Childish. Incredible. Fucking sexy, coming from him: *I must never get drunk in Mick's presence, I swear I'll kiss him, just to get a reaction.*

And besides women, guess what was the other regular, compulsive topic of conversation at the work benches and in the canteen? Oh yes, it wasn't just me who was obsessed about it:

'Know what I read?' asked Mick during one break, not looking at anyone.

'You've advanced to *Janet and John*? Well done son,' said Ginner with a nasty laziness.

'Fuck off. No, I've seen in the paper how one in five of us is fuckin queer. One in five! Fuckin ell.' He thought for a moment and then pointed a lamb-chop finger, counting off the men at the table.

'One.' (himself)

'Two.' (Scott)

'Three.' (Arthur)

'Four.' (Me!)

'Five!' The finger was pointing stiffly at Ginner.

'Fuck off, Micky-boy!' he snarled.

'But it *has* to be!' As far as Mick was concerned, he had carried out a fair count, and the numbers couldn't be wrong. Ginner didn't put him right on the correct use of statistics or proper representative samples, he offered to kick his fuckin head in outside if that was what he wanted. Mick, the man who had warned me not to piss Ginner off, made a grunting sort of apology and the one-in-five thing was forgotten, thank fuck.

I could see why you shouldn't piss Ginner off. There was a lot of Ginner, and most of it in the wrong place. There was not so much of him below the belt (and I suspected that to be true in a variety of ways), but once his spindly legs had climbed up and developed into starved-drumstick thighs and a flabby but somehow meatless arse, he exploded into flesh. His—*ahem*—waistline drooped over his belt, and I mean all round, three hundred and sixty degrees, and his entire upper body wobbled alarmingly with the slightest movement. He had three or four chins, which multiplied into dozens if he lowered his head, perhaps in concentration over his work, and—the man had tits. Quite feminine, round, with a cleavage, and ending in distinct points. *He could have someone's eye out with those*. Although he was an inveterate scruff, he must have chosen with care what he was going to wear, otherwise there'd be some embarrassing nipple-peek going on. But then we come to his arms—and therein lay all of his power: great muscular hawsers, tattooed, thick, rippling, with no spare flesh anywhere. The rest of him was shaped like some enormous mushroom, but then, these perfect arms. If he were like that all over, I'd have been interested, but on second thoughts, no, I'd never trouble Ginner by fancying him. In fact, even if the rest of his body had done the trick, oh, the face! I don't like men who are toothless at thirty, especially not ones who are proud of it. Ugh.

So Ginner and Mick didn't get on too well, but they were agreed on the shop's second-favourite subject: Poofs. Queens. Queers. Arse Bandits. Turd Burglars. 'Backs to the wall!' they'd shout, at the very thought: Christ, what did they think we do? Sneak up behind the unsuspecting and ram our dicks up their smelly arses in the hope of a bit of rough fun? Didn't they think the average *bummos bandido* (yes, very inventive, Ginner) might want something other, something better? And why, for Christ's sake, do men like Ginner automatically assume we want to fuck *them*? Okay, there's a slight flaw in my argument if you consider how I felt about Mick, but the point stands.

I'd expected something better from Arthur. 'Stalwart' was the best word for him; he'd been at the works over thirty years. I wondered what sins he committed in a past life to earn the fate; it was no place to remain so long, the work was useful, but drainingly dull. The erotic Mick once summed it up as 'We Do Things To Things'. That ought to have been our motto and escutcheon, emblazoned over the workshop door and tattooed on our chests. But Arthur was devoted to his craft, he would never leave. He was the archetype of fidelity, espousing what he called 'shop loyalty'.

In this, all of us in the workshop were honour-bound to look after one another; we worked together, took breaks, ate our snappin (Arthur's word) together, and on-many nights went to the boozer too. It was wonderful, shop loyalty, and not just because it meant I got to spend more pulse-pounding minutes eyeing and nosing Mick. As a new and green worker, you were never left alone, never left stranded or dropped in it. You were protected from being picked on or sent for tins of striped paint or boxes of sky-hooks or whatever other bloody silly initiation tricks. Arthur wouldn't let anyone take advantage, and the lads were solid in his support.

The ultimate problem with shop loyalty, though, was that it was a trap. You moved from your workbench to a rickety table at the canteen at break times, then swapped that for an unshiftable beer-stained, bolted-down monster in the evening, and you gazed at the same faces all day and more. *From that, I'll be glad to get away when the time comes, although I'll need to advertise for a new tenant to occupy my fantasies.* But Arthur meant well; I liked Arthur; the sterling sort of steady, dependable bloke, not an unintelligent man, but perhaps unambitious, who finds a niche and stays, contentedly, a steadying influence on younger, more volatile workers, a court of appeal for workshop disputes; without him I reckon Mick and Ginner would have battered each other out of existence. His idea of shop loyalty was all-consuming; thinking I was doing the right thing, I asked him about joining a Trade Union. 'What fer?' was his mildly surprised reply. We called him 'Gaffer', but he had no real power; he had the job-title of 'supervisor' or something like that, but it was his personality, not the imprimatur of the management, that endowed him with his authority and won him respect.

He was fifty, an elderly, craggy fifty, with a diffident way of talking that made his occasional diktats yet more authoritative. When chatting, he had a mannerism of emphasising his point by spinning his index-finger in little loops through the air as if tracking the flight of a drunken bluebottle, and when he wanted to place a special emphasis, accompanied this with a thin whistle, a 'Thwip-thwip!' the better to underscore his point.

I thought about Arthur, although not in the same way I did about Mick. I fancied that one could divine Arthur's working history from his face, as if encoded in its lines. He arrives age sixteen as an apprentice: callow, clumsy, self-conscious. He falls for every cruel trick played on newcomers and burns with silent humiliation; somewhere in his young mind he pledges that one day he will put an end to these stupid games. For a long time, he's got nothing to say to his workmates ('He's a shy one!') but then an older worker, the Gaffer of that day, extends his paternal protection to young Arthur, recognises and encourages his skills, encourages him to speak up, helps him to mature, to spot and fend off the bullies and practical jokers. Arthur becomes one of the lads, no longer an outsider, he's respected for his sound work and his solidarity with fellow labourers. He meets a girl, marries her, but he's still around for a beer with the boys. He watches his children grow up, while at work he spots a new lad who's clearly been sent on some fool's errand: he intercepts him, talks to him, takes him under his wing. And gradually in this way, as the older men fade into retirement, his own mentor amongst them, he is the senior man, he's become the Gaffer, the exemplar of shop loyalty, the man who's never bailed in search of more cash or sold out to the management.

And, probably, I thought, he's looking for a younger man to take his place, anticipating when his breathing grows shallow and arms weak, when a short retirement awaits, along with its inevitable conclusion. I really liked Arthur: his is an eternal and honest story. I struggled, however, to spot a potential replacement. Mick lacked Arthur's depth and thought mainly about himself, when he used his brain at all. Scott? Forget it. We called him The Echo; he'd never had an original thought in his life. Ginner solved problems

72

by hitting them. Perhaps, after all, a host of old and respectable traditions died with Arthur.

I suppose all of this is why I expected better from him about you-know-what, and yet it was a comment of his that summed up the problem at this works and in the world, and which supplied me with a motif. Arthur was recalling some of the workers of yesteryear; the carthorses (compliment), the skivers (insult) and clever dicks (another insult) that came and went, and he was yarning about a 'character' (could be a compliment or an insult) called Smithy. Arthur was fond in his recall of this maverick spirit, but wound up his comments on the man by spinning his finger through the air and saying, 'Truth be known, tho I liked Smithy, I was glad when he left. Always struck me as a bit of a— y'know—*thwip-thwhip*—Willy Woofter.'

I was disappointed, I admit, and yet there was something different in what Arthur was saying; whereas Mick and Ginner (and by echo, Scott) seemed to hate Chocolate Stabbers, Ring Pirates (etc. etc. etc., ad infinitum), Arthur didn't seem outright hostile to 'Willy Woofter', he was just more comfortable in his absence. The others snarled at the thought of the Rectum Robber—the *taker*, you notice, the *thief*, Arthur was tolerantly bemused by Willy Woofter. Some of my friends would say he was just as bad as the others, that prejudice is prejudice and gentler words don't help, but I know I could in some way eventually get through to someone like Arthur, talk to him, reassure him, explain who and what I am: and he wouldn't say, 'That's *your* problem.'

And still, they couldn't keep off the subject. Willy Woofter is always with us.

'It's an illness, innit? God knows how yer treat it, but it's an illness,' moaned Ginner. 'I think yer can only cure it by cutting their fuckin cocks off.'

'Yeah, it's an illness,' agreed Mick, 'and yer can *catch* it!'— at which he grabbed at Scott's balls, making him leap up and away, flailing his arms as if fending off a wasp.

'Where's the fuckin Dettol?' bellowed Ginner, a chant taken up by The Echo. Mick was about to take a swig of tea, but instead held the mug out in front of him, subjecting it to forensic inspection.

'Who ad this mug before me? Was it washed up proper? You can catch stuff off mugs and the like.' He then went round the table, fingers crooked and stiffened together in the mime of giving injections.

'Protection,' he said, pressing my arm, 'But it won't work if you've already got the bug.' He looked straight into my eyes, as if to announce that he'd found the seat of the infection; was that sudden frank look a threat, a guess, an offer of collusion and protection—maybe even a secret confession? No such hope; hetero through and through, the old horse-stinker. In fact, Mick was probably the worst when it came to condemning Willy Woofter. Admittedly such behaviour can be a giveaway itself, you know, someone protesting too much, but I knew in my heart that not a single queer cell lurked in his flesh.

'The way things are goin, it won't just be legal, it'll be fuckin compulsory.' *If only, Micky-boy, if only.*

The problem with most men is that they're convinced *they're* the centre of the universe, and that they're so *it* everyone wants to shag them: and, logically, 'everyone' means, well, everyone, and not just the doe-eyed wet-lipped take-me-now girls on the magazine covers, not just the cackling office girls, smirking and drinking and casting predatory after-work glances, or the unattainable married and attached women who've clearly chosen the wrong man and who need a lesson in love—no, not just them. Our man is so beautiful, so compulsively, addictively sexy he can't help but attract the lustful attentions of Willy Woofter; urrrgh, spew, backs against the fuckin wall, where's the Dettol? He can't have his purity sullied like that!

I've always found it interesting that people tend to refer to anything related to sex as 'dirty', even the good and authorised baby-making type. We'd none of us be here some fur-lined pink-cushioned paradise where we sipped chilled champagne provided by the Mayor in person—wearing a thong—but what we had was cold lager, a postage stamp for a dance floor, and a stack of old plastic chairs on which to relax, unwind and be ourselves. *Not bloody much, Ginner, but I will always prefer it to your obnoxious company.* Oh yes, I know what I should have said—for truth, fairness, justice, honour and Willy Woofter. But I bit my lip, didn't I, not wanting a pasting from an enraged human toadstool.

Things are better now, friends say—liberal, hetero well-meaning friends that is, people who want everything to be better and see every small gain as a major victory. Well, my dears, that just rouses my cynicism and I have to say that if things are better then they're better for you, for your ability to feel better about yourselves, so you can say look what a civilised, tolerant society we are, let's pat ourselves on the back! Clause 28 is dead, it's illegal to discriminate against Willy Woofter at work, Willy Woofter can register his partnership with another Willy Woofter, by jiminy the man's almost a respectable citizen, he's almost normal, the restraints are off, the sky's the limit, Willy Woofter for Pope! But there are plenty of times I just don't see it that way: we're granted a pseudo 'normality', like a tolerance zone for tarts; 'tolerance' itself has been granted late, reluctantly and in as watered-down a form as could be, riddled with reminders that Willy Woofter is not quite the same as his breeding brother. He's better-regarded, but still second-class. And don't forget, liberals of good will and conscience, that for every one of you there's a religious nut or two, waiting to drive out Willy Woofter, to kill or cure him; if they come to power then Willy Woofter's fucked. It's not over, by a long way. So—when am I ever going to be able to relax, unwind and be myself?'

Jim lifted his hand from the taxi door.
    'You can go now.'

without that dirty act, but dirty it remains. If 'normal' sex is viewed like that, what chance does Willy Woofter stand? Willy Woofter, as everyone knows, does it in toilets, so that's double-dirty; isn't Willy Woofter *awful?* And yet have you ever noticed how many loud-mouthed homophobes are frankly obsessed with gay sex, or specifically the mechanisms and minutiae of buggery? I once listened to a House of Lords debate on the radio, in which their peerships delved into the subject in astonishing detail and with a relish for matters rectal that bordered on the pathological. Each speaker intended ostensibly to expound the horrors of homosex, but I believed that they were driven less by moral disapproval than fascinated jealousy. My Lords and Ladies, you're desperate to get it up the butt, aren't you? Admit it, then, for crying out loud, go and do it, get it out of your system, it'll do you a power of good. Shall I come and do the lot of you, and Mick and Ginner and Christ knows who else, to sate your curiosity and put an end to your fears? Will you then leave Willy Woofter and his kind alone? No more restricting laws, no more baseball bats, will we get some peace at last?

I rage like this; it happens to me sometimes. But raging didn't help me then and there; I still couldn't be myself, was still wondering when I'd give myself away or—toilet imagery again, is the English language fundamentally against me?—I'd be flushed out. But I was protected by shop loyalty: with the lads, day in day out, right under their noses, being mates—a bit anyway—and Arthur liked me, so I couldn't be Willy Woofter, could I?

It's the world that's dirty, if you ask me, the world where the jokes are aimed at you: 'There were these two queers and a Paki...' Yes, thank you Mick, next! Even a gentle Arthur figure won't hold the mob back once they know the truth. At least I had the comfort of knowing my time here was limited, that there was somewhere else, a more convivial atmosphere. But what if our Willy Woofter were an ordinary, inexperienced and underconfident lad and not a smart-arse student on his way up the career ladder? What if he was another Arthur, destined to spend his life in the works? My deepest sympathy goes out to the working-class poof, someone who has more chains to break than just admitting the truth about his sexuality, who may struggle so long and so hard with other troubles that he may never realise who and what he is, dating girls with a compliant but puzzled air, spiralling into a marriage never meant to be, and the only advantage that he may avoid being thumped into raw meat by his loyal buddies, because he has become the thing he is not.

The way some people talk it's as if Willy Woofter came into existence because he was permitted to by woolly namby-pambies and spineless politicians who conjured him from a mixture of dirt and water stirred with a stick. But Willy Woofter is no artificial creation, no deviant, no aberration; he has existed throughout time, he is a man, and sometimes he has been the greatest of men. What did I dream as I lay in bed at my digs (yes, digs, because although I had a Mum and Dad living not far, they didn't give house-room to *perverts*)? Do you really think I fantasised about butt-fucking every hetero I laid my eyes on, or I revelled in all my happy memories of encounters with pudgy middle-aged men who didn't think they were being unfaithful to their wives because it was a boy's mouth they'd just come in (I hate their kind, but sometimes better sex is hard to find, if you're shy like me)? Did I plot to screw Scott because he was young and blond and pretty (no, I was so uninterested in Scott. I never even bothered to find out if that was his first name or last. He was intrinsically uninteresting, a wraith)? There had to be something more for me.

For all I daydreamed lazily of a naked Mick, preferably in a sauna or jacuzzi, my real fantasies were different, deeper. I dreamed of romance, oh yes, I dreamed of love, being accepted as me, yes, even of being adored as me. But I was unsure that day would come: not sure I deserved it. Why not? Because I was a coward. I wanted things to be

better for me—for Willy Woofter—but did nothing ab[out] it, nothing active, I waited for someone else to do the j[ob.] Instead, I hid, pretending I was not who I am, what I a[m,] didn't deserve to be recognised, accepted and loved beca[use] I didn't fight for it.

'You won't fuckin believe what this loony fuc[kin] Council's doin now.' Ginner slammed his lumpham[mer] hand down into a pool of beer, sending up a spray [that] soaked my shirt and looked like drying blood. 'The[y're] putting thousands of pounds—*thousands of pounds*—[into] that Poof Palace! I can't believe it; my money—*my f[uckin]* *money*—is goin in taxes to subsidise some queer to g[et] cheap beer in a gay club!'

Everyone around the table agreed that this was fu[ckin] terrible: we're all ratepayers, why can't they subsidis[e our] fuckin beer? Ginner was working himself up over it, a[ngry] enough to hit anybody who faintly contradicted him[, but] there was no chance of that happening. The others wer[e just] as puffed up, and as for me, when I should have spok[en up] and fought the good fight, I said nothing and ape[d their] appalled, goggle-eyed glare, hoping the lads would ass[ume I] shared their moral revulsion. Beers for queers! Bende[rs for] benders! The poor ratepayer!

But I *should* have stood up to Ginner, put him [right.] Made him accept the truth. The 'poof palace' was a [gay] club called RUBYS—'Relax, Unwind, Be Yourself' [its] full title, which I thought appropriate and clever—a[place] where Willy Woofter could enjoy a drink witho[ut the] danger of getting the glass in his face as afters. I was a [regular] there at holiday times and sometimes did bar work[. I] attended the occasional committee meeting, and I [knew] that the 'thousands' we queers were creaming off the [poor] working populace came in the form of a very [small] discretionary loan at a commercial rate, which was t[he only] way to get the club launched, after which we neede[d just] enough Willy Woofters in each week to st[ave off] bankruptcy. Subsidised drinks; my arse. Ginner in [his]

If Frank Speke Does Not Speak Up For Free Speech

Then Who Shall Dare Speak Frankly?

'That's Frank Speke—the clue's in the name. He tells it like it is; no fear, no favour.'

How he would have loved to hear those words, from any of the regulars at Pilot Ken's table, not least from Ken. But... no luck. People so often overlooked the obvious. It was one of the reasons he didn't like people very much.

Frank Speke knew his subject; he had read up on it, immersed himself. Dammit, he was no idiotic all-mouth pub bullshitter, he knew of, understood and supported—though not uncritically, as may be expected—the US First Amendment, its elusive, unwritten British precedents, its windier European iterations, and the efforts of the UN and other august bodies to define and uphold a universal good. He knew his Milton, his Mill and Voltaire (even though the man didn't really quite say that thing that people always quote because they know nothing else of him), he had absorbed as mother's milk the parrhesia of the Pnyx; he revelled in the inspiring example of Free-Born John, he lent his vocal aid to every dissident and dissenter, and above all knew intuitively that what was true mattered and so did the right to say it out loud and without quailing in the face of power. Frank Speke was a truth-teller, and should anyone he encountered come away a little bruised, they would at least come away the better, the truth paid due honours. Naturally, casualties were regrettable, but... for instance, everyone at Ken's table still prickled with guilt if they thought of Uxorio, whereas Frank held his head high. He was not attacking a man but a type, and of that type he had spoken the plainest and most necessary truths. Nothing to feel guilty about. Start feeling like that and the good fight is over.

And there was much to fight. Frank observed the human sprawl in the microcosm of life of the town and the Ring O'Villages, it showed a depressing consistency; what was true in the Bat and Ball, the town and the Ring was also true in the county, the country, every country, the whole idiotic world. He could not restrain his lofty scorn. Time-server rubbed shoulders with time-waster, the overambitious with those who pottered pointlessly day by day, with pub-bores, parasites and pen-pushers, dilettante do-gooders, cheats, thieves, drunks, show-offs, gatemouths, smartarses, crossword solvers. They talked sport, sex, food, beer, telly, bigotry, bollocks. Not a thing was said that was of any account, and should anyone slip into thinking, true speech, the booze would cloud their minds soon and dullness, conformity and quietism reclaim them. Someone had to take a stand, and in this place, at this time, there was a shortage of candidates.

Step up, Frank Speke: nobody else has the courage.

'There's no fight in people anymore, nothing, haven't you noticed? They'll put up with anything, anything at all. They can be trashed, taxed, trodden, mismanaged, bullied, spat on... and not a word, not a flicker. Well, a twitch maybe, and then surrender. Unless there's someone innocent and harmless nearby they can take it out on... As for speaking truth to power, *pah*. The meek shall receive their just reward—pinned to the floor with someone else's boot planted firmly on their throats.' And this was why Frank had to do it, to speak out against those who led supine, sheep-like lives, dumbly facilitating and perpetuating the evils that lurked amongst them, never saying a word against them: the complacent, the complaisant, the merely, meekly compliant, the people who stood in the way of the truth without even knowing their fault.

80

He was no revolutionary, Frank; he would leave such infantile dreaming to irresponsible talk-talkers such as FMC, a man who regarded even the sanctity of free speech a luxury, a toy of the bourgeoisie: a man who advocated the dissolution of the police force (which he alleged was 'fmc' anyway, a tool of the corrupt ruling classes as was everything that he hated, which was nearly everything), but who in a breathtaking mental back-flipping regarded a malignant, cancerous network of secret police and snitch-your-neighbour denunciation as a legitimate, essential tool of statecraft in the perfect revolution of which he ever dreamed. The working classes should not be told how fast they should drive, or constrained from taking one another's property or murdering one another in the streets (all crime, according to FMC, was the oppressed fighting back against their oppressors which didn't, both Frank and Pilot Ken pointed out, account for thugs who belted old ladies over the head for a handful of spare change and other such incidents), but they should perforce be spied on, denounced and put away in icy gulags if they thought or spoke a syllable against the diktat of FMC's fantasy polity.

Support for Frank's own full-blooded principles was in short supply; just look at the table's reaction to the Uxorio business. Ken and Jim paid lip-service to the great freedoms, but they were misfits, dilettantes; they would never uphold the cause *in extremis*. Little Mal came straight from the enemy camp, Frank could imagine him signing bans by the dozen, gagging orders, totting up proscription lists. The others were lightweights and chatterers, inoffensive but unserious. The closest that Frank had to an ally around that table was Emily—what she went through with that theatre made her a fellow spirit indeed, engaged as she was in a constant battle to stage what she thought was artistically justified, and always running up against the censorious, the conservative, the fanatical, the penny-pinchers and just plain stupid, and she fought her corner with dignity and determination. Frank could admire that. Mind you, she wasn't a patch on her mother; Frank remembered the golden period of the Playhouse when Tara was in charge. Her daughter had inherited her skills and determination, but oh my godfathers what bloody rubbish she put on! Frank hadn't been to the theatre in years; but he stood for its freedom to be there, and to put up whatever its director thought best. Frank applied that dictum of Voltaire's, the one he never really dicted.

The one thing—apart from plain talking—for which Frank Speke was noted was his appreciation of authenticity. You were nothing to him if you were not the real thing. Frank maintained that his name was the real thing, and could be quite irritable if anyone suggested that he'd given it a little help. He had tried to shoot a little line that the name showed that he had ancient aristocratic connections. 'The family Hall, the famous one, you know,' he blustered.

'Isn't Speke Hall named after the place, not a family?' Pilot Ken was engaging in his characteristic false modesty, only pretending to ask a question. 'The family name was Morris or something, I think…' He didn't think, he knew, and to add insult, he had that 'you have to know these things if you do crosswords' look. All of which went to prove that Pilot Ken really was a smartarse.

Another more sensitive self-indulgence of Frank's went mercifully undetected; he had made Francis his foremost name, hardening and shortening it as part of its promotion for suitable effect, tweezering 'Richard' out of its place and sliding it along to second in the running, where it could go quietly unmentioned. Richard Francis was not a man Frank wished to offer any memorial—Frank famously did not 'do stories', especially back-stories, and especially not his own. Richard Francis had been diplomat by nature, a conciliator, a consensus-builder. He was known for his patience and respect for all, his ability to consider many points of view, to debate without rancour, to heal breaches and build bridges, even between apparent irreconcilables: even as a kiddie he had shown his skill, arbitrating smoothly between gangs and factions at school, whether the argument at hand was about music or football or broken romances, even stupid haircuts, bringing peace and accord where no one else could. Richard Francis was blessed with the ability to make people feel that they were not 'wrong' as such, and that at long last and at the very least their point of view had been heard and treated as if it mattered. His proud parents said that one day he would go out there and truly set the world to rights. As he grew older, his friends joshingly named him ADR, to cover their astonishment. He saved marriages, helped others turn away from a state of interlocked hostility, pulled friendships from the brink of mistrust verging on vendetta; it was said that he knocked the first three letters off 'misunderstanding' and 'miscommunication'. How he was not a millionaire and the target of vengeful pauperised lawyers was another cause for astonishment. Some joked that they wished for war, just so that they could see what Richard Francis would do to save the day.

No matter what his other achievements, the best thing Richard Francis did, he confidently pronounced, was get married. The gentle maker of bonds found his own heart-bond and, happy man, wanted nothing more. His wife was a different sort of soother; she always steadied Richard Francis if he tottered, shoring him against a self-doubt that grew within him every year, nagging and carping, hollowing him out, telling him that there was no forever—not for admiration, not for friendship—not for anything. Young and fearless of failure, death or destruction, Richard Francis recovered from his every wobble with the loving support of his unfailing wife, and carried on, an arbitrator, healer.

Richard Francis became troubled, however, not just by that undermining inner voice, but by that most problematical of things; the truth. His great discovery had been that almost everyone, no matter how intransigent and intractable, had something they would trade, at a price, for something even more precious—security, a feeling (however illusory) of victory or vindication, of attaining that

83

elusive 'closure', or simply the promise of a quiet life after storms and dissonance. It was Richard Francis's artistry, innate but honed and polished after years of judicious application, his gift, to seek out and find the willingness to make a bargain and end the bickering that dwelt within even the noisiest and most intractable no-no-naysayer. There was something even in the hardest of arguments that was negotiable. Arguably, although he had used it for what nearly all concerned would call the good, Richard Francis had won his successes by diverting others from the truth, abetting them in evading its more destructive effects. In getting them to agree, he also persuaded them to fudge, forget or set aside facts. He had made them feel better, but he had not cured the disease. What, whispered that corrosive inner voice, would happen when the truth came to collect?

This: Richard Francis was in trouble; there was a truth clear in his mind, clearer and plainer than anything. He owed it to his wife to make that truth known to her, but how to tell her such a thing? He had come close to managing it, but never made the breakthrough. In one typical instance, the two of them messed about as they had done years before as young lovers, prodding and tickling one another over the washing up, giggling and growing excited; she kissed him enticingly, draping the damp tea-towel over his shoulders as if investing him with an honour, then drawing it up over his head, whipping it over his face, rubbing it in and laughing.

'What's the best thing you ever did?' she stage-whispered with hammy huskiness.

'Meeting you, finding you, being with you.' It was an unadorned, absolute truth, simple to say.

'The best?' she asked, still smiling but with some playfulness abated; her eyes had a spark not of joy but of mild surprise.

'The absolute best thing.' Richard Francis was speaking truly, but he knew he was also dodging; he had given the correct answer, the answer that had always been the right one, but now she wanted him to say something more, a particular something, a something he did not wish to say because it was not true. They kissed again with the passion of their teen years, and for the moment Richard Francis had avoided the problem, knowing however that it would be back, and soon. He felt himself a coward, because although he had told her nothing but the truth, he had not told her the full truth of his heart. To do so would have imposed a burden, as great truths do. He felt ungenerous because he knew what she wanted him to say, but he was not willing to make her happy by mouthing it. He prayed silently she would never ask him the question directly and openly: if she did, what could he do, how could he answer? She wanted him to add to their usual declaration that their children were also his greatest and proudest achievement, but he was honour-bound to say that they were nothing of the sort: more, he would be honour-bound to say that he did not even like them, not one tiny bit. A great, painful, inconvenient, destructive truth—and he withheld it, he never told her. He had been wrong to do that. She was his wife, his true, great and only love, she deserved the truth and yet he had knowingly deprived her of it. Richard Francis had ducked a difficult conversation, a row, high words, tears. He had suppressed the truth to spare her feelings, his own too, not least that a small, stirring part of him, no longer just self-doubt, but something much more, would have found entertainment in her distress.

Richard Francis's life had been blighted by a mistake; only one, but a devastating one. The arrival of children, quads, no less, was a high price to pay for such a short-lived sensation in the local papers. Two girls, two boys, nice balance people said, dubbing them the Four Blessings (*aaaahhhh!*) and Richard Francis was as smitten as everyone else. His world began to shudder as soon as the children could string a disputatious sentence: with yellowing hindsight, Frank Speke considered that it was practically all over from the first '*he/she started it!*' They were inseparable companions, the four, but only in the way of gladiators awaiting the games. Richard Francis, the arbitrator, the conciliator, the arch-peacemaker, was powerless to stop the whining, the fighting, the bullying, the permutations of battle, two-against two, three-against one, four against the beleaguered Richard Francis. Nothing worked, everything he did, every perspective he offered, every single ADR skill he exercised served only to fire them up, worsen their struggles. Their sole united front was against their father. Their ascent from the pettiness of childhood simply made their fighting more bitter, accompanied by an uncanny mutual understanding that only deepened their innate sense of internecine grievance, not to mention entitlement; the only things on which they agreed. Before they were five years old, a frazzled Richard Francis had renamed them the Four Horsemen, the *non-negotiables*, and he put on his tin hat, covered his ears and retired from the game of diplomacy; that nagging self-doubt had now gained its full voice and was well on the way to becoming something else, though it did not yet have a name.

Richard Francis was relieved, but somehow peevish, silently jealous, to find that the sole voice of peace and reason to which the Four would listen belonged to their gentle mother.

They were fractious, factional and yet still united whenever an attempt was made to put an end to their squabbles or to play one against the others. His growing cynicism about his own issue was not something that brought the least measure of satisfaction to Richard Francis, and nor was the criticism of his beloved wife that surfaced in his mind, never to achieve active expression, whenever she attempted to pacify the Horsemen. Her method, in Richard Francis's increasingly hardened opinion, amounted in the final analysis to pleading, please-please, for the sake of family peace, for the sake of a quiet Christmas, for the sake of getting tonight's meal over without a fight, please, for your mother's sake, if you love me. Don't do it, Richard Francis wanted to tell her, never plead, never appease, it never works. And so it proved, more and more as the Four moved towards adolescence; pleading failed, begging failed, trying desperately to match the Four yell for yell—that failed too. Their mother's successes had been, to be brutally honest, patchy and the durability of even her most successful interventions never guaranteed. Over the fraught years she did secure concessions where her husband, the natural, skilled diplomatist failed, humiliated, giving Richard Francis periods of relative if unstable peace, during which he could bide his time until the Four turned sixteen; at the stroke of that midnight, he would exercise his new-minted legal right to turf the little blighters out.

Non-negotiables; self-centred and impossible, they were a daily trial to Richard Francis, they upset his equilibrium and diminished his satisfaction with life, but they were no threat to his existence per se. Such a threat, unthinkable previously, difficult to face, and impossible to resolve, came in the unexpected form of the ultimate non-negotiable, and after this descended on him, Richard Francis was no more. Pilot Ken would pontificate about the word 'ultimate'. People who used it didn't understand its meaning, he said, and those who used and knowingly abused the word were usually politicians or the snake-oil charlatans of the advertising world. But, on this occasion, the word 'ultimate' could be used with precision and the word-bending smartarse could get stuffed. Richard Francis had faced no greater menace and, ultimately, he was overwhelmed by it; even Frank Speke recalled the phenomenon with an abiding horror that justified the weapons-grade deployment of that word. Recall was not welcome to Frank Speke; reminders were unwelcome intruders: recall and horror were often one and the same. Reminders: recall: pallor: skin: horror, the horror of the ultimate non-negotiable.

The skin, the pallor. Frank was never much of an admirer of Wayne's. He regarded him as a loutish dipso who, tongue-loose with alcohol, mistook freedom of speech for licence to say anything, no matter how crude, incendiary or brutally offensive. Speak freely but with precision, speak about what is important, eschew trivia, those were Frank's principles. Wayne degraded and befouled these lofty aims by blurting out half-chewed thoughts, unformed opinions, unfunny funnies, witticisms without a whit of wit, scattergun insults, often as he was teetering on the verge of utter incoherence. But what troubled Frank the most in those last weeks was the skin; the pallor. Wayne hadn't long to go, but he was still battling away, fending off death day by day just so that he could have one more night at the bar-rail. It seemed a petty cause to Frank, certainly nothing to die for, yet that was precisely what Wayne was doing. As his condition deteriorated, so did his temper and also, Frank shuddered, his skin. It passed through phases, declining from Wayne's natural rustic weathered colouring to a sun-starved and unhealthy whiteness then deteriorating to unattractive greying, candle-wax shades, and the bruised grey-yellow of his impending end. Frank wasn't troubled about Wayne's fate; the man had chosen and he had been free to do so. It was that jaundiced, dying skin that troubled Frank; the unsought reminder of the ultimate non-negotiable. Falling ill out of nowhere, his beloved wife had declined rapidly through the same awful stages. No will to live, no fighting spirit, no cutting-edge medicine or positivity of mind could hold it back—least of all pleading and bargaining with invisible forces in which his wife never lost faith but whose absence or culpable inertia made Richard Francis curse and abandon them.

The conduct of the Four Horsemen during their mother's short and final illness brought Richard Francis to the precipice: age had not mellowed their malignancy, they were more entrenched, self-centred, combative, cunning, entitled than at any time during their young lives. They would agree on nothing, cooperate on nothing. Everything was the excuse not just for a fight but pitched battle. Even turns to sit with their mother as her end came closer were fought over, sometimes as if they were prized favours distributed by an all-powerful monarch, other times sharply and spitefully rejected as if the four had been asked to wash the dishes or polish their shoes. Richard Francis, weakened and distracted, tried to emulate his wife's gentle methods— but he ended up just as she had, pleading, surrendering all advantage, and finally begging in the face of intransigence. The extremity of the Four came to outbid and outlast all mourning, there were squabbles, scowls and silence at the funeral, and Richard Francis despaired.

Richard Francis's life had become unbearable: though he contemplated it in passing, he regarded it as nothing but cowardice to propose to put an end to that life. Seeing his agitation and depression, some friends thought that he was considering 'joining' his wife, but had they asked him he would have made it plain that he didn't believe she had gone anywhere, the end was the end. Which was in itself a good reason for clinging on to life, if you are of the firm impression that you only ever have the one go. Self-destruction being unthinkable, what else was there? Richard Francis's solution was to resign: not to surrender his life, but to hand over control to a new and entirely different self, someone who held Richard Francis's great achievements to be nugatory, who repudiated his weaknesses and would never waver in the face of the truth. To hell with diplomacy, persuasion, bargain-making: people needed telling, hard and quick and true, it might just change them.

Richard Francis was a failure, a loser, a man who had tried to appease a pantheon of capricious gods as they pulled, wilfully, in wildly contrary directions. It could not be done; it was the very definition of a waste of time. It had taken—what, forty?—years for this to become so brutally apparent to the idealistic dimwit, and so he was forced to agree to his own annulment, for his existence to be quietly erased and for Frank Speke to take his place. People had called it a mid-life crisis, but the nascent Frank paid them no heed, it was after all their own brick-wall stupidity that had finally confounded poor Richard Francis and goaded Frank to being, their blinding, blinded conceit, their inability to get it. And, at the same time was birthed The Imp: they had both been a long time coming, forming slowly within Richard Francis, seeing him flag and fail, growing stronger as he faltered and finally arbitrated himself out of existence. Some small spirit of Richard Francis still lived, in the form of the to-and-fro, the ever-shifting balance of power between Frank and The Imp. He would sometimes persuade it to rein in its worst desires in return for some lesser gratification, and it would sometimes persuade him to take a back seat because it wanted to scratch an impish itch. But other than that, Richard Francis was gone, buried, good riddance.

Nobody at Ken's table, nobody in the town or the Ring O'Villages, knew any of this: not even when full of drink, not even when filled with an unbearable, need to share some of it, had Frank said a word. It could be a struggle but it was a pushover compared to his on-off battles with The Imp. Frank Speke would not deal in back-stories; no. But whether or not we acknowledge them, stories are there. They build and grow, they have sequels and codas and sometimes unwelcome echoes. For Frank, another unwelcome echo of the ultimate non-negotiable came again in the form of Wayne. He had even less time to go now; he was no longer working and his ploughman's frame of erst was diminished, perished and thin, and yet still he stuck doggedly to his regular arrivals at The Bat And Ball, staying as long as he could, downing whatever he could, make him even more ill though it did. In his waning state, he had somehow decided that various people needed to be given 'Some ome truths', which he delivered with a mirthless, man-eating smile on his gaunt and haunting face. Friends and acquaintances gave him a wide berth, so devastating were the 'ome truths' he pronounced. Secrets, confidences, old confessions, the eavesdroppings of years of being there, none were sacred to Wayne as the shadows fell and time pressed. So angry, so virulent did he become that for a short time Frank toyed with the idea that The Imp had deserted him and found a new abode.

Wayne could have been an ally in the cause, Frank ruefully mused, but he was lacking in the mental discipline required for the task; Pilot Ken called him a force of nature, but that was just words, words, words. Frank cared deep-down about what he said, why he said it, about whom, it was his aim to wield truth as a weapon for the betterment of all; he intended to change the world, and to be there to see it changed and improved, but Wayne had rejected such an option, all he sought was a weapon: full-stop. Wayne didn't represent freedom of speech; he represented its chaotic antithesis. He was say-anything, not say-truth. Certainly, he would have cried fire in a crowded theatre, just for the rush, the thrill of chaos, just for a grim laugh on the gallows.

Frank had been having a good evening. He had dispatched several foes during a rhetorical running battle to which they had contributed nothing and of which they knew nothing, a fact that diminished his satisfaction not an iota. The gatemouths at the bar who talked computers, computers, computers without knowing what they were talking about—people who believed they had one foot in the future, whereas they were planted foursquare in irrelevance: the barking golf club toffs who came slumming it, putting on airs as they stood at the bar-rail surveying their inferiors before they noticed the stares they were drawing and withdrew with celerity and ruffled dignity, to general amusement: the peach-fluff amateurs on a pub-crawl, fit to puke on their third pint.

Wayne curled a lip in contempt cloaked as amusement; 'You're all talk, you. Welded to your fookin pub chair, havin a pop at the ole wide world to get back at it cos yer a stupid, ugly, lonely ole fart oo no one wants.' Delivered of his barb and apparently satisfied, Wayne slunk toward the bar: Frank showed no reaction before he stood and walked unhurriedly to the Gents. He swished water over his hands from that stupid tap he could never figure out how to work properly, and patted at his face, not looking at his reflection in the over-lit mirror above the sink. The water on his face stung a little and he scrubbed at it with a coarse paper towel. As Frank returned to the table, Pilot Ken was explaining in technical terms why the gatemouths knew nothing about computers, and Frank retook his seat, vindicated in his attack, still wondering if The Imp was now in the possession of another.

Wayne's Pyzin Cup

'Kenny, Kenny! Kenny, hey Kenny!'

JC's voice, usually either a tarry gurgle or a corncrake's fullest, most crakeish cry, was a thin, urgent hiss. The self-styled singin pot-man had arrested his erratic zigzags between randomly-chosen tables and the bar and was calling Pilot Ken with a bubbling, blatant desire to spill someone else's beans. Ken, on his way from the bar with pints for himself and Jim, drew JC from both the bar and his table by walking towards the now-silent juke box, placing the brimming glasses on a narrow shelf that ran beneath the machine.

'What d'you want, JC?' Ken failed to sound even-toned; he had noticed an intense tete-a-tete between Evil Mand and Wayne and he hadn't liked the look of it, not least the unusually pasty expression on Mand's face.

'Bin lissnin, I eard, Wayne, it's Wayne, he's bin dire-nosed!' JC, inasmuch as he comprehended discretion, was trying to be discreet, but without the background hum of many conversations his grating voice, now raised again in the excitement of having a scoop, would have been audible in most of the Ring O'Villages. There was no point in attempting to shush him, the old man would never have understood and may well have become annoyed, and louder.

'I eard it, eard it, Wayne's bin dire-nosed, it's is liver, if e don't ave it took out e's a dead-un!'

'If they take it out and don't put something in its place, he's a dead-un too,' added Pilot Ken sourly, inwardly calculating how long he would have to keep JC occupied before the eavesdropped news lost its excitement and the old man's mind threaded back to its customary state of fogged, churning chaos.

'Young innee?'

'Young for what?'

'To die of the...' JC tipped his wrist back twice. 'I gotta be twice is age, more, and it ain't done me!'

Yet.

Ken kept JC busy a few more minutes, keeping him away from Wayne, Mand or, indeed, anyone, and just as his ploy seemed to have been blessed, Jim came barrelling over, in search of his drink.

'Jim! Jim! Eh, Jim!' JC broke away from Ken, dodging his instinctive blocking-move with astonishing agility, and in a moment was at Jim's side, dwarfed, squinting upwards.

'Jim, eh, Jim!'

'What?'

'Pay yer Poll Tax Jim, pay yer fuckin Poll Tax, that's what, pay it eh!' He broke into giggling.

Ken almost flopped down with relief: having discharged his burden of hot gossip, the old man had forgotten.

Back at their table, Ken confided quietly in to Jim, and they both sat and worried—what to do, how to handle this: *how to protect Wayne?* The core of the Cabinet agonised. It was Wayne who came to their rescue. Disengaging from Mand, he strolled to Ken and Jim and plonked himself down with easy familiarity.

'Jus bin tellin the lass, I gotta get meself a new wotnot or invest in a patch o'ground,' he announced, in the manner of someone who was examining abundant options at his leisure.

'When are you going in?' asked Jim, weakly.

'Goin in?'

'To get it done... the op... you're not are you?'

'Clever lad, top o the class.'

'But if you don't...'

'Don't start up tellin me what I already knows. I don't want no lecture-lecture-lecture from no one, I got all that from the whitecoats. An no big eyes an croccy tears and "Oh Wayne" stuff, neither, just ad ter talk the lass out o that. I got a choice. I'm usin it. I'm goin nowhere, I'm havin me beers while I can, and when I'm done I'm done. No point goin through all the blood an guts an pills an docs, cos I sh'd only come back here, new liver and all, and get started again. So as thass the case, why stop?'

'But if you…' Jim's nascent protest was crushed by a contemptuous look from Wayne.

'It's pyzin, this stuff,' Wayne regarded his glass thoughtfully and without malice, 'Pyzin. Killin us all, every one, drop by bittersweet drop.' He drank off most of the pint in one draught. 'Pyzin.' He finished, set off to the bar once again and returned with a refreshed glass and a frankly wicked expression.

'You wantin I should go now, Kenny?' Wayne grinned over the lip of his pint.

'Eh?'

'Well, I'd be getting in your way. I know how this all works Kenny, I can't be ere when you get everyone together, convene your li'l social welfare committee like, an worry and stress over what we goin t'do bout Wayne, how cun we help Wayne, ow do we save im? That'll be the lot of you, moment I'm out the door, werretin and wonderin what t'do for the best. Do we keep an eye on im, ow do we stop im drinkin, should we refuse t'buy drinks for 'im, fer is own good? I can see it all, the debates, the discussions, the high words an high sentiments, the fuckin ethics—an you cannot deny it. You an Jim I reckon will fuss yourselves alf to death, but in the end you'll do what's right, real carin blokes both, an I'm not bein funny. The ole grumpy bugger, now he believes in lettin people go to hell their own way, so he'll do the right thing too; the Commie gobshite's too tight to buy for anyone else anyway, an that Little Mal, well, he'll need a bloody committee decision, a fuckin vote, mebbe two or three, who knows which way he'll go… not sure about your girlfriends either, I always found women a bit nursey, a bit do-as-I say. Pomo? Too broke, him. Could never buy a round even if he wasn't too shamed to show up. I knows

95

about ow much e owes you, Kenny. Reckon e would if e could though. Decent lad, bit wet.'

'Wayne...'

'Hear me out. I done a deal with Mand: long as I don't make her break no law, then I get to have my wish. She serves a drunk man; she breaks the law—but if she serves a dyin man she breaks no law. Then I'm here so she can keep an eye. She won't interfere, she's promised. Now you must too. You're a good bloke Kenny, ol Jim too, you're well-meaners, people like you for it, but I han't much time for well-meaners. Y'can't solve people like crossword clues, they're messy and don't fit the boxes. Do as I want, leave me to meself. Be a pal.'

'Wayne—always assuming we agree—is this a secret business?'

'Nope. Plain and open as y'like. Besides, making a dramatic out o it would only spread it sooner, i'the wrong way—yeah?'

'Yeah.' Both Ken and Jim had been thinking of the need to head off JC and were relieved at there being no need to muzzle his eager rattletrap of a mouth.

'Or I could always just take meself off t the Wing, if that'd suit y'better?'

The worst thing for Ken was that this was a genuine offer, gently mocking but without bitterness. He had long ago labelled The Angel's Wing, The Waiting Room, where the worn-out husks of once-humans, near-shades, gathered for a long, slow one for the road. To be a regular at the Wing was to resign from life: talk was of the past, and like all nostalgia, dishonest, delusional—and comforting, like death's pre-med. The two pubs were rivals in a curious, off-kilter way, but there was a slow one-way traffic between the two, a seepage: drinkers passed over to the Wing from the Bat and Ball, but it was a rarity for them ever to make their way back.

'I'll stay ere, see me time out, lessin anyone starts the lecturin an the like. That happens, I go off to find some peace.'

'Blackmail,' sighed Jim, flatly, unhappily.

'If yer like. But we got an understandin, yes?' Wayne smiled, and the gleam from his jagged teeth put a momentary shaft of fear in Jim.

'Cunning bastard that Wayne,' grumbled Ken after Wayne had moved to spread his tidings table by table. 'He got us over a barrel, just like he did with Danny Deebee over Julie.'

'If someone wants something badly enough, he'll find a way. Even… even that.'

Evil Mand was troubled; troubled and trapped. It was the eternal lot of the barkeep to oversee many a patron's decline into shadows, and Wayne was not her only case. She had also inherited Chris and Dave—labelled by Frank Speke as 'career piss-artists—long career'—from her predecessors, who had inherited them from Danny Deebee just as he had inherited them, and so on down the line. Although they lacked Wayne's declared militant manifesto, they were traversing the same route: Dave was genially drinking himself into an amicable stupor every day; Chris, by contrast. was hard and disputatious, her perpetual scattergun whisky-rage often too much for other regulars, leaving Chris and Dave at a two-table in silent boozy gloom. Just as with Wayne, Mand felt responsible for them; if she turfed them out they would go somewhere worse.

In keeping with Mand and most of the regulars, Pilot Ken had always found it hard to work out an angle on Wayne; he appeared at the pub straight after work, drank enough to kill three ordinary drinkers, tottered off home and then came back and did it all again the next day; his quiz nights became a local legend, and no matter how kaylied he became he behaved better and often talked more sense than the average fizzy-water sipper, no matter how earnest and pontifical that sober sipper may have been. He never spoke of home, rarely of work, he was a pub-creature, alive and complete the moment he stepped through the door, happy from his first deep gulp. He was, in short, an enigma, yet another pub puzzle. Jim concurred, but with a rider to the effect that 'getting an angle' on Wayne was a waste of time, he had to be accepted as was, or not at all. Frank Speke took a simple approach; his pre-label for Wayne, never challenged or altered, was 'The Soakaway'.

He was large man; large enough to easily persuade chatterers at the quiz to put a sock in it and discourage those who wished to argue over the answers—but to put the largeness in perspective, two of him would have made one Jim. He was framed powerfully; squat, broad burden-bearing shoulders, gatherer's arms and hands. He looked to many—who had never seen such a sight, one long-lost even in the bucolic Ring O'Villages—as if he should be in charge of a team of slow-nodding Shires as he guided a plough to make deep furrows in the orange-brown soil. A man out of his time, perhaps; the face that came with this strongman ensemble was open, pleasant and boyish for his forty-five avowed years, and his smile could lend him a gap-toothed pre-adolescent aspect—but only when he smiled just-so. His spaced, pointed teeth, should his mood sour, could become cunning, animal-like, filled with spiteful glee when he grew argumentative. And if he really didn't like someone, those teeth would become predatory, shark-like, bloodthirsty. People had a tendency to treat Wayne as an amiable dimwit, a true old-fashioned bumpkin, encouraged in this foolishness by his dipsomania and burring, not-from-here accent. Mistake.

Wayne tipped his first pint at fourteen, strutting into his local with the confidence of a strapping youth. He hadn't even been questioned, barely looked at, as if he were a long-established regular. He grew up, worked hard, went to the pub. That was sufficient: that is, it became sufficient. He entertained dreams and ambitions, but not long after the age of twenty abandoned them, realising that the more you wished and wanted, the more someone somewhere would work against you, seeking to deny you, frustrate you; the moment you set your heart on something, they determined to deny you. Wayne decided that there were choices: fight, retreat, or go to the pub; Wayne chose that which never frustrated or let him down. Wayne had a peculiar power— Ken called it his sideways affability. People always assumed he was someone else's mate, and this gifted him an uncommonly useful social advantage. He was welcome in any group, and nobody minded if his secret was uncovered, he had been part of the gang from the moment he set foot in the pub. Not a mixer, perhaps, but a natural blender.

There was a Wayne-tale known to everyone, a story so handed-round it was worn, polished smooth, containing no surprises and yet retold with relish. True stories, as true, at least, as any told behind an ale-house door: for example, Wayne was at the doctor's, having a medical. Inevitably, up came the question.

'Units innit, tha's how you counts um? Well lessee… twennyfive? Thirty?'

'Now that's quite a lot for a week. Try to cut it down.'

'A week?' bellows Wayne, 'Thassa *night!*'

The medico's opinion of that response was never recorded, and anyway at that point in the story it was time for the appreciative cackles, especially if Wayne was the storyteller. Oh, and there was that time—with fuzzy probability more than one—when Wayne fancied a takeaway at closing time one blow-blizzard night and snowshoed up the high street, popping into a place, making a home-delivery order, leaving, forgetting he'd done it and then doing five or six encores until he stubbed his toe on his own doorstep. Wayne crashed out to the wide, and, knowing him of old, the delivery people left their burdens on his doorstep, thinking he would open the door eventually. Which he did, but only the next morning when his mind was a tabula rasa and he was setting off for work:

he tumbled over a snowed-in, solid-ice pile of curry and chow mein, flat on his face, breaking his nose and wrist.

'How much had you supped, eh?' snarked an A and E knowitall.

'I were *sober*, thankin you,' Wayne sniped back smartly, a nominal truth.

Just like Pilot Ken, Wayne felt a natural affinity for the Bat and Ball, and would gravitate there in preference to all others. His loyalty had its limits however: at one time, Danny Deebee closed the pub for a month at short notice because he had forgotten he had booked himself a holiday and hadn't time, or was too mean, to arrange cover. Wayne denounced Danny Deebee as a fool, took refuge at The Angel's Wing, intending to drift back once the idiot got the B and B started again, if he was capable. But while double-booked stupidity could be tolerated with a heavy sigh, Wayne led the walkout when the furore over Julie broke out.

Julie had started work for Danny a few weeks before the holiday debacle, winning hearts among the regulars because although young and small (she had to bring a library-step to reach the optics, and performed interesting little flying leaps from the stool to grab bottles from the top shelf, never hurting herself, never breaking anything) she was no pushover, giving as good as she got from mouthy barflies and spurning the interventions of the ineffectual Danny or the hovering, solicitous Ken and Jim. Like everyone else, Julie was caught on the hop by Danny Deebee's holiday, but she had an economic shock to face too. 'You're casual labour,' she was told offhandedly. 'No work, no pay. And if you so much as try to get another job you're not coming back. End of.' Pilot Ken wished great harm on people who employed phrases such as 'End of.'

'Why not let the girl run the place rather than shut it?' pleaded Julie's champion—not Saint Ken but Wayne The Soakaway. 'She'll be fine, there's always me, Ken, Jim, we can back er up. An I predict she won't need none of us. Capable wench.'

Danny refused silently, not looking up.

'At least pay her for the month, then, we all know—you best of all—it's her only dibs, she's got a kiddie to look arter and no fella about.'

Danny finally deigned to speak, spinning some lame tale that Julie had been given 'fair warning'.

'No she a'nt,' said Wayne heavily, 'None of us has.'

'Look: I'm putting up a sign stating that the pub is closing for remedial work. I like the sound of that, "re-mee-dee-al". Everyone can either await my return or clear off. Okay?'

'Okay,' said Wayne. Danny really should have paid attention to his tone.

To Danny's not very secret, tight-smile delight, Wayne and all the regulars were there on the dot as the Bat and Ball opened its doors once more. All seemed normal except a whiff of lingering resentment, but the non-appearance of Julie at her next shift set matters in motion again.

'Whur's the girl?' asked Wayne, on his fifth trip to the bar in as many minutes.

'Not coming.' Danny was cold and cagey.

'Not well? Kiddie not so good?'

'Not coming. Not coming again, not tonight, not at all. I told her to wait till I got back and she could have her job—but she's been doing casual at the Wing. I don't like disloyalty. And you Launcelots didn't help either, nagging me like that. I can do better than her, and if I can't find someone who'll do what I say, I'll run this place alone, I...'

A glass banged down: Wayne was at Ken's table in two strides, gesticulating. Moments later, the pub was half-empty. Led by Wayne, who no one had ever before seen in such a passion, the boycott of Danny Deebee had begun.

Three days later, Wayne reappeared at the bar of the Bat and Ball.

'D'ya give in yet?' his voice was chased around the silent pub by hollow echoes.

'You bastard,' said Danny Deebee's face, mouth and body.

'Yer, but d'you give in yet?'

'Get out, Wayne.'

'Goin, not comin back—none of us is till you give in.'

'Out!'

'Goin.'

Days later, the telephone rang, scattering shards of silvery sound around the almost-empty Bat and Ball.

'Give in yet?' came a voice, the moment Danny Deebee picked up the phone. Danny's subsequent bridling, blustering, ignominious collapse became Wayne's party piece after the regulars returned in triumph. Wayne stood over his defeated enemy as he made an abject call to Julie.

'She... says she's happy where she is and I can sod off,' gasped the abject Danny, 'I can't believe it!'

'Muppet,' grunted Wayne happily, between his meat-grinding teeth.

'I love a happy ending,' whispered Ken to Jim.

Jim was fingertapping on the bar; Pilot Ken, partly to distract himself from his irritation at this tic, was absently push-pushing at a glossy leaflet, trying to restore it to its place in the elegant fan-like arrangement in front of him. Ken became markedly less distracted and absent as he realised what was on the leaflets; his hand descended on Jim's, more forcefully than perhaps warranted.

'What?' yelped Jim, sucking on his fingers in fine slapstick style.

'There was this woman I once met...' began Ken, still looking at the flyers.

'God, Ken, not another tale of your exotic ex-girlfriends? I never got over the snake-dancer, never mind the dope peddler.'

'No, this was just an acquaintance, long ago, a rather appealing middle-aged woman who worked as the chaplain at a hospice; I can't recall much of the conversation but do remember being impressed by her gentleness and principled refusal to thrust her religion on others. But most impressive was her protection of her charges, keeping away the peddlers of death-bed conversions; she said, "It's important to keep the vultures away as the shadows fall."'

'What makes you think of her now?'

'Look at these.'

'Someone left them here?'

'Deliberately, fanned out like a gambler's cards. I think someone has been here who hasn't put so much as his shadow through the door in a long time. He's been here— these are his calling-cards—and he wasn't looking for a drink.'

'Tony the Convert,' groaned Jim.

'None other. Brace yourself James; it's vulture time.'

'And with the flap of black wings he circles down towards the prone man,' muttered Ken; unsmiling, with a gloomy nod to Jim, he noted the arrival of Tony the Convert, who was casting about, trying not to be noticed, making a bad job of it, blatant and self-conscious, moving like a man in unknown, hostile territory, a man doing what he had to do, expecting a violent reward from every shadow.

'I detect a numinous glow. It's his halo,' suggested Jim sarcastically 'It'll light his way, guide and protect him in this den of iniquity. Bless.'

'I could do with that if ever I go back in to the PH Bar.' Ken nodded towards the creeping, hovering creature, 'Perhaps I should have more sympathy. But I don't. I've had enough; it's time to put an end to the hunt.'

He raised a harsh tone and gestured theatrically to catch the interloper's attention. 'He isn't here, Tony, you've chosen the wrong time—again. You look as if you need a raincoat with a turned-up collar; a big hat; shades, perhaps? Nope—it doesn't work. Give it up.'

'Hello Ken, I'm looking for a friend...'

'Ah no, mate, no. God doesn't like fibbers Tony; you should know that. You haven't been in here in years; oh, outside, preaching against the demon drink, but not in here doing battle with it. Not lately anyway. Eh?' Ken was sorry for that last bit, it was spiteful. But again, he was feeling spiteful. 'Now stop looking for Wayne, he's not here and I'm not telling you where he is. I'll tell him you dropped by, now clear off.'

Tony the Convert ceased to stoop; he towered over Ken, as if about to preach. It was more him than the attempt at stealth; he was hardly a man to move around unnoticed and still less one who wished to. He was accustomed to attracting, wanting attention, for he had a message. His suffering at being unable to preach at the Bat and Ball added a painful aspect to his awkward, gangling movements. His face was that of a sufferer, a born martyr. Tony had known what it meant to be fond, in grotesque excess, of the booze and fags and many other things too; with a show of strength and bravery he had broken the hold of every addiction, and yet all this delivered him, in Ken's opinion, to yet another overwhelming craving.

'Come for your fix?'

'May God forgive you for such thoughts,' snapped Tony the Convert.

'Your god forgives no one, I've noticed, that's part of my point. People's gods often reflect their personalities rather closely. Almost as if the deity was... internal... an invention.'

'May God forgive y...'

'Forget it, Tony. Give it up. He won't want to see you. Give it up.'

'Ken, you know I can't.'

'No. You can't. Addiction is a terrible thing. Y'know Tony, you are the Augustine of our little locale—give me sobriety and satiety Lord, but not yet, eh?'

'I must see him,' said the grim anchorite.

'Well don't stalk him, stop creeping about. I'll ask him. I'll explain why, and I'll be plain as day about your motives. If he says no, the answer's no. And even if he says yes, if there's too much lecture-lecture, he'll just walk. And you will have to accept that.'

'Ask him.'

'I will, if you're gone from here in five seconds flat.'

Wing-flutter and flap, the vultureman, godman was gone.

Ken was astonished when Wayne agreed equably to Tony's request, and yet more amazed when Wayne told him of his conditions. It was to be at the Bat and Ball—but of course—and they were to sit at a table out of the line of sight of Ken's; no regulars were to be permitted anywhere near, JC especially was to stay clear and not attempt eavesdropping by 'jus collectin them glarses', Tony the Convert was to fund all drinks for Wayne and for Wayne's chosen representative—none other than Pilot Ken in person. Any reluctance to top up the booze would count against the evangelist, as would ostentatious, virtue-signalling sipping of fizzy water.

'So I'm what in this set-up? Chairman; referee? Facilitator?'

'Ooo, "facilitator" is good; got that off Little Mal and his silly bloody meetings eh Ken?'

'Probably so.'

'One thing y'can do is stop me takin is bloody ead off if e overdoes it with the oly waters.'

'Other than that, I stay out of it?'

'As you say.'

'I shall begin with a short prayer.' Tony the Convert composed himself, hands meshed, eyes closing in ostentatious self-satisfied serenity.

'Short an silent, Tony.' Ken heard Wayne's warning growl and hoped that for his own sake the holyman would play a better hand.

'Do you not pray?' asked the Covert sharply; apparently, he was no reader of people, and a slow learner to boot.

'Only for closin time never to come.' Lucky Tony, Wayne had decided to be flip.

'All the better that I have come to save your soul.'

Oh for goodness sa... Ken's thought was cut through by Wayne's much less playful response.

'You've come ere to arst me somethin. Now ask it and ask nice, less it with the savin, I doesn't want any o'that.'

'Very well, I mean that I wish to guide your... you to safety.'

'C'mon then, you wanna tell me there's something better for me: get on wi it. Don't dress it up an spare me the fancy words. Make yer pitch, be quick.'

Treated more as a salesman than a saviour, Tony the Convert was already on the back foot. 'I speak from experience Wayne; I once knew the allure of the bottle—and worse. I couldn't defeat those urges and if you'd asked me then, I'd have said I didn't want to defeat them, I was happy, so I claimed. But those pleasures were false friends, and by and by were killing me.'

'Good story; all the best stories use "by and by". Go on.'

'There seemed to be no hope, nothing and no one could pull me back from the brink: but then I found love.'

'Was she fit?'

'I mean the love of Christ, Wayne. I am just telling you how I found hope, a greater love, and the promise of another and a better life.'

'This life's enuff fer me.'

'I am talking about Paradise, the better life by far that awaits us—if we reject sin and the devil, embrace God.'

'You got your paradise, I got mine.'

'Paradise is not for us to fashion; it is for us to work to deserve it.'

'Spose…' began Wayne.

'Suppose?' echoed The Convert, hunching forward, encouraging, close-listening; well done, at bloody last, thought Ken.

'Spose this is paradise, here—close to it as a git like me can get. S'pose it's not just all I can ave but all I wants. S'pose when I die, I just shifts over a dimension, and pops up here, its version of here. Paradise enough for me.'

'Wayne, you are playing around with blasphemous thoughts.'

'I can make up me own afterlife. One as suits me. You got yours, off the peg you got it, all made up for you. I can make my own up if I want one. I dunt get much choice about how I has to live. Got a borin job to pay the rent and the like, stupid-long hours an not much pay, all I got is a decent drink at the end of it. An that's about it, there's nothin more, not for me. There's nothin comin neither, before someone says some crap about you never know what's comin round the corner. So I got me nights an me pyzin cup, an make do wi that.'

'It is not enough just to know the love of heaven, to enjoy its bounty you must free yourself of sin. It is a duty, to set aside our sins, to make amends.'

'Fuckin ell, it must ave taken *you* a good while to do that, our Tone!'

'We all must work hard if we are to free ourselves of the sins of our past,' continued The Convert, to Ken's amusement, 'and we must have pure intentions. Wayne, show me that your intentions are pure.'

'Show me yours are pure, Tone. Hit the bar.'

'Wayne, to come to the love of heaven, perhaps you should think about what… evil… is driving you in your current behaviour?' Ken winced.

'What if it's not evil, what if there's none of your bogeys, good or evil, workin here, what if it's a choice, the choice of a man?' barked Wayne, passion undulating beneath his words. 'What if it's the best thing available, *my choice?*'

Tony was open-mouthed. 'How could such a thing be a choice? How could it be so?'

'Cos there's nothin more for me, sure o that. They take this glass out of me hand and there's nothin at all; livin just becomes breathin, breathin an waitin. So I choose—end the waitin. It's the only choice I got, the only control.'

'Wayne, the philosopher of death. Bloody hell,' breathed Ken.

'But… why? How can going on living seem so pointless to you?'

At last—the question we all want answered. You took you time, Tone.

'Daytime, me, I'm just a donkey. Wakes up a donkey, goes an gets harnessed, gets loaded as a donkey, pulls and labours as a donkey, goes home and sleeps, wakes up as a donkey, endless donkey days, wassapoint? I'm only a man, I'm only me, when the donkeyin stops and I gets here. There's nuthin else. Donkeys just do—they dunt ave t remember what they done. Endless donkey days, just endless. Tell you what made it clear, made me realise ow stupid it all was—it wus the Bollocks Board.'

'Bollocks board?' Tony the Convert worked over the words as if tonguing a lump of poison.

'Named it that, reckon that's the sort of thing Kenny would've called it, so I borried the idea. Noticeboard at work: y'know, the bosses put it up, ole cork board with bits o paper pinned up, notices, build-ups for the boss's fav'rit charity, whist drives, I dunno, sometimes come-one-come-all for a works shindig, maybe even bits for sale or swaps, bit o business amongst us shopfloor lot, y'know—but, what d'we get? It got took over. It wasn't ours no more, it wasn't *for* us, no, it was at us. No more bring'n'buys, no more party invites or charabanc trips, instead we got words, words writ

108

big, messages from the top to the bottom, and you can make book it wasn't about pay rises or bonuses. I gets in one day and there's this block-caps shouter sayin:

"'NOTHING IS IMPOSSIBLE TO A WILLING HEART".

'An I thinks wass all this about? Wassit mean? Then day after day the same bloody thing, bloody pieces of paper with these slogans in magic marker.

"'ALL WHO HAVE ACCOMPLISHED GREAT THINGS HAVE HAD A GREAT AIM AND FIXED THEIR EYES ON A GOAL WHICH WAS A HIGH ONE — WHICH SOMETIMES SEEMED IMPOSSIBLE".

"'Motivational" they called them, as to get everyone workin harder an happier, so they'd have it: more like threats that's what I says; be like we tells you or you'm out. An then there was this one:

"'THE PRIME CAUSE OF UNHAPPINESS IS NEVER THE SITUATION BUT YOUR THOUGHTS ABOUT IT".

'See whut they did there? It dunt take much of a fool to work out what what they meant—if yer dunt like what's appenin to yer, it's yer own fault. Change yer thoughts, cos we in't changin.

"PEOPLE OFTEN SAY THAT MOTIVATION DOESN'T LAST. WELL NEITHER DOES BATHING—THAT'S WHY WE RECOMMEND IT DAILY".

'Oh god! The sheer bloody *bollocks!* If I could just splain how my spirits crash whenever I go in an see a new one on that board… for gawd's sake, we're donkeys every one on us, move shite around a damn warehouse, what for do we need all this? One of the bigwigs must have had a Big Book of Bollocks that they got some poor put-upon sec'try to copy in her best handwritin. Somehow those writeups, they sneak into your mind, you start obeyin, they're… law. And people don't realise what's happenin to em. So many people dunt realise what's being done to em. There was another a while back:

"'A DIAMOND IS A LUMP OF COAL THAT DID WELL UNDER PRESSURE".

'Now I didn like tha at all. Know what it said to me? We're gonna squeeze you, squeeze you tight and hard an it'll improve you up, cos yer crap.

'And—"IF YOU LOOK AT LIFE IN BLACK AND WHITE, YOU MISS ALL ITS BEAUTIFUL COLOURS".

'Couldn't help it, I adds "But your TV licence is cheaper". That bit got cut off, double-quick. They didn't like it, backchat, like. The bollocks stayed, mind. Spend time and money on what the bosses want, give it all up for bollocks; bollocks costs em naught, gets em lots. Bollocks becomes law, an people don't realise whass happenin, they just do as wanted.

"'CHANGE THE WAY YOU LOOK AT THINGS AND THE THINGS YOU LOOK AT WILL CHANGE".

'They bloody hope, eh? Thing is, our works has got the sickness; it's all about: this town's got it, the Ring too, probably everyone. They know summat's wrong, but dunno what to do, or mebbe dunt care—so they just pin up the bollocks on the board—and wait fur us to take the blame for not donkeyin hard enuff and lose us jobs. Like ever, they won't lose theirs, they'll screw what they can out o'us, pitch us out, then move on elsewhere and carry on making their ackers no matter. I heard Little Mal talkin about it with his council mates, they were here, "managed decline" they called it, the town's goin down an the best they can give us is a soft landin. There'll be no rescues...' Wayne glared at Tony '...and no fuckin miracles.'

He brightened momentarily as another beer arrived.

'Went in the office on site, what d'yer know but I found the book they used—the Bible of Bollocks...' He grinned as Tony the Convert grimaced. 'All them stupid slogans were

110

in there, them an hundreds more, so much that there could be booster bollocks on the board long after we'd bin out in th dumper. I wus so tempted to steal it, burn it, ave an accident with the office shredder...

'Any road, it were when they put up "WORK:MORE WORK: BETTER WORK". That's when I knew it was all up. They were gonna squeeze us one last time then that'd be it. Pee forty-fives all round, and off out to find that there int no other jobs out there. All over.'

'But can't you see.' Tony the Convert was urgent and impassioned. 'There are miracles, hope—that's exactly what I can bring you to! You have described hopelessness, a void—you can fill that void, with the word of God!'

'So you say mate, but to me all that religious stuff, yours, anyone else's, it's just one more Bollocks Board. If you gotta feed people bullshit in magic marker just t'keep em goin then nothin's worth anythin. So there's nothin waitin round the corner, no bright tomorrer, jus me an me pyzin cup, an if I'm lucky, people who'll be good to me and let me be.'

The evening did not end well: Tony the Convert, appalled, drew himself gangling out of his chair, then gestured angrily over Wayne's head, throwing his arms about and taking in Pilot Ken in the compass of his agitated whirlings.

'I have never heard such... heresy from a man in my life, such offences against the truth of God! In the name of Jesus Christ...' Tony spun, opening his arms to the pub, playing to an attentive gallery; the showman in him took a beat, tried to gauge his crowd, and in that moment he was lost.

'Yew think yer im, don't yer?' Wayne's voice was loud and plaintive.

'What?'

'Im, you think yer im. Like some dumbo politicians ponce round and talk like they're bloody Churchill, think they are bloody Churchill—you think you're im!'

'I wish to be like him, I wish to do his work.' Tony, his momentum stymied, gulped, clasping at his dignity.

'Nah,' grunted Wayne, 'it's more'n that: less, rather. I'm just a scalp for your collection. You don't care a cuss oth'wise.'

'Wayne, that is not so!' But Tony was rattled. Wayne bared his serried sharkteeth at Ken wickedly, triumphantly.

'They calls you Tony the Convert, but you wants more'n that. You wants to be Tony the Converter, fishin for men an duckin heads in th'river and all that. Thass the name you want. "Look Lord, I saved Wayne I did, where's me badge?"'

Tony the Convert twitched, an anger-twitch, a pulsing, pressured-nerve tic.

'Get gone, Tone. No deal.'

'I shall pray for y…'

'Nah mate. Don't bother. Really.'

Wayne was a hero of the local for a short time after his up-and-downer with the Convert, but in retrospect the ill-tempered final exchange was just another sign of his decline; he became touchier, more of a loner, instead of responding to provocation he sought it; the quiz night lost its popularity as Wayne became disagreeable even with those who followed his rules. His skin tone sallowed, and yet still he came and nobody could make themselves stop him.

Ken's hospice acquaintance, he recalled, had also remarked about people's need to communicate in the face of impending death.

'Most want to say four things—"I forgive you"; "Please forgive me"; "I love you" and "Goodbye".'

Ken always thought of this whenever he spoke to Wayne, whose messages to the world were somewhat different. Spit it out, he told himself, why be just a dead-and-gone who never said his piece? He had already gifted his advice to Frank Speke: as time drained he also cornered others, and let them have it. To Gina it was 'Stay wi yer husband an stop pissin him about'—to Emily, just 'Stop pissing him about'—which left a question of stress, which 'him' was meant? To Jim Wayne said, 'Y still worry about what people think o you. Stop it. They are scum and their

112

opinions are but nothin.' He spoke to Pilot Ken too, but Ken told nobody what was said.

The service took place at the usual venue, Pilot Ken and Evil Mand were once again archly complimented on how good they looked together in their posh outfits and there was a great spread back at the Bat and Ball. JC shambled to Pilot Ken, dusted in crumbs and with tiny cucumber pieces in his ragged beard.

'Kenny, Kenny, hey Kenny, where's Wayne? He'd of liked this ere, free food n all!'

'Where do you think he is, JC?' Ken realised that his question could be taken as a metaphysical, philosophical one. He thought for a moment of Wayne in his other-world, his paradise, where Wayne was a new Prometheus—every day his liver destroyed, but renewed with every dawn. JC, however, was not musing metaphysics or philosophy. Ken could see the old man's eyes behind his thick, rippling distorting lenses; they rolled slowly upwards as if following the stately rise of a plume of smoke. JC's mouth opened a little way and from it issued a croak, a snatch of a hymn, 'Slow to chide an swiff to bless,' but the mournful sound decayed as it began, degenerating in to 'Nyerrr yaee-arr, nyerrr yaee-arr!' Turning back to the buffet table, JC picked up another batch and shed more crumbs on himself and the floor. As Pilot Ken turned, JC's voice picked up again, filled with a renewed urgency.

'Kenny, Kenny, hey Kenny—pay yer Poll Tax mate, pay yer fuckin Poll Tax, pay it mate, pay it up, make sure yer do it.'

The old man had forgotten.

The next day was quiet, the pub almost empty all day.

Not that, as it's deathly (8) Pilot Ken sighed over the clue.

'Difficult one?' asked Jim.

'No, not at all. Just sort of untimely.'

The Theatre Is Dark

How do you build a ghost? Not the sort the stage crew could put together—simple white sheets for a kiddies' show, a cocktail of light, shadow and misdirection for the grownups—but the sort that was supposed to haunt the Playhouse? Out of halfmemories and semidark, rumours, bloody lies; add generous dashes of guilt and gullibility. That's how. There is no fucking ghost here; that's a tired, hack story from a PR man who's sold his little pass to the enemy. Oh, he's butter-wouldn't-melt at the moment, but I'll catch him out one day soon and knock him into next year. And there will be a next year, there will be a next season. Just to scotch another irritating, lingering rumour.

Emily kissed Pilot Ken gently on the cheek, brushed at a piece of fluff on his coat lapel—a silly thing to do, his lapels and collar were all fluff anyway—and watched him swing open the door and leave, waving a tiny bye-bye as he turned to his right to make for the shopping centre, the short-cut to his destination. The steel-framed glass door stuck—yet again—as it swung back: Emily had to drag it shut and it protested in a groaning, juddering, ringing. Another minor problem to add to the long can't-be-paid-for repairs list; two out of the four main doors now played up, and both the others were showing disturbing signs.

It had happened as she greeted Ken an hour before, it was the grating of the door that had given away the presence of another arrival who, left to himself, would almost certainly have gone unnoticed. He was a small man with sharp, snout-like features and tint glittering eyes full of self-interested enquiry who, after a nervous glance at the betrayer door, scuttled to the nearest shadow or approximation, trying not to trade so much as the sliver of a glance with the couple in the lobby as he made his furtive way to the swinging, silent door of the PH Bar. Ken had arrived in a good mood and although his face screwed up with obvious disapproval as he saw this human rodent arrive, scurrying for a bolt-hole, he couldn't help but alarm the creature with a hale, ironic tone.

'Good day to you, Scamp.'

The creature stopped, turned, looked alarmed but then dissimulated a smile.

'And to you Kenny. And yer friend.'

The PH Bar door flapped quietly as Scamp vanished inside.

'If you want to make this place classier,' said Ken, as they walked slowly to the Foyer Restaurant, 'close that cesspit down, fumigate it and then nail the door shut. Only, unfortunately, I am all in favour of the place remaining open as it keeps him and his ilk from poisoning the atmosphere at respectable establishments.'

'Catering's nothing to do with me.' Emily smiled. 'Nor is environmental health. Anyway, you know why that bar's there; it may be a dive, but it pays. Steady income stream. Money-money-money-money. I just make theatrical decisions, artistic decisions. Theatre? Art? *Phut.* This is the Playhouse. Here Mammon rules.' The door of the restaurant folded around them like a curtain.

Emily laughed at herself as she watched Ken go; it was almost a stock scene of a woman seeing her husband off to work, but it was she who was returning to work, and Ken was almost certainly returning to the Bat And Ball. And he was not her husband or anything else—unless you subscribed to some of the wilder rumours that coursed the pub.

'Nice lunch then Ken?'

'Had another little nibble, eh, Kenny?'

And so forth. Emily didn't go back to work at once; not to her tiny office at the top of the building, at least. A thinking-space was needed, not a penpushing one; she had chosen the tiny room just off the studio-theatre as her office because it sat at the top of the building, approached by steep stairs, an added isolation that encouraged her to bear down on the paperwork and discouraged others from 'just popping in' with gossip, trivial complaints or talk of fucking ghosts. The office was Emily's declared, owned space, but her true den, her retreat, was secret, undeclared. She walked furtively back through the foyer, up the stairs past the parade of framed pictures highlighting the past triumphs of the Playhouse, then in to the silent, lightless auditorium. She had to grope her way to the Producer's Chair, a venerable high-backed winged monster set into a small alcove at the very back of the auditorium, behind the back row. Emily settled and at once was comfortable and relaxed, her body at rest but her mind alive.

Several people bent on 'improvements' had suggested removing the chair; Emily refused sternly. You can innovate, modernise, update anything, but the chair stays put. Take it away when I die, not before. The chair had been in place many years, it was there for the director of a show to slip into unobtrusively during performances, to see what the audience was seeing, to test the atmosphere and offer pointers to the cast as the run progressed—one or two visiting directors even managed a crafty snooze in the comforting darkness, though whether that demonstrated despair or confidence in their cast, nobody knew. Emily used the chair frequently, observing rehearsals, sampling shows, and like now for silent solo meditations, as had her mother in years gone by. Nobody was taking it.

As Emily's eyes grew accustomed to the less-than-half-light of the still auditorium she could make out some of the rows of seats and the steps running between them, which plunged into more profound darkness just below, darkness her eyes still could not penetrate. The square arch of the proscenium gaped more in her recall than in sight; old plays, past performers passed and paraded, threading through the lightlessness, criss-crossing one another easily and without sound. Ghosts. Some of Emily's earliest memories were of

116

sitting in this auditorium; she remembered being frightened by the first pantomime she ever saw, she had clung to her mother with clammy hands, afraid of the noisy grotesques who thudded heavy-footed across the echoing stage, able to conjure an obedient, shouting hysteria from everyone around her. Slowly she grew accustomed to the frantic mummery, a little bored with the constant repetition, fell asleep. But she was not sleepy now in the still, soundless ambience. The theatre was dark yet there was a lingering trace of life, performance, hot lights and the smell of people seated close together, rows of eyes following every move on stage.

Memories took Emily backstage too; kneehigh, she was staying close to her mother as she toured the dressing-rooms, which that night were filled with tassels, chaps, check shirts, cowboy hats, feathered headdresses and the strong smell of thick, dark makeup. Tara introduced her to one of the cowboys, and with a boldness that took her by surprise, Emily asked if she could hold his gun; this was agreed at a nod from her mother and on a solemn promise that the little girl would not attempt to pull the trigger. 'It will make a terrible noise,' said the cowboy mildly, lowering his hand as Emily attempted to pick the gun up; his caution proved wise, Emily had expected the gun to be hollow and light, a plastic toy, but it was huge, coldly and solidly metallic and of such a weight she could barely lift it with both hands. The cowboy laughed gently, rescued the gun from her failing grasp, slipping it into the long black holster at his hip. His face was ruddy, shiny, the dressing-room lights drew out sparkles and aura-glows to accompany his slightest movements.

'Is it *real?*' asked Emily, awed. 'Are you going to shoot someone?'

'Not tonight,' chuckled the cowboy, 'but I fire it off over my head during the show. Cover your ears, it's loud.'

Huh, thought Emily in the chair, men in makeup, I never knew why people made such a fuss about it, not when it was a part of my life from the very start. I always wondered why men on the street looked so pasty. Mother had once bought her a box of her own stage-makeup, coloured sticks in little wrappers as if they were chocolate bars; the foil was golden, the thick stick-tips felt cool on her skin as she drew bizarre designs on her face, only bothering to consult a mirror once her work was done. The box was a wonder, so beautiful, the size of a large shoebox made with a stacked lid like a little roof, the light-coloured wood of its sides and lid beautified with intricate inlaid lines and swirls, Emily read them with her fingers as if she were discovering a new language. But though she had loved the makeup, the box, the thrill of dressing up, she had never fancied a role before the lights: the bug had not bitten her that way, and in that she differed from her mother. Where was that treasure-box now? Somewhere safe, but the too-safe sort of safe, the sort of safe that would require the house to be stripped to bare laths to find it. One day, perhaps... a shadow shifted, a whisper hissed, Emily could hear movement elsewhere in the building, far off, faint. That stupid door screeched as someone came, or went. Emily caught herself worrying at her nails: it's not attractive, I know, but how to stop? It makes me look frightened and nervous when I'm not—it shows weakness. This is no time to show weakness.

No ghosts then, but the magic-lantern show continued, summoned at will: the figures on the stage, insubstantial and yet there, stirred, crisscrossed, blended, separated, interacted, interplayed, acted out scenes sometimes linked, sometimes simultaneous, crossing and recrossing the apron, upstage, down, stage right, stage left, the bounds of time; people appeared as they are now, as they were years before, sometimes both at once. Not ghosts, not phantoms; thoughts and memories, called to the stage by Emily, under her control in the calling, but once before her the privileges of the chair were curtailed, and the performers would accept no prompts, no directions or rewrites; she was an onlooker, an audience member only.

Scene: The Bat And Ball. Emily's first appearance there. Pilot Ken, Gina, Jim, Frank are at the table engaged in their conversations [unheard] as a spotlight picks out Emily to emphasise her newness and isolation. The spot widens to include a man seated next to Emily: he is leaning forward rather too much and she is trying not to shrink from him.

'Theatre? "Artistic Director"?' Disgust and anger were the only things keeping this man conscious; his eyes were watery slits and Emily could have sworn he was asleep half the time, even when speaking. He reeked of drink from his clothes, skin, hair, breath; why he wasn't face-down on the table was a mystery to Emily, but he was keeping grimly going, tilting his wrist and making aggressive, almost automated conversation.

'Theatre,' the man repeated. 'Theatre. What fuckin use is your theatre to the working-class families on my estate? Uh?'

The 'uh' was a gale of fermented waste product. Jim leaned over as if to offer protection or intervention, but Emily waved him away. Instead, she prepared and served a response of spun sugar. 'I don't know; what would they like to see?'

He may have been on the verge of alcoholic lights-out, but this man was not to be mocked. His sleepy eyes widened and water was ousted by fire. 'What have you and your fuckin middle-class theatre ever done for...'

This man was not to be mocked but Emily was not to be browbeaten. 'Three recent benefit concerts for local causes, free theatre workshops for youngsters from the estates, free tickets or concession-prices for most performances for low-waged and pensioners,' she snapped; but it was as if she had not spoken.

'But what is your fuckin theatre doing, what good is it?'

'I just told you.'

'Your fuckin theatre would do better as a shelter for the homeless, or a food bank, or just a fuckin car park; somethin fuckin useful anyway. Noel fuckin Coward and Shakespeare, maybe a fuckin light opera, nothing that means anything, nothing that helps...'

'Three recent benefit concerts for local causes, free theatre workshops for youngsters from the estates, free tickets or concession-prices for most performances for low-waged and pensioners.'

Emily considered rhapsodising on dreams, the free flight of imagination, travel to other worlds, both physical and mental alternatives from an inexpensive theatre seat, but didn't, firstly as it sounded like second-rate puffery, but also because this man simply was not listening.

'Just fuckin middle class, fuckin middle class... theatre should be there to arouse the revolutionary consciousness of the workers, educate them, get them to think about rising against their oppressors...'

'Rather than just "thinking"? Actually, we did an evening of Soviet drama a few years back, it was very funny; boy meets tractor, falls in love, devotes himself to Stakhanovite labour, makes windy speeches, dies heroically, if pointlessly, Soviet Union collapses...'

'It's not fuckin funny, you fuckin middle class...'

Scene: The Playhouse, interior, nearly all seats are full, the house lights are up, curtain is closed; five figures are seated at a long table, facing the audience. The table is draped with the symbol of the council workers' union.

There was no stagecraft—not the usual kind anyway, no performances ditto—no subtlety or shifts of light; no shadows, no hidden corners; everyone equal. It was the same pattern every time: speeches from the platform, questions from the floor, or rather the rake of seats, a show of hands, purely indicative, binding votes were secret. Another part of the floor show was when a figure would rise from his seat during question-time, but unlike others he was not asking a short question, indeed he was not minded to put questions of any sort. He straightened, pulled at the lapels of his ill-fitting jacket as he cleared his throat with the determination of a street-corner orator, a barricades preacher, plunged his hand in his inner breast pocket and produced a sheaf of cue-cards: closely-typed cue cards. Before he could speak, a groan swept the auditorium, a deep moan of well-accustomed despair, from the proscenium through the stalls to the circle to the gods. Sober, absolutely concentrated, FMC would let every word resound, he had learned to use the theatre's carefully designed acoustics to their best advantage. He ignored, possibly did not even register, the howls of pain at his every Marxian cliché, the knowing cackles at his every call for a strike, the vigorous games of bullshit bingo so obviously taking place under his nose.

Scene: A void (white backdrop, strongly backlit) against which stand two figures in silhouette; the WHISPERER and the ASPIRANT.
    'How are things at The Regal?'
    'Going down the drain. Plughole. Nothing I can do, it's all out of control. The place will be a car park or something, and fairly soon. No idea what I'll do after. Exit one career.'
    'You've got good ideas, the right approach. You'll find something soon.'
    'Don't suppose there's any vacancies at your end?'
    'You can't quote me of course, but there's talk of change—the need for new blood, new ideas: energy. Vision.'
    'Tara Peterson's not moving on, is she? She is that place, she's there for life.'
    'One of the new ideas is that there are no jobs for life. Tara is a legend, but there's a feeling she's done all she can, she's tired, the well is dry.'
    'But I know she's already talking about the programme for next season…'

'Tara doesn't realise the reality. There's a new funding model, she can't accept it. Her reputation is impressive, but she's losing box office, and artistic temperament, not to mention artistic tantrums, are no good in the face of that. We need someone who can accept the new reality, work with it. Be artistic but without the temper.'

'How soon?'

'Her name still carries weight; she's still got support. She'll get her next season but it will only confirm what we already know. Stay in touch, eh?'

Scene reprise: Emily vs FMC at the Bat and Ball

'So, what have you done for the unemployed on your estate? Are you their leader? Did they elect you? Do they know you're their leader?'

'Listen, you fuckin middle-class bitch…'

Emily leaned over to him, deep into his stinking aura, and breathed 'Never mind that. Would you like to come outside?'

'What?' he still exhaled pure fumes, but now he was paying attention.

'For a dramatic interlude.'

'What?'

'I haven't punched anyone for thirty years, not since I knocked my sister's front tooth out. Now I'm so angry I'm going to push your fuckin workin class face in and drag it out of your arse.'

But FMC was out to the wide, his head flopped forward, chin on chest.

Pilot Ken became angry when he heard about this encounter, which annoyed Emily. What was the use of leaping to her defence after the fact? She was deeply fond of Ken, regarded him as one of the best of men, but even he couldn't help but occasionally imply that she was incapable of fighting her own battles. She calmed Ken down and lunch went on peaceably. But he became angry again when he heard about her meeting that morning. Ken offered to 'have a word' with Little Mal, so incensed was he, and though tempted to allow someone to berate, and preferably belt, Mal, Emily again testily demanded the right to decide her own response, and to lead the fight.

Scene: The Bat And Ball—could be any night
'Dickens! As in what-the.' Pilot Ken dropped his pen and removed his half-moon glasses with a firm flourish, a gesture of triumph over another convoluted crossword clue.
'Genius,' spake Frank Speke.

Ken's crossword clue had sparked the latest round of a perennial parlour game: name a genius who was not a bastard. To date, nobody had ever thought of an acknowledged genius who wasn't also an inadequate individual, an insufferable colleague, a bad parent, a terrible spouse, a selfish, troublesome and unreliable friend. Suggestions were made, as were arguments, agreement was never reached, the discussion died to embers and then rekindled. Musical genius, political genius, inspired artistry, a heavenly facility with the pen, a case was made for all, but even where genius was admitted, there remained the second qualification.

'Genius,' repeated Frank Speke sharply in his most authoritative do-not argue voice, 'Visionary, social reformer.': the search was over as far as Frank was concerned. Gina, as ever, was ready to ignore Frank's strictures on her free speech; 'Wife abuser, cheating, sadistic torturer.' Frank glowered his fiercest anti-PC glower but he had never been able to browbeat Gina.

'When Lenin was dying,' chipped in an amazingly sober FMC, 'his wife sat by his bed and read him stories. He enjoyed Jack London but waved away Dickens; full of bourgeois sentiment.' Pilot Ken chuckled; another candidate proposed and then monstered in short order. Emily never played the game, but it always set her thinking, a stream of melancholy, unsettling thoughts, always of the same name and face. For Emily, Ken's competition was won, and yet nobody ever spoke the name: artist, director, artistic director too, thank you very much, actor, writer, administrator, exemplary parent, friend. And genius. Sometimes unsung, sometimes too-much sung. People never could see what was under their noses.

SCENE: *Playhouse past. The curtain has fallen on A Night At Every Theatre. Emily, age seventeen, is in the Producer's Chair as a favour, as the house is packed.*

'Encore! Encore!'

'Author!'

The heat and noise stirred memories in Emily of her wave of childish, uncomprehending fear at the unruly racket of look-out-behind-you and drag-dame shrieks; she felt closed in, pinned by the applause, threatened by the shouts as if they would stifle her, steal her breath. The exit, where's the door? Oh; right next to me, I'm at the back. Stop panicking.

'Author! Author!'

'Author!' the voices were whooping, insistent. Join in— applaud! Emily beat her hands in a different time to everyone else. The curtains parted and the ragtag cast took another bow; with syncopated movements they assembled in two ranks, arms extended to the rear of the stage to summon, then gliding forward to usher, the beaming author.

'The other writers send their apologies...' began Tara. Laughline, well delivered. So come on girl, laugh.

People of discernment had never ceased in their acclaim of Tara's production of Shaffer's *Sleuth*, which she directed, also taking a double role; all declared that they had seen no better work pro or am. She could have been an accomplished writer too, but the same discerning people held that she didn't take that aspect of her talent *seriously*. As the satyr-play conclusion of *An Evening At Every Theatre*, a fundraising selection-box of scenes from all-time favourites,

124

Tara wrote and directed the superlatively silly *Pintermime*, in which Shakespearean characters in full-ruff finery would wander on a stage set for John Osbourne, interrupt a kitchen-sink argument, declaim a fragment of a famous soliloquy in broad local argot then burst into tears, fleeing the stage; several characters remained on the apron of the stage in grim, tell-all silence; performers in togas and ill-fitting Greek tragicomic masks blundered into the scenery, fell offstage and then tried all over; Jacobean revengers pursued one another with long knives, circling and swiping, occasionally expiring from ingesting Spanish salads; two tramps waited patiently, unmoving, by a withered tree; middle-aged men skittered at random across the stage grabbing desperately at sagging bags. This ludicrous free-form mash-up received distinctly sniffy notices but everyone else who saw adored it. Tara was heaped with bouquets, a new one every time she attempted to quit the spotlight, and Emily knew the party would go on for hours, raucous and self-congratulatory, gushdarling-gush. 'Emily-Emily-Emily, you must be so *proud* of her!' Yes of course I am, when can I go home?

The chair, in the quiet dark, conjured admissions. I *was* proud, but I was seventeen, embarrassed by the fuss, confused by the storm; that's not fair but allright-allright, I was carried away by my imagination, I wasn't jealous as such, but why wasn't it me on that stage reaping that applause author-author-author? I saw my future on that stage, but wanted to quick-cut from aspiration to applause without doing the bloody hard work that came in between. I kept it all bottled: Mum would have understood, she probably did, she could always see through me. I soon found I could never lift a pen, not to make new words, and never to rival my mother, even though she didn't take her talent seriously.

Emily got round to doing the bloody work: given the nature of her mentor there was little choice. Turbulent, disputatious, oppositional, the conflict grew as Emily gained experience and honed her burgeoning skills against the unyielding whetstone of Tara's perfectionism. Sam Delgado called it the Apprenticeship of Fire; Sam, the Playhouse's masterly Stage Manager, had worked with Tara for years, Emily believed his every Beckettian wrinkle to be sculpted by the strain of that association. As Emily slammed out of the Studio Theatre where shrill echoes still played around the walls and ceiling, Sam put out an arm to halt her stalking, stamping progress.

'Well,' rolled his gentle, cultured voice, 'you're still alive. Which makes me suspect your mum is not...' It worked; Emily smiled; she couldn't stop herself. How to tell him that what he'd heard was nothing compared to the screaming rows of high adolescence, you embarrass me, you and your showoff luvviebunch, *you're the worst mother in history, no wonder dad took off, you're never there for me, you ought to be, choose me or the fucking theatre...*

'Runs a tight ship, does Tara. Sometimes it's difficult.'

'People who boast about running a tight ship are bullies and incompetents, sheltering their inadequacy behind macho words. Sheer crap.' Emily trampled fiercely on his avuncular empathy.

'Humph. Chip off the ol... nevermind.' Sam smiled amiably and tried not to give the impression of hurrying away. Such a lovely man; an occasional actor too, none other than the gun-toting cowboy of infant recall. He died on the same day as Tara—in a different place and from a different cause, but however thin it was sufficient gruel to feed the ghost-builders.

Scene: Emily in the Producer's Chair. Side View. Tara straddles the last chair of the backrow, facing her. Their heads are strongly spot-lit, the chairs barely visible, they are in separate islands of light. The atmosphere is tense, but their voices never rise.

'I've got to tell you: the new show is... superb. You're ready to go it alone.'

'Ooo, I can take the stabilisers off?'

'I mean it. You're ready. The question is for what?'

'Meaning? Are we about to "have a talk"?'

'Yes. Perhaps not the one you're thinking of. Emily you're ready, for anything. I want this theatre in safe hands, and yours are very safe, the best I know. But... I've also had to admit that you may not want to stay here. Don't look at me like that; I'm saying that you are good, you are excellent, you could take my place in due course, or you could strike out for yourself, another town, bigger, more prestigious theatres, London even. Yes, you are that good. Providing you understand you'd be moving from a placid lake with the odd pike in it, to a churning ocean full of sharks.'

'Strike out?'

'Emily, I've been selfish; all I've thought of is to train someone to take my place, and I have to admit to myself that mother's footsteps may not be enough for you. You've never said anything, but we can't put it off too long. This place calls me, but you may not feel the same. If you're going to commit, or to get away, you'll need to decide soon.'

'Why now? What's going on?'

'Something tells me I need to know. Not now but soon; as soon as possible.'

'You're on about me taking over? You're talking as if...'

'It's not so much about me. It's more about the big fish... circling.'

Long pause.

Blackout.

Scene—Emily's office at the top of the Playhouse building. Three people, two men and a woman, sit upright and confident, dominating the tiny room. Emily sits at her desk but appears uncomfortable and out of place, like a nervous interviewee or errant schoolgirl.

From the point of view of a director, Emily thought admiringly from the depths of the Producer's Chair, it was an object lesson in how to make a ghost- an unseen presence, an immanence, that may be more accurate; no names, no literality, not even the merest hint or inference; and yet...

Emily had paraded the shiny, natty little delegation through the foyer, up the stairs and on a brutal forced-march tour backstage, as rapid and rigorous as that of the over-excited participants in *An Evening With God*. That was a favourite recent squib of hers that had commenced with the audience being enjoined from the stage to search the auditorium (making sure to look under seats) and then to comb the building for any hide-and-seek deities (a process that caused quite a ruckus in the PH Bar). On returning to their seats they were given lucky-dip drinks, which were either 'holy water' or 'communion wine', until an unremarkable figure in an upper-tier seat was identified as none other than God and escorted to the stage by eager helpers and there subjected to a withering fire of questions, the responses to which showed that the deity was a question-dodging, blame-throwing waters-muddying consummate politician. Provoked to outrage, a member of the audience (an actor, planted, of course) bellowed 'This is an outrage! Get God!' prompting a rush at the stage and a hurly-burly pursuit of the small figure, who proved to be as elusive in motion as in speech; the chase went on backstage until the athletic Almighty was discovered, untouchable, in a nest of knotted ropes in the flies, swinging most high and alternately hurling down curses and small bags of sweets from the folds of His shimmering robe.

The three nights of the show were picketed noisily by Tony the Convert and a small band of evangelicals, none of whom was familiar to Emily as she hovered near the ticket office, worrying about the effect of the blockade on her audience and take. Tony and his acolytes stood close to the doors, shouting loudly, placard-waving, leafleting, kneeling in hammy attitudes of prayer and extending their arms across the span of the propped-open doors as people tried to pass; no incidents broke out however, the restraining arms were dropped the moment it was clear the theatregoer was determined to enter, and the yelling was uncoordinated, barely comprehensible. Some punters may even have thought it was a little pre-show entertainment; there were uncertain smiles as people ran the bawling barricade.

Now, here's an interesting scene developing, thought Emily, as she recognised the head-down lone figure on a direct heading for the door covered by Tony the Convert; FMC was coming in for a night of bourgeois culture and he did not look minded to be stopped by what he'd doubtless call Cross-creepers. This could be a row worth a listening-in; Emily edged closer to the door, muttering discreet good evenings as people filtered past her. Tony the Convert and FMC locked eyes: they knew one another. Tony extended his arm, not across the door this time but in a pointing gesture, fingers almost touching the other man's chest. 'If you proceed,' preachified Tony, 'you make a mockery of God himself!' Emily edged a little closer, waiting for the tirade of obscenity and vilification. FMC pushed Tony's hand away, their eyes still locked, as if…

'Ridiculous,' snapped FMC, breaking the lock and marching into the theatre with renewed determination. Curiously disappointed, Emily remained in place, telling herself she was ensuring that none of her customers would be molested, but in truth hoping that someone, *someone* would give Tony what-for. Just before the main doors were closed, Emily slipped outside, stalked up to the departing Tony, tapped him on the shoulder, and before he had pivoted to look her in the face, asked, 'How do you know it's your god up there?'

'There is only our God,' retorted Tony with flat certainty.

'Sounds avant-gardee, Em, very cuttin-edge.' cackled Frank Speke, back in the pub. It was his way of providing support.

'It was shit,' pronounced FMC. 'But no fucker stops me going where I want.'

Emily pushed the pace still further, hoping that the final clamber would at last tarnish their sheen of self-confidence and indefatigable rectitude; their uneven breathing as they reached one more, yet narrower, set of steps gave her hope as their feet taptapped out of time with one another up the resonant metal steps. Emily had chosen her office with care; this was a working-space, a paper-shuffling space, a small afterthought of a room at the top of the building, off and above the tiny Studio theatre. It was a private room, almost secret, which was just that bit too much trouble to clamber up with petty complaints, carpings, gossip or idle talk of stupid ghosts. Her forced-march stratagem failed; the trio seated themselves without invitation, catching their breath with ease, retaining their irritating image, that of bank clerks who boast that they are 'bankers' or of corrupt coppers; neatsuits, gleamshoes, faces that said 'so I lied'; their cold indifference, their glossy self-confidence, reduced not one iota.

Emily resented their failure to resent her deliberately neglecting to offer coffee; perhaps three-in-one oil would have suited them better. She eliminated their names from her memory; they were, after all, ciphers, placeholders. They had a leader, nominated by Emily; the one who talked the most, absent their ineffable principal.

'This is wonderful building, a classic of modernity.' The female talking suit spoke as a connoisseur who had somehow lost her enthusiasm and subsisted as skeletally forensic.

'It won awards in the 1960s,' Emily replied, aware of the ambiguity of that accolade.

'And the theatre—award-winning also, with a fine reputation and a remarkable history.'

'Remarkable, but relatively brief,' chipped in the smaller man.

'Brief, but ongoing.' Damn; I sounded angry. Never let them know you're angry.

'The photographs on the staircase; mostly of your late mother's time here, yes?'

'I am very proud of my mother's time here.' And now I sound pettish and defensive. Emily felt the hair rising on the back of her neck.

The three unwanted visitors exchanged momentary glances and in unison adopted a 'to business' adults-in-the-room attitude. In unison, on cue; they were admirably scripted, directed from afar. In her head, Emily riffled through the script; it was familiar. It was one of regrettable hard times, empty pockets, multimedia temptations that drew away audiences, the slow death of the live show. There was to be much talk of 'Going forward', and yet they would make no progress. These were people of the future, of vision; cut-your cloth people, for the future meant do more with less, and you'll be surprised how much better things will be. They were not there to waste time; they were there to be listened to, and with respect. Tempers were kept, voices moderate and even, expressive but not overly animated. There was nothing and no one to attack. It was so frustrating, they never put a foot wrong, and in their mildness, goaded Emily to a blind fury: do something, say something, something I can react to you bastards! Their smoothwords, their buzzwords, were scripted to perfection, rehearsed, although the process couldn't have been too arduous for the performers, because they were speaking from the heart; the words had been prearranged for them, but the sentiments were innate, each a believer, a carrier, even before they had digested their lines. Scripted: and Emily knew who had plied the pen. 'Bums on seats' was never said, but boil the fine phrases down and there it was. 'Value for money' made an appearance, and Emily did not have to wait long for 'managed decline' to slither in. It was nobody's fault, every cause in the town was a fine and noble one, and yet these days there was so little in the pot, so much competition; look at the Library, the Children's Centre, the on-your doorstep offices in the local shopping hatches, they too need our help—would you deprive them? Once again, words were loudly unspoken.

'Democratic retrenchment,' Emily cut across the speaker.

'Why yes.' The speaker blinked, refusing to recognise her satirical tone, that she was trying to tell him that she recognised the cockerel-crow of his controller.

Practical, nay, pragmatic, suggestions were made by the earnest realists: perhaps there should be a few more *popular* bookings, a little less, ah, modernity, and, ah, the avoidance of unnecessary controversy such as *An Audience With God?* Go dark for longer; increase drinks sales; close the restaurant; cut the number of original plays and things people don't know; experimentation, innovation, they are not popular, they are of the past, the playthings of ghosts. Tribute bands, they paid well; Psychic Nights (Bollocks Nights, Pilot Ken would say), celeb-rich pantos for the tinsel touch.

'We believe in the future of the Playhouse,' smiled the leader, 'we foresee something… broaden the appeal, offer an immersive experience, more interactivity,'—Emily was sure that these were just spouted words, divorced from meaning—'a creative hub, an Arts Centre, a centre of cultural excellence in the town.'

Are you trying to imply that, to date, this has not been a centre of bloody excellence? Emily wondered if there was sufficient space in the vast backstage to conceal three bodies. Hm, no: four. My mother built this place—gave it birth anyway, won it friends and funds, and a reputation as both a showcase for established talent and a nursery for the upcoming, a theatre that people wanted to come to; it sold out without selling out. Mum had the advantage of a rising tide, now I must cope with the ebb. Now it's managed decline—slow subsidence and collapse. I've put my own stamp on the theatre, I've been praised for my 'progressive tastes', though that's a double-edged sword, but the crowds are dwindling and the stars don't want to come any more.

Our town is now spoken of—sneered at—as a cultural backwater. And all this is democratic bloody retrenchment making it so. We used to be a 'pocket haven' of the arts. What has gone wrong? Not a fringe theatre, more hanging-by-a-thread theatre. In the old days it was just the religious nuts who tried to close us down, now the parade of villains was far less flamboyant, darker—bureaucrats, boredom and bankruptcy. Moneymen and cutters, idiots who talk of a 'tight ship', meaning a leaky vessel, threadbare and tatty. Why must cuts be made? They never say—they just must.

Emily shrank away from the hackneyed hero-villain simplicities, but if the enemy was sieging, where were the allies? Pomo the Clown, who dreamed of a solo show at the Playhouse, offered himself, telling Emily that the two of them were the last bastions of culture. Pomo: at least he was a free agent, albeit a broke one. No high expectations imposed by a glorious history.

And there is my choice. If I take the cuts now, I may be called excellent even as I debase this place. Bloody hell. The Playhouse is under siege; once it was Tony The Convert and his little army of piety—but now there is a real enemy at the gates, in fact through the creaking, shrieking gates and eating away at us from within. The rundown theatre in the rundown town. The dark theatre in the dark town. Emily thought of her gloomy lunches with the head of the Town Library, prognosticating who would meet the cutting blades first. More signals to the young; your town, your town is running down, leave here or live in a desert.

The begging-bowl scene had been played before. The crosstalk act went on; just like the Music Hall acts of old, they toured place to place, varying the routine hardly at all. They did not need to. When Tara Peterson had heard it run through, she nodded indulgently at the suggestions for running her theatre, only breaking in on her visitors' enthusiasm by drawling languidly, 'I'm not fond of marionette shows.'

'Are they so very popular these days?'

133

'Puppetry is timeless.'

Tara also took full advantage of the Playhouse's award-winning windows, daubing their striking height and width with stark, white fury **CLOSING DOWN?** The letters, in ghost-outline, remained visible for months after the funders, catcalled, accused and petitioned, backed down, intimidated and horrified by a power they did not understand. They sent people to clean the windows and eliminate the embarrassing incident from history. But such acts of resistance were subject to the law of diminishing returns: they're back: what do I do? Mum, what do I do? What if they've learned from last time?

Fighting her disinclination to see the visitors out, for that would show such disrespect—and besides who knew where they might poke their shiny noses if not escorted off the premises?—Emily herded them out of her office, clattered them down the steps, down the wider stairs to the footstep-smothering deep carpet of the Circle landing, to the broad landing leading to the Stalls, down to the lobby past the photographs, the time-frames of a glorious past haunted by the uncertainty of the future. 'I hear tell you have a ghost in this theatre?' The leader of the invaders was almost smiling, almost conversational. 'That's quite a selling point. You might wish to think about that.' Emily hauled the heavy door open; it wailed ear-splitting notes of protest, and Emily leapt back as a figure flashed by her, a scuttling rodent that had lurked just behind the group, leaving a foul wake of stale alcohol that was nearly enough to put her off the thought of that giant G and T that had sustained her for the last hour.

Theatre, Arts Centre, Creative Hub, call it what you fucking want, just get your hands off it; let me, us, keep it, intact and working, a living thing; an inheritance, not a modern ruin abandoned by all except stupid, hopeful ghost builders.

The Cabinet in Exile

I fuckin said to fuckin Jim
I'd go the fuckin pub with im
I fuckin didn't fuckin know
The fuckin fucker wouldn't go!
And so I'm fuckin sittin ere
Starin at me fuckin beer
When fuck me, what's that fuckin row
That fuckin fucks me ears now?
This fuckin music's fuckin shite:
Fuckin ell, it's disco nite!
E fuckin knew this, fuckin Jim,
I'll wipe the fuckin floor with im;
You let me down, Jim, let's be blunt,
You fuckin fuckin fuckin…

'With apologies to the author of the original,' added Ken mildly, after this doggerel tirade.

'Apologies to us too I should hope!' Little Mal could be so, so prissy. 'Erm, precisely what was the point of that little epic?' he whined querulously. Jim, meanwhile, lolled back in his seat, head tipped, letting the ceiling have the full force of his laughter.

'The Ballad of Last Thursday Night, by Ken! And a fairly accurate picture too!' Jim continued to chuckle as he patted his mate on the shoulder, 'I'm so sorry Ken, I'd double-booked meself and forgot all about it—and I'd also forgotten that The Flag's started looking for younger customers, bit like the Bat-And.'

'But…' persisted Mal, 'what was the point of all those excess fucks?'

'Is there such a thing? I've never known you turn one down!' teased Jim.

'Don't be obtuse,' commanded Mal, which just left Jim cackling in to his beer, 'Come on Ken, what's it all about?'

'Have a think,' said Ken, now quiet and quite serious, 'on a quick word-count, how much shorter could you have made my poem by cutting out the "excess fucks" as you call em?'

'About twenty words. Oh but then it wouldn't scan would it Mr Shakespeare?'

'Just making a point,' said Ken peaceably.

'That's The Flag crossed off the list, then. One has to admit Ken's campaign to stamp out swearing in pubs won't get much of a hearing in there…'

'Stupid crusade,' pronounced FMC. 'Fighting against the tide at best. And anyway, if he's that lily-livered he should stay out of pubs, his objections are…'

'Oh-let-me-guess!'

'I'm only saying what's true.'

'Have you checked that the Party still thinks that? It does tend to change its mind quite a bit.'

'Fuck off!'

'Oh, and news just in—Joe Stalin's dead.'

'Fuck off!'

If someone conscientious and steady of hand were to plot out the rough circle known as the Ring O'Villages and then a coiled descent into town via well-chosen public houses, the result would be a jagged spiral dotted with waterhole stop-offs. Jim was steady-handed and conscientious, and he flourished his work before the others, ruining an OS map that he had lifted from an obscure shelf at the Bat And Ball before he and the rest of the Cabinet were finally repulsed by the reformist zealots who took over from the hapless Danny Deebee.

'It looks,' sniffed Little Mal, 'like the blueprint for barbed wire.'

'The search-pattern that will help us find our home from home.'

'We hope.'

This disconsolate Odyssey began in a world as yet innocent of Evil Mand, not long after the seizure of The Bat And Ball by Mr and Mrs Whitepaint: for once this was not Frank Speke's label, but a group effort. The new landpersons (that was Frank's) were two relatively young people, but who both sported white-streaked hair, greasy-stiff and raked back as if by a wild wind, their faces bearing the etiolated look of forgotten prisoners. Frank's suggestion of 'the albinoids' was rejected for sounding like an illness; Frank sulked and sought a way to blame some form of political correctness. The Whitepaints, at first perfectly friendly but remarkably slow to serve, were a relief after the dither and chaos of their predecessor. Very soon, however, they became notably less welcoming; slower than ever to the pumps, likelier to serve favoured latecomers while Ken and the others were left to wait. The regulars' favourite beers were taken off, inferior wine selected, prices increased, opening hours messed about. The newcomers achieved what Danny could not manage, ousting Julie with forensic ruthlessness: the outrage of the Cabinet and Wayne was of no avail this time, not least because any proposed walkout/boycott suited the newcomers' plans to Machiavellian perfection. With frictionless insouciance, Mr and Mrs W informed Pilot Ken that the Bat And Ball was to be renamed, refurbed and rebranded, with giant tv screens, a powerful PA, a 'performance area', a sporty, dancey air, contrivances to lure a younger clientele. 'We'll be clearing out the over-40s,' Ken was told, as if he were some aspiring apprentice drinker seeking a sympathetic spot. The Paints were without malice, displaying only the crushing artlessness of those who do not care a jot.

The Cabinet met in emergency session: at once, as with all cabinets, splits appeared and widened, disagreements became arguments became shouting contests followed by some low-lying, undying resentments. In short, nobody could agree what pub to settle on, absent the Bat and Ball. Some places ruled themselves out by repute alone, some by one exploratory visit. Their wild-west reception at the Silver Crow, for instance, a house struck mute by malice at the sound of strangers' footsteps, where their movements were followed by hostile eyes—eventual gunplay there later confirmed its reputation. Pilot Ken stalked away from the Tudor Arms when the regulars formed an impenetrable block at the bar; strangers would be served over their heads or not at all—preferably not at all. The experience in the Tudor led Ken to assess candidate pubs in accordance with their methods of making newcomers unwelcome: there was always the classic, old-school 'that's old Fred's corner' approach, but it had many interesting variants. In the Tudor it was 'what we have we hold'; the company was treated elsewhere to 'they shall not pass'; 'the cluster by the pumps', 'the spearhead', 'Hannibal at Cannae', '4-4-2'; 'The Maginot', 'The Home Guard'. 'They knows you're from the Bat an they thinks yer snobs,' Wayne informed them bluntly. 'S'a common enuff view of the people at the Bat, in the town and the Ring.'

In a short club-shaped side-road, a small crew of adventurers stood waiting for the 393 bus; a Dayrider would take them out to the Ring O'Villages and back again, to explore the unknown—the semi-unknown anyway. Emily couldn't help but stare at the head of the club, where the Playhouse dominated, its gleaming glass modernity, bright posters and limelight promise pulling all eyes joyfully away from the brutalist, windowless concrete walls of the abutting shopping centre. It was odd to look at the place as an outsider, watch it in its slumber, long before any performers arrived for rehearsals, the restaurant lit its ovens or the bar opened its swinging door. Emily gasped as she was nudged too hard by a suddenly chatty Frank Speke, who diverted her attention across the road, opposite the bus stop, to a brand-new building, a gravity-defying oddity that resembled an inverted pyramid on a square stand. It was a block of flats for try-out tenants, an attempt to prepare youngsters for managing their own homes, but it was already turning into a bottleneck as there were fewer and fewer places to move on to; nothing was being built and the existing housing stock weather-beaten, stained, powdery-concrete, perished-plastic, neglected, cash-starved, rundown.

'That used to be the Stage Door pub,' Frank began dreamily, his tone hardening, 'Predecessor of the PH Bar. The local scumbags and hangers-on used to gather there, too.'

'Ghosts,' whispered Emily.

'This town is fucked.' Frank didn't seem to hear her, his thoughts following their own track.

Pilot Ken heard them and shuddered. The club-head of the little road was the playground for twirling cold winds, dust-devils of dirt and litter, clanking cans. The town could be tickled into prettiness if the sun would only shine in the right way, but often enough the old orb was not obliging; the place had a greyness not repellent, but in no way attractive; even Spring's blossoms could look autumn-sapped. The sky looked used, tired. This town is not fucked, but oh boy there's something amiss. The town was a statement, an act of modernism, the embodiment of a long-dead architect's futuristic optimism, but the statement's forward-facing force had been eroded by years of falling short, not failure exactly but close enough, a council obsessed with tinkertoys such as bloody democratic retrenchment, and a string of governments that summoned up indifference for the cocky municipality at best, listing towards quiet and not-so-quiet hostility, carefully-managed reputational damage via compliant media, draining the town by degrees with slow, calculated fiscal bloodletting.

The growl of an engine drifted into earshot. 'Thought Wayne was coming with us?' Frank sounded anxious, looking around for a latecomer.

'Worry not.' Emily smiled. 'He's already at the door of target pub number one.'

Lonnie Dolan of The Wheatsheaf swung open his heavy front door, taking in the sight of a bright midmorning and Wayne's semi-silhouette.

'You've got a fuckin drink problem,' snarked Lonnie.

'It's called your beer,' drawled Wayne. 'Now giss some.'

By the time his colleagues arrived Wayne, with sideways affability, was one of the locals, and had to shake his head like a dog to remind himself not to join the flying wedge deployed by his new pals to fend the newcomers from the bar.

The snub-nosed single-decker 393 arrived empty from the bus station; Ken stumbled slightly as he boarded, Frank laughed harshly, Jim and Emily competed to be the helper-out. Ken sat pressed against the window by Jim's bulk, wondering, wondering as the bus began the barbed-wire spiral out of town. The next stop was just outside the town centre, affording Ken a sideview of the long broad walk with the town hall looming over it. The streets looked to Ken like tight, strangulated veins. Our national smallness, thought Ken, here in microcosm: why do we not create space, grand squares like those beautiful prospects of the old European cities. In this town we don't even take after our own capital, barring its crippling prices. How mean our little spaces are. How mean we are. A fine way to start this jaunt; sort yourself out, Kenneth.

'That used to be a pub, and that.' Frank Speke pointed to a garage where once creaked The Hanging Gate. Ken remembered, but it had been boarded and scaffolded before he could cross its threshold. The Smithfield was now a helpful car park. The bus swung briefly back towards the town centre, halting at the Photo Op. This was at the foot of the Water Steps, which looked up towards an imposing view of the Town Hall. Also close to the Registry Office were stepped terraces of whitened concrete, each with its discrete area of shaded seating boxed in by small hedges and bisected by the fall of water from a small pond at the top, near the doors of the Town Hall. Every other terrace featured a small fountain in its own oblong pool, each area enhanced with cheerful seasonal plantings; at the foot was a bigger, square pond with the biggest fountain, and it was here tourists and newlyweds could have their finest snaps taken, among the play of light, breeze and tinkling water. That was the original concept, and very nice too. The pool at the base was now stagnant, green-tinged, and the fountains sputtered only rarely. Locals avoided the 'Slime Steps' as they deteriorated, and on fine days whenever the doors of the PH Bar were closed, the only tinkling came from Scamp and his cronies as they guzzled their takeaway tins and fouled the stilled waters further. The recumbent bodies of the PH drunks adorned the benches, spicing the air with snores and belches, and occasionally two of them, Fred and Wilma, could be seen on top of one another, humping semi-consciously. They were left to move themselves on. So-near beauty, silted with neglect, then given over to degenerates, thought Ken sourly; the town had been built to a plan, overseen by a committee of the great and good, there had been a share of the public purse to make the place attractive. What had happened—the plan got lost, the committee decayed into internal bickering, the purse pickpocketed?

A few stops later, Frank's graveyard finger pointed to the site of Syd's Bar, now an Indian Restaurant under the cosh and offering loyalty cards and complicated mealdeals. The Sutherland Arms was rubble just outside town awaiting a never-come bypass. The Marsh Head was reconfigured as flats for oldfolk—perhaps the Whitepaints intended it as the final destination of their outcast over-40s; The Crossways of erst was a 'gentlemen's club', collapsing, seedy, desperate; remember the queues when Gio's opened? Now look.

'There are rumours that The Wing is in trouble too,' added Frank, sepulchrally.

Ken grunted. 'How does a pub die, when it's already undead?'

Emily taptapped Ken on his shoulder; wordlessly she pointed as they passed an undistinguished bunkerlike structure attached like an unimaginative afterthought to a low-rise red-brick block. Across the largest window of the small building was a large blue-white hoarding— COMMERCIAL LET: CALL AGENT.

'The TestBed.' Emily sighed.

'Bloody noise factory, y'can hear it from the Bat sometimes. Good riddance.'

'Not your scene, Frank? Bit indie for you perhaps? Try the Hi-NRG at our club,' teased Jim.

'No bloody thank you.'

Ken twisted around to shoot a sympathetic glance at Emily; he could read her thoughts too well. A small local venue that punched above its weight with a reputation for nurturing talent; respected and, on the town's tiny scale, legendary. But it had proved no match for Democratic Retrenchment.

'Drugs hole too,' muttered Frank dismissively, his words only just clambering over the engine growl.

'And now all they'll have is the drugs.' Emily's eyes flashed.

The 393 pulled past the railway station, an orphan structure kept arms-length from the town centre as if disowned—its isolation was a flaw in the original town design, as Frank was delighted to point out, 'They were cocking this town up before a single brick was laid.'—and across the town boundary to the Ring, where Ken's gaze was greeted by empty fields patched with pools of greyish water: should there not be sheep, cows, crops—something? Long, stark roads, sharp corners, no convenient stop-offs.

'It was good intentions o course; the best,' said Frank. 'There was a plan. But you can't just shove down a swathe of lookalike dollyboxes and call it a town, much less a "community". They were doling out from above, y'see, Lord Bountiful, and they thought people ought to be grateful. It took a while for the message to seep up to them.' Ken smiled at his reflection, up-close in the window; the smile looked crooked and unattractive, more a wince of passing pain. Frank was playing one of his best-loved roles; the senior citizen, the senex, the tour guide, the Man Who Knows.

Ken remembered their very first meeting: 'You from here?' demanded Frank peremptory.

'I live at River Meado…'

Frank cut across Ken, 'I didn't ask where you lived, I asked are you *from* here.'

Ken stumbled over his own tongue, flushed, and found himself excusing his failure to be town born and bred. It took a time for Ken to recover and vow to get back at this bloke: Little Mal revealed with casual malice that Frank liked to give out that he had lived in the town since it was built, but it was another of his self-aggrandising fictions. Ken saved that one for later use.

At the town border they had passed, ghostly, the abandoned gin factory, the town's earliest comer and its first deserter. The stills used to be visible through the six enormous square factory frontage windows; their coppery surfaces, lit yellow-orange at night, looked like the chemistry kit of an infant giant. They were an object of pride, a local attraction: there remained some remnants of respect—those windows, a perfect target, were still intact, unscathed. The first workers to come to the town were gin-makers and bottlers, they lived in 'dollyboxes' on quaintly-named estates, each with its own purpose-built pub. So: is our town built on alcohol? Instilled with gin and with pub names pre-planned, that was the original design; but plans and names change. Time advances, abrades.

Nearby older towns, by contrast, had drink designed out of them by progressive, pious teetotallers of the late nineteenth century. Pubs crept into those consecrated demesnes, latterly, furtively and adopting unusual names as disguises. In some places they were still quite the rarity. Gina was of the opinion that broken homes and beaten wives may have had something to do with the decisions of the pious: Frank was quick to point out that such things didn't dry up with prohibition. Good old booze; fuel of the town, and of the farmers and agric workers who once abounded in the Ring O'Villages with its Ring O'Pubs.

The pub is the hub, remember? And we can't settle on one. If only someone decent would turpentine the Whitepaints, restore The Bat And Ball. Ken's mind slipped back to when the pub became his hub: his cousin took him to the boozer and introduced him to his friends as an 'apprentice', to laughter, but laughter spiced with cruelty. Everyone has to start somewhere. At fifteen, Ken felt exposed, obvious, a wrongdoer. He never braved the bar and insisted on soft drinks; shandies appeared, sweet and safe, and Ken eased into the ethos of The Hercules.

The shandies became darker by degrees, bitterer by gradations; Ken scarcely noticed. The place called him; the poorly-polished dark wood of tables and chairs, the appalling once-thick red carpet with its scuffs and burns, the warm metallic sheen of the half-lit bar top, the spaces filled with suggestive shadows, the click and thud of the pool table from which came the only strong light, the smell of cheap beer heavily overlaid with bitter-foul smoke—Ken was as yet far from his lecture about his lack of suitability for pub life, almost as far as he was from his discovery of Guinness and the crossword—even the appalling, dry cheese cobs on offer under dirty glass domes, it was all a confirmation to Ken; he had never made it to the more respectable variety. His visits became more frequent as he left school, found a job, lost his hair; a few eyebrows arched knowingly when his eighteenth was celebrated in the Hercules, a night capped by a large Scotch, the first he had been able to swallow without gagging, but he dropped the glass as his head snapped back from the recoil, he gazed with woozy side-eyed guilt at the minatory figure behind the bar; Davina, who governed all with terror verging on lovability, and allured Ken with a sexless fascination at her half-demonic face and sardonic, sickle smile. A sharp nail jabbed at Ken's shoulder and he swung clumsily to face his fate. 'You fucking stupid fucking cunt.' Davina's voice and smile were slow, poisoned honey. 'Happy Birthday dear.'

'That used to be a pub,' intoned Frank once more. The Hercules used to be a pub too; Ken couldn't remember what was there these days, it had been a long time. I wonder, if we settle on a new place, if we could save it from joining Frank's list of moribund boozers? So many are going under these days. We can't save them all. Frank blames the government, any government, for any-many reasons. FMC blames the pubcos, their ripsnorting, snout-snuffling greed: he has a point but as ever with him there's a greedy capitalist to blame. There are, there must be, other reasons. Our pubs are dying, our shops are closing, our people are giving up, not to mention getting out as and when they can. Are the pubs dying for the same reason as the high street? Or are we just getting healthier in our habits, has the town deserted the booze that built it? And do we hate our town because it's dying, or is it dying because we hate it?

'I s'pose you girls are just looking for a place as serves a nice cold Chard'nay, where the men don't go on about footie too much, keep their voices down and never use vulgar words for lady parts.' Frank Speke, at the first emergency meeting, awaited a reaction with impish eagerness; he relished Gina's stoic expression, but Emily flinched, thus giving Frank his true gratification. She had previously told Ken to stop Frank saying 'that word' or she would never come to the Bat and Ball again; this led to an extended loggerhead between the champion of freedom of speech and the 'feminist maniac'. The Imp targeted Emily from then on, and wanted a word—just one word—with her.

'I don't want a footie place either, no sporty pubs,' interrupted Jim, 'And both me and Ken don't like freedom of speech of *that* sort, Frank.'

'Neither Ken nor I, you mean?'

'Jim says fuck off, Frank,' Emily rejoindered tartly.

'I don't want music,' pronounced Frank, ignoring her, 'I want to be able to talk.'

'Not necessarily to *listen*...' whispered Ken to Emily, who giggled and shell-liked the crack to Jim.

'FMC wants to find the people's pub that's deepest red. He thinks that somewhere he will find the wellspring of his revolution,' Jim told the group.

'The Prole and Sickle?' growled Frank.

'FMC was seen in the Golf Club bar last week,' interjected Little Mal casually. 'Quite the regular, he's become, after eighteen holes. He avoids me, as you may imagine, but he's been seen buttering up the Membership Secretary—apparently he's playing as the guest of a member, but wants the full thing. '

'Plus Fours? Funny hat?' Ken was hopeful.

'No, but I took some sneaky photos of the bum-kissing in the members' bar.'

'No doubt your fellow members will be all *fore* the revolution,' Ken called over the roar of approbation.

'Oh my god,' whispered Jim to Gina, 'I'll owe the little weasel a pint. Several in fact. Mal will enjoy a rare thing in his life, at least for a while: popularity.'

Jim and Frank steered their way across the curiously sloping floor of The Blackfriars and took seats in a gloomy, silent corner.

'Have you noticed how much more difficult it is to have a conversation when we're not at the Bat And Ball?'

'Yes.'

The day out in the Ring proved beyond doubt that even its best pubs were too distant in every sense, and a note of indignity was added for the slightly unsteady explorers as they awaited rescue by the returning 393. A vile wind cut cruelly and as the bus failed to show, they quietly regretted not having just one last wee before they left the Dusty Miller. Regrets mounted to discomfort and then aching desperation, and a relay was organised to ensure at least one of them was there to hold the bus; if it came. Another twenty minutes went by; Emily was about to call for another relay when the encouraging sound of an engine preceded a small white van on is erratic way around the corner. Wayne stepped into the road, threw up his arm PC Plod style, and was nearly killed: he addressed the driver in the very same manner as Davina had addressed Ken in long-lost days. 'Gissalift Terry!' he bellowed, pulling open the rear doors and ushering his drinking pals into the seatless semidark within; a strong metal grille protected the driver. Wayne slammed the doors and took his place in the passenger seat. 'Cheers mate.' He grinned spikily at Terry, and then bared his teeth great-white at his friends.

'Ang on. Terry's done about ten at the Tudor. Always does, always drives. Daft bastard. Ome James, an don't spare the orsepower.'

'Lucky I came,' bellowed Terry to his passengers, his head turned to them owl-style, almost horror-film style. 'That bus don't run after one-thirty Sat'dy. They cut the service and ain't changed the timetable yet—fuck!'

The expletive was aimed at the car that Terry grazed as he turned his owl-head back to the road. The journey was only a few miles, but there was discomfort, disorientation and a few more brief moments of terror for the drinkers thrown together—frequently—in the back of the van.

The barbed-wire spiral was traversed, there was touchdown in town, and still there was no agreement. Gina persuaded the group to try Gio's wine bar in the centre of town; spacious, clean, well-lit and perfectly empty, the place scored well with her and Emily; Jim was nervous, out of place, fussed over the price of the beer and threw a high-camp swoon at the price of the wine; FMC scorned the venture, as did Wayne. Pilot Ken iffed and ahhed, then opted to visit his mother on the day of the trip. Mart made a rare appearance in support of Gina, and although a latecomer, Nev arrived to be with Emily. Frank Speke made

147

sure of his own attendance, certain as he was of an enjoyable disaster.

Husband spoke to wife, boyfriend to girlfriend, Jim sat uncomfortably with Little Mal, and Frank sat in splendid isolation which was penetrated once, and briefly, by Gina.

'What is it that holds us together?' she mused, 'After all, we're a ragtag lot; barely a shred in common. A doesn't get on with B, X would clash fatally with Y were K not there. Was it just The Bat And Ball? If it was it's over; off we go, flaking off to here and there, never to meet again. I'd like to think there's some hope.'

Frank Speke sighed heavily, but unlike Gina he was not saddened but exasperated. 'We're only pub-friends, we pass one another in the street and barely know who brushed by; should the balloon go up we would cut one another dead in quite another way without conscience or apology. It's not much of a loss if you use your reason, stop letting emotion take over. And don't think the emollient immanence of Saint Ken will save matters either—here or anywhere else.'

Jim squirmed, pinned by the glitter-eyed malice of his enforced companion, who was taking advantage of Ken's absence. 'Considering, no matter how much he goes on about them, how not one of Ken's old girlfriends has shown up, and he's never had one since we've known him, do you ever wonder if...'

'He's had a... complicated past. Some of it pretty funny, you must admit—going to tea with the posh girlfriend and her parents and finding he "was devoid of any social graces whatsoevah!" That was when he picked up his fish knife and didn't know...' A meat-cleaver gesture from Mal put the second-hand anecdote out of its misery. 'Things are a bit simpler now. With Ken. No ongoing entanglements, far as I know.' Jim heard his own sheepishness, and hated himself. Mal's smile retained an abattoir sheen. 'He's discovered the beauteous pain of the one-way romance. The way to love a woman forever is to choose one who is forever beyond your grasp; you can then indulge in endless dewy-eyed heartache

148

and, most of all, maximise your drinking time. Anyway, James, speaking of ongoing entanglements, what about you? How many blokes are you running at the moment?'

'Five,' admitted Jim quietly, not desiring to discuss the complications of his own life.

'You're just being greedy. There's lonely men out there and you're hogging the pool.'

'You're not lonely are you Mal? You're still with Raf...ael?'

'Of course,' snapped Mal, angry at being reminded that his boyfriend had been barred by Danny Deebee after 'things went missing' and was disrespectfully dubbed 'Raffles'.

The door of the Playhouse screeched like a pissed-off banshee as Jim pushed it open, struggling against its stubborn unwillingness. Ken cringed; he had really hoped for an unobtrusive entrance. FMC followed Ken, scowling at the theatre foyer, the box office, the door of the restaurant, the parade of smiling faces behind glass ranged across the foyer and up the stairs. Bloody hell, thought Ken, we're here at his insistence and already he's looking for enemies. Passing from the relative plushness of the foyer to the stygian darkness of the PH Bar, FMC relaxed; this, for him, was more like it. Stark, dark, bare, stinky, this place was a little fermented hell, thought Ken, what can FMC see in it? A secret hole in which to brew up his stupid revolution? Anyway, whatever he thinks, this will not be our new home from home. It is a dingy dump.

Ken ordered drinks, nodding in vague acknowledgment to the barman. They didn't even keep decent beer, but why should they, given that the sole purpose of the place was to serve the cheapest possible moonshine to the sleaziest clientele? Ken joined Jim and FMC at a corner table, hunching his shoulders, his back to the bar, hoping not to be seen. But—no such luck, they had been spied the moment they came in. Two pieces of shadow split from the far wall and idled over, unafraid of the intrusion of light, inserting themselves either side of Ken. Another hovered behind them, as if deciding whether to come forward and take a risk, or melt back into the safety of the gloom. Next to Scamp was a far younger man, practically a baby in drinkers' terms, known as Gizmo. The lad had nothing to say; his head lolled and the lights were out, he had sat down because it was easier than remaining standing. Gizmo appeared minimally aware, and this was his daily state, it was clear: he had drunk his real name away, nobody knew it any more, if they ever had. Behind him was Hank, another of the dubious regulars here; Jim recognised him, Ken had pointed him out at a distance, a tall and ragged tramp of a man with a bald dome and exploding back-hair, which came into view on the rare occasions light caught hold of it. Jim thought that Hank looked like a ragged troubadour; tonight, he was a ragged troubadour with a shining black eye. The black eye indicated to Ken that Hank had suffered recent contact with the leader of this little gang, the Major, whose absence indicated he was blotto and crashed out somewhere already, or had suddenly taken one of his regular little trips to hospital—possibly attached to a prison.

'Ello Kenny, not your usual hangout then eh?' said the older of the two seated men, a small grey-hair who though slight was wiry-tough, his aged, lined face made oddly childlike by a wide gap in his front teeth; he had glittery, main-chance eyes, and as always a touch of the *Norvegicus* about him.

'Hello Scamp.' Ken's voice was flat and unfriendly. Ken always thought of Scamp as someone who was beaten every day as a boy, a situation which had continued through to the present day.

'Gonna buy us a drink then?' smirked Scamp; Gizmo's head twitched, indicating faraway assent, and Hank hovered a little closer, to make sure he was not left out if anything came of this gambit.

'Ooze yer mates?' Scamp was cheerful in the face of a head-shake from Ken, who then conducted introductions that were curt as opposed to courteous.

'Well then,' Scamp looked straight at FMC, 'now we're all mates ow about you buyin us a drink?'

FMC did, misreading or ignoring Ken's body-language and quelling glare.

'We can't afford much drinks at the prices they charges, even here.' Scamp bit into his new pint. 'We get nothin these days, our kind, that's cos they're forever givin all that money to the...'

'Don't, Scamp. Just don't.' Ken headed him off before he could warm to his theme.

'If that's yer attitude, Kenny...'

'It's my attitude and it's always my attitude. And don't forget it. Don't try your bullshit on me.' Ken sensed that FMC was irritated with the way he spoke to Scamp; no doubt the People's Champion would speak in their defence soon.

'Anyway, are yer bored with the Batty or somethin?' jeered Scamp. Jim gave him a look, but decided there was nothing meant except the pub; Scamp was probably too stupid for word games of that sort.

'We're looking around; the Bat-And isn't all it used to be.'

'Good place here,' burped Scamp. 'They look arter yer.'

Ken shot Jim an appalled look. The conversation stuttered, faded, until Scamp, with a leering grin, revived another of his favourite tropes.

'Tell you wha I heard from Ronnie, goes up the Angel's Wing, e tells me that every week e gets a chitteh from the dole an he takes it to the Wing, free beer he gets, s like a prescription, free beer all week!'

'Chitteh?' said Jim.

'Chitteh. Piece o'paper. If yer doctor signs one sayin you're alc'olic, you get three undred pound a week an free beer.'

'Bollocks,' said Ken flatly.

'S a fact.'

'Scamp, it's no more a fact now than when it was when you last came out with it—last time our paths crossed, and the time before that and the time before that.'

'Ronnie...' protested Scamp.

'Is a drunk and a liar, just like you Scamp. You pillocks sit in bars and tell one another these stupid lies—look, if Ronnie gets free beer from the dole, why can't you?'

'If I went down the dole, they'd give me a chitteh...'

'You'd be there every damn day if they did! If you really went to the dole, they'd tell you to get a fucking job, that's why you don't go!'

'Mebbe they just do the chitteh for them up the Wing...'

'Crap, Scamp.'

'Lissen Kenny, watch y'self or you're gonna get a...'

Jim cleared his throat lightly and Scamp, realising he was at a tactical disadvantage, fell resentfully silent. Gizmo, looking like a delivery-boy from a lost age, disorientated in time and place, pitched backwards off his stool; his head thudded on the hard floor. He was retrieved by bruised, hovering Hank, and they resumed the form of shadows. The visitors drank up quickly and stood.

'Nice talking to you Scamp.'

'Fuck off Kenny.'

'As you say, you old charmer.'

Outside, the searchers bickered as they tried to discuss where next. 'Come on then FMC, tell me that's the bar of your dreams and I'm just a fuckin middle-class snob. Those boys are your boys, yes?'

'The bar's a shithole and they're fuckin scum. He who will not work shall not eat.'

'The Bible?'

'Lenin.'

'Surely the Bible.'

'It's both,' said Jim. 'Let's try The Hare.'

152

To achieve their objective, the searchers had to cross Shortcut Square; straight lines through an empty space to another place; footfall was all the square now knew. Its former focus, the TownCentre Kinema, was fronted with sheets of corrugated metal flanked by time-frozen posters. Ken remembered the place in full health, when the Kinema glowed, the offices of the local paper snoozed next door, a cafe spilled tables and chairs across the straight lines, a bank and a building society nursed nest eggs, solicitors lurked in quiet deep-pile offices, a florist, a candle shop and a pet shop mingled exotic odours; shoppers crisscrossed under sunlight or lamplight, business never quite boomed but for a while it bloomed.

Twenty years ago, trends being what they are, the square was awash with estate agent frontages, but it wasn't long before the newcomers rolled down their blinds or smeared their windows and their trade transferred to the solicitors and the local court rooms, conveniently located above the bank. The shops, the café, the TCK fell away, not all at once, but the loss of one weakened the others, slow-falling dominoes. Now Frank Speke could gesture at the ground floor of abandoned Waymer House and mutter, 'that used to be a pub,' as his group crossed the uncluttered North-South line between two square arches.

Ken liked the beer at The Hare: the pub was voted down, however. 'Needs to decide if it's a bar, a restaurant or a creche.' Jim's verdict.

'George Orwell wrote about his ideal pub—oh, shut up you!' having begun sunnily, Ken roared at FMC as strangulated sounds leaked from his gullet. Cabinet splits continued, fissures deepened, a desperate compromise of a rolling chairpersonship was proposed; the group to go to the venue decided by that day's petty dictator. To the relief of all, the plan was never implemented, as news filtered through of developments at The Bat And Ball. The Whitepaints, by all reports, had lost their initial fervid momentum, appeared to have lost interest, all their refurbishments and thematic innovations suspended and then forgotten, many having never scrabbled past the planning stage. Reliable information was scarce; Wayne claimed to have 'dropped by', only to be ignored by Mrs Whitepaint, who took herself off to the back room for long enough for Wayne to thumb-twiddle, lose patience, sidle behind the bar, self-serve and drink up before laying eyes on the landlady again, or another customer.

Unabashed by the sceptical reception of his tale, Wayne was the source of the next news, and initial disbelief was dispelled by several corroborating stories. 'The Whiteys is gone. Brewery's put in a new woman, she's already thrown out a mob o' Young Conservatives for being "toffee-nosed noiseniks" an she's flattened Harry Lamford for yellin at her barmaid.'

'Flattened?'

'Decked. Chinned. One punch.'

'This we must see,' said Pilot Ken happily.

Pomo The Clown and The Joke of Life

'There's no money in it.'

Pomo the Clown sighed as he picked up the old hat he had brought along; he even shook it, knowing there would be no responding chink of coins. That was blind optimism for you. He knew it was one of his flaws. One of.

'There's no money in it.'

He spoke to himself; it was a literal here-and-now fact, a general one too, and the gateway to an irritating memory. He gathered his props and moved from the empty shop doorway: his limbs stiff and cold, in spite of the fact that he had been moving, performing, for three hours. He could have carried on, but what was the point? Few passers-by had paid attention, and of that minority even fewer had shown appreciation, not even in the form of the smallest of coins. No one gave a toss. Ha; a joke, and a truth. The joke of life.

It had always been a hard choice, opting in to a difficult life, to be a clown. To be ignored was painful but survivable; the most difficult thing was to face the unforgiving realisation that your heart's love, the craft to which you were born, had lost its power over people, its elemental attraction, and that it was now coldly unwanted, a relic of lost yesterdays. No: Pomo shook the defeatist nonsense out if his head. He was still seeking his audience, they were there somewhere, it was early days, he was only finding his way in a self-taught apprenticeship. Yes: his career would blossom, one day. Remember Grock—at one time the highest-paid entertainer.

Still, he had to admit, laughter was in a poor state; it needed a conservator, a rescuer, it needed Pomo. Too much laughter was fake, forced, cruel, sneering, all too often uncomprehending, it was a sound made by people who didn't understand where it came from, and too many didn't bloody well like it. Too often it was a bark, a yap, the beginnings of a feral howl; it wasn't laughter at all. It was a hard world in to which to be born a clown.

The shop door was empty because the shop was empty, the hat was empty because pockets were empty and the street was emptying. This, the town's main street, was a generous broad walk, concrete-slabbed, studded with planters that were meant to sprout cheerful arrays of flowers; metal benches, steely bright when first fixed for tired shoppers to rest and people-watchers to make their observations at ease: in its heyday you could have called the town bustling, still seen a faint flicker of its former market-day come-and-go from time to time, but with increasing rarity. The shops closed, their windows papered or smeared to conceal the emptiness; to Pomo, this seemed a false chrysalis, a pretence that something new would emerge, it was a stubborn and ineffectual denial of death. The planters became less and less cared-for, then they were abandoned, weed-ridden, worse than dead. The shiny benches lost their lustre, neglected, damaged, nobody wanted to sit on the dull, dirty coldly unappealing things, and, well, who knew what happened when the thinning crowds went home and night set in.

The western arm of the street was dominated by the Town Hall, designed to impress and inspire; in this it failed. Its brushed-concrete brutalism was deemed cutting-edge and indeed award-winning when built, but like the seats in the street the sheen was short-lived. Known widely as 'Pisa', the Town Hall shed some of its concrete coating and word went round it was leaning out of true, sinking, toppling slowly, eventually to tumble and crush a random sample of the townsfolk, showering the shopping-walk with rubble and dust. The Eastern bookend for the slowly-shutting shops was the market, fading, failing stall by stall, its characteristic cries and sales-barks diminishing as month followed month. Its food-stalls had been eaten by the supermarkets, who then came for the clothing stalls, the baby-goods stall, the meat van, the music stall; they were vanishing, curling up, slow, inevitable folding.

With all that going on, wouldn't you think people would want some diversion, fun? There should be room in the world for a clown, someone who could bring out a smile back on weary faces, give heart to the worn-down. God bless all clowns. People talked admiringly of passion, drive, ambition and devotion, but they didn't mean it. The word people tended to use most of Pomo was 'idealist'. Very few of them didn't mean 'idiot', he mused sadly.

If he could rely on nothing else, Pomo could rely on his skills; his sense of balance would never fail him, every fall he took was planned, controlled, executed with consummate choreography. He was never jarred, never injured, always moving smoothly, ready for the next trick or tumble. The sticks would fall together and balance, the padded bean-balls drop into his waiting hands, everything would work to perfection even if his arms, legs, whole body seemed a crazy whirl of random activity. Never putting a foot wrong, that was it. What did go wrong was... people. The occasional lout would attempt to snatch a stick or a ball from mid-air, some even attempted to shove Pomo over, making a crude grab for the hat at the same time—tough, boys, there's no money in it—but Pomo could dodge and duck, he only fell if he had planned to and he never dropped or lost any stick or ball. Seeing the grey, joyless faces of the adults and teenagers, Pomo tried to appeal to the simple innocence of the small children, those in whom wonder still had a safe and reliable home, but he found that even those who smiled and strained to stay to watch were held back by hovering, over-cautious parents. And sometimes by a diffidence that Pomo had never experienced as a little one who watched the jugglers and street-clowns. The instincts of joy and wonder were still there with these children, but they were inhibited, hampered by a nameless fear, a learned fear, fright that had been trained into them. So—he could rely on his

157

performances, but no longer his audience. The magic was gone from the air and the money from his pockets.

His most recent paying gig—just a few days back, but it seemed so long ago—while it had paid well, confirmed much of what was wrong. It was a birthday party for a little boy; Pomo had prepared well, plenty of balloons to become animals, lots of little treats to produce by happy clown-magic, oodles of funny mime and gentle slapstick, he knew what would appeal to that little group, he looked forward to conjuring their smiles. The party was in a church hall and the children gathered in a circle, awaiting the entertainment. Pomo popped into the Gents to make sure his costume was only crooked where it was intended to be and that his cheerful-clown face was perfectly made up. He picked up his bag of tricks and treats and sauntered gaily to the hall, into the centre of the circle of waiting children to perform his usual opening.

'Hello, hello, hello, I'm Pomo, Pomo the Clown!' This came with planned-clumsy dance steps that spun him around, and as he spun he lobbed sweets in gentle curving flights into the ready hands of his audience. A scuffle or two broke out as sweets fell into disputed territory, but they were soon quelled. Pomo moved on to the juggling-song that he had invented.

'One-twooooo, One-twoooo,' he sang easily as two cushioned balls cycled slowly between his hands.

'One-two-three, One-two-threeee,' he sang slightly more quickly as a third ball appeared from nowhere.

'One-two-three-four, One-two-three-fourrrr.' Pomo's hands and the song sped up as ball after ball added itself to the increasing whirl, becoming a blur. Pomo could keep this going for ages, but he remembered the short attention spans of children and brought his speeding hands to a halt, singing a *ta-daaaa* and bowing slightly, harvesting the applause. It was starting well.

'And today we are all here to say Happy Birthday to Sam!' Pomo produced a special, enormous treat from his

I must award credit to my father: no, he did not inspire and support me, what's more he still does not—nor does he hold me back. He is neutral, in all things, even as regards his own. I draw from his experiences, not least his first and greatest disappointment, the beginning of a lifelong sequence. He also nursed infant dreams of being a clown: knew the fun, the thrill of the fall, practiced in secret, painting his face but wiping away all trace before others saw.

His parents took him, at his urging, to the circus, and not just any circus but Blackpool Tower, to see the most famous clown in the world. He felt a nip of disappointment when he realised that the Circus was not at the top of the Tower, which he had taken for granted. This was forgotten when he saw the clown, that famous clown, roving up and down the aisles as the crowd settled in their places, picking out excited children and talking to them in his rich, accented voice. He felt his throat close and tongue swell as the clown approached him, clumping down the steps, the bowler hat, merry-madeup face, red nose and glittering eyes. 'You looking forward?' The clown smiled as the eager boy nodded. 'Wass your favourite?'

'The pie in the face, are you going to do the pie in the face?'

'Aww, we doan do that no more. Thass too old-fashion. No more the pies.' The magic drained from clowning at that moment; the Circus was magical, the clowns excellent, but—no pies.

Poor dad: put down, pained, quiet. Such a small thing, so early in life, so devastating. He still loved clowning, he does to this day, but after that queer knock, it was even more a secret shame to him. Sometimes the urge was irrepressible, but he was never anything better than court jester to loutish schoolmates, later to workplace bullies. Perhaps, by instinct, he felt the draining, the failure of laughter's mission. What a young age to lose his grip on his only future. He never dared hope for anything again, he surrendered expectation. If something nice came along, he would take it, thank-you, but he never made anything happen, never willed anything to be. Inert, harmless, everything in his life was whatever fell to him; 'Schnorrer', gramma called him and mother told her hush. I didn't ask; I thought it meant sleepy, maybe lazy.

Trying to persuade him that I could make a go of clowning was like beating your head against a sponge. He neither blocked nor

baggy-trouser pocket and bent to the birthday-boy, who, instead of seizing the offering with greedy delight covered his face with his small hands and shook.

'Ahhh Sam, are you a little bit shy? Never mind, let Pomo cheer you up—watch this!'

But Sam was not watching, he remained, face in hands, rocking back and forth in childish distress, and was rigid with terror as his mother dashed to his rescue, picking him up and sweeping him out of the circle.

'Aaaaaaaahhhhh!' bawled the birthday-boy, capping this with a fusillade of hysterical shrieks that scraped horribly at Pomo's ears. As the woman hurried her son away, she shot a look at—at Pomo, he thought at first, but no—someone over Pomo's shoulder; birthday-boy's daddy, no less.

'Uh. That didn't work out well,' mumbled the young man into his stubble.

'Pardon?'

'I was hoping it would cure him… or something. He's frit of clowns, always has been, I sort of thought that if he had one all of his own, he would… y'know… it was a sort of experiment.'

Renewed shrieking came from another room, as if in fervent dispute of the shaky theory. It grew louder, swamping the woman's coos and imprecations.

'I'm gonna cop it now.' The young father was steeped in guilt. 'And I told her you was a magician.'

'I'm… sorry.'

'Not your fault mate. Here's your dosh. Not your fault it didn't come off.'

Pomo left quickly and drove home, sitting in full costume and makeup; he had not completed the performance, it seemed wrong to attempt to take them off. What a weird gig. Never before had he been used as—what, a test animal? Nor could he shake off the creeping feeling that there was another dimension to the whole business— the husband had not enjoyed the child's terror, but there was somehow a gleam in his eye when he watched and heard his wife; Pomo had been used as part of some ongoing war-game between the adults. Ha, no wonder he wanted an audience that was infantile for all the proper reasons.

Pomo had a hazy recollection of once being told it was hard to conjure magic, true earth-magic and not quick-hand stage pretences, in this cynical world; the reason was that there had been, in ancient times, an elemental substance woven into every wisp of air that acted as a catalyst, an enabler, to aid the spell-castings of those wise and learned in lore. Unbeknown to the witches and wizards as they worked their arts, this magic-filled air was like any mine or quarry, it was finite, exhaustible, and over the centuries the unwary drew upon that ineffable substance until it was drained, rarefied, and finally irretrievably exhausted. Young and credulous, Pomo had wondered; was that what rendered the practitioners of the old ways so helpless in the face of the fanatical witch-burners, unable to conceal themselves or fly to safety?

Whatever its truth, Pomo appropriated the story: for him, however, the magic-aiding substance that was once so bountiful and was now exploited to the point of exhaustion was laughter. Laughter, and indeed kindness and generosity, were lost Earth-elements: this much was apparent to Pomo the Clown. This was no lament of the sadness of a clown; far from it. Sadness, meanness, selfishness and cruelty walked free in the world, but not in the breast of the new Grock. He considered himself a happy, complete and fulfilled man, the keeper and protector of that which the world had very nearly lost. He was the conservator of laughter, nursing it through its gravest crisis, at a time when its lack threatened to darken the world.

Today, the mystical ether had been thin indeed, pickings slim: all right then, non-existent. After three hours of trying hard and facing chilly indifference and sub-zero stares, Pomo was thirsty; how he would love a beer. He felt the pull of the pub, strong, almost irresistible. The town, built on ground that was generally flat as a board, sank a little

beyond the market place, he felt himself drawn to the incline that would take him through a small subway and the continued downward curve at the foot of which was the Bat and Ball. Pilot Ken reckoned—*theory alert!*—that space curved towards pubs.

'It's Einstein wanting a beer,' he would explain, 'he sets off towards the Bat and Ball, finds himself speeding up, faster with every step. By the time he clatters down the steps into the car park he's accelerated to near light-speed because of the pucker in space-time created by the pub, and by the time he arrives in the bar he's travelling so fast he is barely visible, everyone seems to be treacle-waders relative to him—he hovers, increasingly agitated, at the bar but they seem never to get near serving him; this is called the beer frustration effect.' I will use that one day, if I ever change my mind and expand to a talking act for adults—I'll credit Ken of course, it will all be part of paying him back. Paying him back. Pomo halted, resisting gravity's pull. There was a reason he couldn't go to the pub, apart from empty pockets. Were he brave enough he would be bought a pint by Pilot Ken, maybe Emily too, but he would have to endure their accusing silence, not to mention Frank Speke's open assaults on his impecuniosity.

Everything In Life Is A Controlled Fall: perhaps it was presumptuous to have begun his autobiography when not yet thirty and unknown, but Pomo knew that some z-listers had two, perhaps three selfie-books out by such an age, and they had a great deal less to tell the world.

I felt the call at an early age. No sooner had I learned to walk straight and stop falling than I learned again how to fall; but this time to work with the descent, to master gravity, make it do my bidding and, most importantly, harness it to the manufacture of laughter. Such mastery can never be absolute—a fall is a fall—but to learn how to land, to roll, to be gainly but appear its opposite; the gracefulness of a cat disguised as a helpless tumble. The ground is hard, nasty and unforgiving, but they must believe you have hit it.

encouraged me; like everyone else he just said, 'There's no money in it.' At the time of writing, he is perfectly, inertly correct. But times of writing change. I will not be stopped. Disappointment is a downfall, but one to be rolled out of, on to your feet boy, huphoi. People, too many people, are like my dad; they let things happen. They moan a bit, sometimes even get a little bit shouty, but that's all. When Pisa topples on them, they will shrug. 'Bound to appen.'

Not all falls are controlled; you have to keep your concentration. I broke my collarbone once, trying out a tumble, showing off to girls. Come on, I was only six. 'Watch me do this!'—big fall, crack, ow. The wrong sort of laughter. I was more careful after, I respected the fall, invented my own drop-and-roll routines, learned my craft, went to the Circus again and again, but always without dad—he wasn't going there again. I hadn't the heart to tell him when the clowns did pie-in-the-face. I've not only created my own brand of falls, I've made a pie-flipper, useful for a solo artist, it works on the principle of a pedal-bin, hit it right and you get the desired effect. Mis-hit and it's creamy groin time, but that gets a laugh too, within acceptable definitions.

If only the show at the Fun Day had worked: clowning in the sunshine, eager infant faces, adults modestly mellowed by booze, but not lairy. Typical Danny to deliver such a consummate cock-up. Would have been free beer too, post-show, but he welched, no show, no freebies. But I tried. That will all get its own chapter one day; when I'm ready.

'What d'you call a man under a wheelbarrow?' asked Frank Speke archly, unprompted.

'Eh?' Ken wrinkled his brow.

'The correct form of response is "I don't know, what do you call..." Et cetera.'

'Very well, I don't know, what do you call a man under a wheelbarrow?'

'A mechanic.'

'That's not funny!'

'It was funny, until your woke-brigade got hold of it. The "man" was once an "Irishman," but that's not allowed anymore. I suppose I'm lucky I can even say "man"…'

'FMC claims Irish antecedents.'

'Only so he can praise bloody terrorists, the idiot.'

'I mean it's lucky he's not here; you'd set him off on a rant.'

'God! Don't tell this joke, it's offensive, don't tell that joke, you'll upset Jim, you'll upset Nev, you'll get the bra-burners up in arms, you'll have Tony The Convert blockading your doors: we're scared we might bloody well laugh at the wrong thing and get five years in a PC camp for re-education…' Frank grumbled.

'Laughter shouldn't be used to bully. Right, Pomo?'

'Who made Funnybones a bloody expert?'

'Come on Frank, he knows a bit about what's worth a chuckle…'

'Does he hell.'

Everyone looked to Pomo for response, for comment, but he was mute.

'What is funny anyway?' interjected Jim, diplomatically deflecting attention from Pomo, misinterpreting his silence. 'Seems to me everyone will have a different opinion. For me, it's…'

'Drag acts,' sneered Frank.

'Can't stand them,' snapped Jim primly. 'No funny in them for me. I like sitcoms.'

'Hate sitcoms.' Gina sniffed. 'Predictable, dull. Give me standup, improv, something satirical.'

'Please don't say "edgy" or I may have to kill you,' snarled Frank Speke.

'Spike Milligan. Monty Python,' said Ken, 'stuff like that, something crazy.'

'Jokes, just jokes, good, solid jokes, with a beginning, a middle, a punchline, no fancypants pretensions, no "meanings", no politics and sod anyone who's "offended".' Frank flew his colours.

'Still nothing to say, Pomo?' Ken nudged the clown.

'What can *he* say? Big shoes, red noses, buckets of water and flan-flinging, that's his bloody limit. He's got nothing to teach anyone about humour. Any four-year-old knows his world inside-out.'

Pomo remained silent: his thoughts remained on laughter, its plight.

'All right, got another one for you: Why did God create jugglers?'

'So the stamp collectors could have someone to laugh at,' was the choral, jaded response.

'You only tell that one when Pomo's around. And it's not very funny either, Frank,' chided Pilot Ken.

'It is. You just won't allow it.'

That was the problem with jokes: awkward, spiky, teetering constructions; once pieced together they had to be delivered properly, with timing, elan, pizzazz, or they flopped fatally, embarrassingly. And even done well, they had to be 'got', and people who failed the test felt excluded, humiliated. Not to mention those who were offended, the victims. Where Frank was concerned, every joke required a butt, and the laughter elicited was only satisfying when knowing and heartless; Pomo had never been comfortable with the humour of embarrassment, of humiliation.

That despatched most British humour in a stroke; Jim's sitcoms, Frank's jokes, Gina's satire, Shakespeare and all. Ken's 'zany' was more appealing, but still there were traps, disappointment and lurking horrors. Words were the problem, they were a barrier, and all too often a weapon, the resulting laughter cruel and cold. Without words, what was left? Action, colour, mime, mummery, the purity of clowning; laughter's refuge. Big shoes, red noses, buckets of water and flan-flinging; any four-year-old knew that world inside out. But that was what was good about it: a universal language, no need of words, the simplicity left few unreached, many elevated, none hurt.

The greatness of clowning is vested forever in the circus, but I also have an enduring adoration for the film comedies of the pre-sound era. This is the second-best legacy from my father: he didn't dare unleash the clown, but he could not conceal his admiration of others, he became a collector, avid, compulsive, of old comedies, the golden silents. I shared that admiration, I felt the allure of the films, it was good to share that with my father, his surviving enthusiasm, albeit the embers of his abiding passion. There is a special innocence about the pancaked faces, heavy-rimmed eyes and dark lips of early films, the blameless simplicity of the moves, the chases, the pratfalls, double wing, clutch, kick and scram, the plunges into water or mud or molasses, the eternal truth of the little guy winning against the big snarling heavy no matter what the odds, walking away with the girl as the screen narrows to a circle and then closes on itself, a spot, a tight dot, darkness, the end. There is no malice or cruelty in this shimmering universe; the worst is a bandaged, gouty foot suffering stick-whacks, door-slams, dog-bites, all sorts of other indignities before the reel runs out. But the pain is pantomime, unreal, there's no harm, no hurt.

Best of all, of course, are the wonderful pie-fights, Dad could not give them up altogether, and of that I'm glad. Perhaps pace the clown at the circus, they became over-used, 'We doan do that no more,' but oh, the glory, the funny, funny glory. There is a film, The Battle of the Century, the holy grail for my father, the animating genius of which was to make 'the pie picture to end all pie pictures'. Pies fly and splatter, a delirious chaos of crust and cream, faces covered, a street is taken up with frantic, innocent, harmless combat, the purest, most life-affirming fun. Rumour has it there were ten thousand pies used in that movie, perhaps more. This movie is a legend among those who know; and yet poor Dad has never seen more than clips, mere teasers, much of the film lost years ago. Dad thinks it will never be found, he despairs quietly, he will be robbed of this too. I tell him chin up, you never know, people are finding old film-cans in attics and garages and goodness knows where, and sometimes a lost gem is returned. Maybe one day he will win his battle.

The arrival of sound did not add a dimension to the movies, it encouraged the clumsy, the witless, the blunderbuss of dialogue.

Except for a lucky few whose tones carried well on the scratchy soundtracks, it killed the careers of towering talents, geniuses of move and mime; people who should have been showered with honours were discarded, forgotten, fed on scraps, left to fade. Dad feels that loss too, he bears their hurt, those who are beyond caring. I disagree with his passivity, but agree with the essentials of his world: all this is something worth protecting, nurturing, passing on to grateful future generations. When every witty barb and cutting quip is blunted, when every smart remark has become meaningless, when all words are dead and gone, mute clowning will still reach out, connect, inspire, brighten lives and satisfy souls.

Laughter! It scattered like steel shards at the far end of the street. Momentarily jealous, as if he had been robbed, Pomo checked himself; that sound, its metallic edge, it told him that it was the wrong sort of laughter, and that Nug was near the Town Hall, standing on a low wall, a form of street punctuation that marked the end of the High Street and the beginning of the civic pale. Nug would be holding up a home-made placard—SAVE THE TOWN HALL!—and his small audience was not laughing but jeering. Perhaps that metallic sound had not been unpleasant laughter alone, but coins hurled in scornful mockery. Huh, thought Pomo, there's money in it for Nug but not me.

Nug, Dennis Nugent to allow his correct name, was no laughter-seeker: indeed, it irritated him deeply, he would not be pleased to steal from Pomo. He was there, as ofttimes, to vent his grievances, chiefly a demand for his 'true entitlement'. In his late sixties and probably far beyond, Nug asserted that his pension had been 'stolen away' and replaced with a pittance, a sliver of his deserts; he was also often to be seen with another placard: 188 CARSWELL IS SOVEREIGN TERRITORY. He considered his council house to be his, 'Clean and free of false impositions by natural right', refusing to pay rent, local levies, gas or electricity bills; JC could have found useful occupation by berating Nug to 'Pay yer Poll Tax!'

Nug's passionate desire was for justice, restitution, for the heads of those who had conspired against him—variously and variably, members of his family, the council, Little Mal and the local MP. Whenever he sought or was offered help, legal or voluntary, Nug was betrayed; he uncovered a masquerading conspirator every time. Nug was not trying to rescue Pisa from its tumbledown doom for aesthetic or political reasons; he believed its collapse was sought by the conspirators so that the evidence of their malfeasance could be buried in the ruins.

A plastic bag skittered down the main street, a tumbleweed for our times, and at its cue Pomo the Clown packed his trappings. He was tired and fancied a… *Pack the van, pack the van, do it carefully now, there will be other days and better audiences.* He fancied a… *No, get the van home first, old van, third-hand or more, but still, it won't do to drive and…* you know. Ahhhh, he wanted to go down to the Bat and Ball, but… too embarrassing, he had promised Pilot Ken he'd have some of that money to pay back his borrowings, but… the money from the gig had vanished instantly, it had crossed his palm into unstoppable oblivion. Ken would never mention the money, he would buy Pomo a pint, but someone else would say something—Frank Speke, for sure. He always did. The engine coughed, threatening rebellion, but then expressed a more even, biddable tone. As Pomo drew away, passers-by saw the cheerful home-made signs on the sides of the van:

'POMO MORELLI:
SERIOUS ABOUT CLOWNING'

Nev and the unwanted honorary

'Oh look, Token's come in.'

'Frank…'

'He don't mind being called that, so neither should you. That's patronising, Kenny. Sides, he says it's nowt but the truth.'

'Frank…'

'I c'd call him summat else. How about Bame? Heheheh!'

Pilot Ken sighed, not prepared to open up another old Frank-controversy. Frank Speke, glowing with satisfaction, greeted 'Token' affably, but he was nevertheless concealing inner turmoil, a roiling presence: The Imp wanted a word. Just one. Enraged by Frank's tickle-stomached delicacy it plucked at his ribs, beat its fists against his breastbone, danced and fizzed on the tip of his tongue like a mouthful of sour champagne. One word, just… one…

Jim greeted Nev warmly, Emily stood and kissed him, creating a space and pulling up a chair next to her, fending off a meaningful look from Gina with the slightest shake of the head; Pilot Ken was amiable as ever, buying Nev a pint. Yet there was a tension, a frisson between the two men. Nev Batham could have crushed Pilot Ken with just three words: Nev remembered those words as clearly as, surely, did the man who had spoken them. No matter how delighted he was to see Nev, Ken feared those words, was reminded of them, always. He knew Nev was a kind man, a thoughtful one too, a man of intelligence and integrity who would never act out of egregious spite or vengefulness; and yet still he feared. Knowing Ken's thoughts, Nev felt bemusedly guilty, as if he had a knife in his pocket he had no intention of using, and yet the knife was there, and an unused knife is as sharp as any other. Any sensitive soul who detected an atmosphere between Nev and Ken invariably ascribed it to a certain other cause and then

169

promptly forgot it. Neither Ken nor Nev could forget the true cause, neither could mention it to the other. The matter could never be discussed, cleared up, forgiven. Nev felt terrible about it; Ken felt terrible about it.

'Ken's been asking after you. He wonders why we hardly ever see you.'

Emily hovered as Nev set the table at his flat for supper; she seemed nervous, flustered, and Nev didn't like himself for giving in to the temptation to tease her. 'You see me pretty much every day.'

'He's worried we've done something wrong.'

'Nobody's done anything wrong.'

'It's Frank, isn't it?'

'Dear old Frankie. He's cute, he amuses me: he's so desperate.'

'Ken would like you to feel more a part of things.'

'Is that the laying down of my rival for your affections? The Sun King thinks my orbit is too remote and he says, "Friend, go higher!"'

'Oh Nev...'

'Okay, okay, joking apart; it's hard to explain. I've nothing against any of them, not Ken, not Frank, not Lenin's Ghost, not even Gina when she bends your ear and calls me a commitmentophobe, and I sometimes think she means commitment to the group, the pub; to Ken. You know I'm not a big drinker, you know the calls on my time, I'm flat-out busy, my career matters to me and I admit it. I don't stop you going, no reason to, I'll come in whenever I'm free and I'm not fit to drop.'

'Nev, that's not the real reason.'

No. The real reason had to do with the complexities surrounding three little words, a business that began not with Ken but years before, with the spade in the sandpit.

Nev's first appearance at the pub, straight from work and besuited, had been memorable for the attack launched on him by FMC. Forewarned by Emily, Nev was more than

170

ready: gargling drunk at 6pm and smelling as if he had been steeped in vinegar, FMC kicked off.

'Lawyer,' FMC grated, accusingly.

'Solicitor.' Nev steered him, judiciously.

'What you wanna be a lawyer for? It's so...' Nev smiled politely as Jim mimed a hand-crank.

'He was a promising lad but he had no positive role model.' Frank Speke mimicked PC piety. 'So he grew up to be a lawyer.' Among the laughter, Emily and Ken noticed Nev's lips move, reading 'Oh God.'; but there was no 'Oh God', it was 'Oh, George.'

'Why does anyone work?' Nev's tone was light, bantering, 'I want a nice life for me and my family, I mean when I get married.' He shot a sly look at Emily, 'Besides I enjoy the law, it's a challenge, you can really *achieve* something for people.'

'There'll be no need for fuckin lawyers; the people will be the law, fuckin lawyers will be dead and gone...'

'So, you're like Dick the Butcher?'

'Hah?' FMC flailed, wafting an ethanol reek across the table.

'Shakespeare character.'

'Shakespeare? Shit.' FMC's voice snapped with rage.

'A dick anyway.' The Imp amused itself in the absence of true satisfaction, as Frank Speke idled. Ken, Emily, Gina and Jim cackled; Nev remained composed.

'Fuckin lawyers, always twistin people's words, fuckin cheatin workin people, fuckin families, evictin judges, we fuckin hate you, you'll all be dead...' It was possible to make a few trips to the bar and back while FMC stumbled on, cataloguing the griefs of his wounded, imagined people, in increasingly mangled language. It would soon end, as it always did, in outright incoherence and alcoholic amnesia.

Nev found it a relief, almost a joy to be so attacked. It took him away from the everyday, the questions, the teenytiny incursions into personal space, the knife-edge fight-flight reactions to his presence, his existence. From the spade in the sandpit, the thing of which he could not speak, not to Pilot Ken, though it would relieve poor Ken's niggling guilt, nor to Emily, to whom it would explain so much. FMC, meanwhile, had a surprise for his mocking audience; instead of spiralling into incoherence he regained a steely, hateful eloquence and, in an uncharacteristic flourish he changed tack, to general shock and Nev's deep chagrin. The spade in the sandpit. Huh, a sodding spade.

Nev had thoroughly enjoyed the afternoon; the sky had been unusually clear, summer-blue, warm-hot, shadows were short and sharply edged. The playing-field stretched like an endless bucolic meadow, rolled into light-green dark-green strips, dotted with the run-ups and sand pits for the jumps, the nets and distance markers for the discus, shot and javelin, the huge, stretched loops of the running track, hurdles stacked at its side ready for action. Helpful instructors stood by every net and run-up, others scurried around organising short races, taking names, notes. Nev had enjoyed trying out the track events and he flattered himself he had been quietly noticed, but he had enjoyed learning the jumps most.

He tried the high-jump last, enjoyed it most of all, once he had grasped the technique. 'You gonna limbo under it?' catcalled a pink-faced figure in an overstuffed white t-shirt and concertina shorts as it puffed by leaving a contrail of sweat. Nev ignored the sally, he made it a point to disregard idiots. Nev cleared the awkwardly-lodged bar time after time as it was raised to heights he thought he could never reach. On his last jump he brushed it, he could hear the bar's thin whisper of protest, but it didn't fall. It was perhaps because he was distracted by not wanting the bar to fall that he didn't manage his landing so well, overshooting the centre of the thick plastic mat in the middle of the sand-pit, landing heavily and awkwardly, thrusting his feet in to the sand at the edge of the pit. As he stood to smile in triumph at the instructor, Nev felt a vicious, biting pain at his right ankle. He flopped back on the plastic mat and stared at his ankle as it gushed blood from a curiously symmetrical, oblong wound. As he sat, Nev could see the spade half-buried in the sand, its edge jutting up as if it were a lurking, camouflaged hunter. Who the hell had left that there, why wasn't it spotted, why did it have to be me who landed on it? The instructor hurried towards the pavilion, muttering about the medical kit. Nev remained where he was, feeling foolish, biting his lip against the pain. He had thought himself alone, but a shadow fell across him, a brusque voice came from a silhouette that blocked the sun.

'Get a plaster on that. You'll live.'

'Sir.' Nev knew the voice, it was the chief coach, known for his love of athletics, his sardonic tongue and hatred of skivers.

'I don't know you; what are you called, son?' the coach nodded curtly as Nev blurted his name. 'Well, Mr Batham, team practice proper begins next Monday, pavilion, four-thirty sharp. We'll see what you can really do. And I don't accept excuses and I don't give second chances, all right?'

'Sir.'

'You'll live, son. Get it cleaned properly though. And who left that fucking spade there anyway?'

'*Why... why* aren't you angry? Why aren't you *doing* something?' demanded FMC.

'I never said I wasn't. But if I'm angry it's not your kind of angry. I'm not part of your movement, mate. I've chosen my way.'

'After what we did? We protected you!'

'What on earth are you on about, FMC?' interjected Ken.

'Cable Street, Battle of Cable Street, we protected them from the enemy, we fought them off the streets, drove em off, without us his lot would be...' inarticulacy reclaimed FMC and he gurgled to a halt.

'That was nearly a hundred years ago, what's it got to do with you or Nev?' demanded Emily, her contempt for FMC lending her voice an edge. She broke off and laughed when she heard what Jim was singing to himself. 'As soon as this pub closes, as soon as this pub closes, as soon as this pub clooooo-sesssss—the revolution starts!' It was the signature tune he used whenever he spotted FMC. Nev remained above the laughter, and at arm's length from anger too. But the spade in the sandpit was at the fore of his mind. 'Sorry "we" have been such a burden to you,' Nev told FMC as mildly as he could. 'Perhaps I'm sullen, rather than angry. Half-devil and half-child, huh? But I'm no child. I want to go off and make my own decisions, free from anyone's help and without having to thank the white saviour. And if that brings me to being, let's say, a free-market law-and-order Conservative, that's my choice. I wouldn't change it just because of something your great-grandad did for someone else a hundred years ago.'

FMC spluttered.

Part of Nev's problem, he was often told, was oversensitivity. Nev wasn't proud of the way that he overheard things; yet overhear he did. Always the same things, in point of fact. Remarks at school, whispered up close or hooted at a distance, things said at work, always small but significant, a client referred to, just-heard, as 'one of Nev's lot', for instance; FMC's tirade—for all his angry rebelliousness he was a *bwana* demanding gratitude; the events that followed the spade in the sandpit, yes, those most of all. Even at The Bat And Ball, with Nev at the bar, overhearing Frank Speke who, like the others, intended to be heard. 'Come on Kenny, Nev's allus reminding us that he's a… allus reminding us he's "equal", bad as Jim, chip on his shoulder, that's what it is. Besides, he doesn't mean "equal" at all, he means "better". People as talk like that, that's what they mean, every time.'

'Perhaps he'd be more at ease if we stopped reminding him, treating him as an outsider. Why not treat him as one of us, an…'

Please don't say it, Ken, no matter how well you mean.

Oh, George. There were better, happier times. Olly, George and me studied together, and although it was The Quiet Room, Olly would sneak in a radio and the three of us were steeped in Test Cricket and cricket-test.

'We're thrashin em, Nev!' grinned George as the visitors caned the hosts.

'*Traitahs!*' shrieked Olly in a pepperpot tone, '*Traitahs! I'm tellin on ya!*'

'Cri-cket love-ly cri-cket!'

'*You traitahs!*'

If fortunes flowed the other way, George would clasp Olly around the shoulders and in a warm, plummy voice boom, 'We're beating them Olly dear boy. It's a great day to be English, man.'

'*Bladdy fair-weather friends! I'm tellin on ya!*'

George would tell us about the magic island; long off happy days. The sunseasand parts of his spiel all very alluring, but I loved best hearing about the childhood mango-scrumping trips, the stern barber-uncle taking his cold clippers to a squirming George, bellowing 'Boy, be still!' the day a boatload of gange caught fire in the bay, when the sea front was lined with devotees breathing deep, and abstainer George 'went all wobbly' and got double vision. I always thought the magic island was more a thing of the mind, a notion that helped bar it to me; Olly, always happier with the concrete, said it sounded like a fab spot for hollibobs. It was a sad day when we had to stop studying and get out there, face reality. Where Olly is now, I'm unsure. My fault. I wonder if he ever took that holiday. I know where George is, got his phone number, but somehow… well, that's my fault too. *Oh George.*

Nev and Jim shared a fellow-feeling, and often compared notes. 'It's the way people keep picking at what you are, driving you back to it even if you wish to forget or flee,' Jim would say, provoking a judicious nod from Nev. 'Never a brother, always an Other.' Jim wore a bright-green 'gay vegetarian' badge on his lapel, a toxicity-monitor of how much outrage, self-defensive offence it would generate, and the results were remarkable. Nev didn't need a badge. Jim told Nev his taxi story: Nev had his own, shorter tale. Travelling in winter darkness, he was lectured by the driver on the inevitable: incomers, outsiders, Others. 'They only come here to take what's ours,' the driver told the obviously educated man in the back seat. Nev asked him to stop, paid him on the nail, let streetlight fall across his face and swung open the back door. 'Actually, we're coming back for what you lot looted from us. Replevin is the legal term. Look it up.'

'It's a good group here, mind.' Jim was keen to offer exemptions. 'Ken especially.' Yes, thought Nev; Ken especially, apart from three little words.

Perhaps I've idealised George rather. Confluence of hero-worship and envy. I saw another me: future-me; better-me. Why George never went into the restaurant trade I'll never know, he'd have been minted. International, ecumenical, he could do it all: fried plantain, cou-cou, curry, pasta, moimoi, steak and chips, peppersoup, conkies, bread and butter pudding; name it. Plus whenever I went to his to eat, though he didn't touch booze there would be a bottle of wine on the table, and not one grabbed random-quick, closed-eyed. If he came to me to tolerate my burnt offerings, he'd bring a good red. If Olly came too, we would tease him as always, but in the end he, like me, was another of George's adopted children. Widowed, George had raised three of his own plus three more taken on when dear friends died young. I called him a saint but all that did was embarrass him. I never saw him tired, self-pitying, resentful or anything else I met in the mirror on a daily basis.

As Nev clambered on the team bus, the back seats were already full and there was a semi-riotous air suffused with bellicose banter, bawdy songs and shouted aisle-to-aisle conversation. Nev hesitated, unsure where to sit.

'It stinks in ere!' a snarky voice projected over the hubbub, which died away as if ordered to do so.

'Shouldn't of farted then mate,' came a giggled retort; there was a short and violent fracas between the speakers and the victor spoke up again.

'It *stinks* in ere!'

'Yeh,' agreed the vanquished, 'stinks.'

Nev hesitated still; his mouth dry.

'Pull that trigger!' roared a voice; a chorus swelled in response, but it fell away, a wave that had lost its crest, distracted by a clumping, a slight swaying of the chassis, as the head coach made his way up the steps to count heads and set off.

'All right you lot, I know what's going on. Siddown Neville.'

Nev slumped in to the nearest seat, without dignity.

'You're all here because you're winners—*shuddup at the back!*—I want winners, tryers, people who're concentrating. There's a championship to win and if you don't do all you can you're off my team and there's an end to it.'

The answering rumble of assent was full enough to Nev, but the head coach detected a mutinous undertow in the tide of voices. Having half sat, the older man, putting on a weary expression, hauled himself upright once more, pushing hard on the headrest of the seat in front of him.

'Very well,' he sighed, 'as of this moment and for the duration of the championship, I decree that Mr Batham is an honorary white man. Satisfied?'

Nev slumped further as a fragile silence took hold.

George credited his goodness to God, saw no merit in himself and would hear no more about it. Nev rejected the faith, called it 'their religion'. He thought that he had provoked George to wrath, but his answer was gentle as

177

ever. 'It's a truth they gave to us even as they abused it. We took it home and cherished it, restored it.' George's belief maintained and sustained him, unlike others, whose religion racks and tortures them, mentioning no names Tony The Convert.

The problem with a flat map was that it splayed the world, squashed everything at top and bottom, you didn't know where you were; and there was always the fear of falling off the edge. The teacher's finger took flight, hovered mid-ocean.

'Does anyone know where Neville comes from?'

'About three streets from me, Miss.' Eric Willott was a ha-ha boy, anything for a laugh. Nev's skin prickled horribly. The teacher tried again; the finger hovered; hesitation was followed by a nervous, hand-half-up response from one timorous child. Teacher's finger floated to the low-ish left of the oblong world, hovered over a hunched-up landmass, but there it did not land with the expected fingertip peck; instead, it swung halfway across the world as if pulled by wild wind and tide.

'From here.'

'Why?' snarled one sourface child; but only Nev heard, as Eric called away attention by making a poopoowoosh noise, mouth against hand: but he had overplayed his ha-ha hand, he was lucky not to be slapped down literally. Nev didn't know whether to feel important, self-conscious or both.

That was Primary School. He had it easy there. Relatively. Even so, Nev came to realise that the 'Why?' had been misplaced; it should have come earlier and from him. The teacher had delicately avoided that why; perhaps the class was too young for such a truth. At Secondary they dubbed him Enoch, sneering bitterly in their occluded comprehension. Bad taste. In the mouth too. The only other child at the Secondary who wasn't the colour of a neglected candle was Paul Black, who had a reputation for a short fuse and getting into fights. But what else was he going to do when he was stuck amongst those people and his name was bloody Black? He was older than Nev and had little to do with him; so much for hopes of a protector. The only thing of any significance said by Paul Black to Nev was, 'You're just like them.' That had stayed with him, it stuck in his skin and smarted, as badly as did the bountybar barbs of his London relatives. It's hard to be one who makes his own way, Nev told himself.

'Sometimes I think the ones who want to be your friend are worse than the others,' muttered Nev, not proud of his embittered tone. 'The I'mnotas; the wheedlers who use you to prop up their cred.'

Jim shoulder-shifted mild dissent. 'I'd rather be faghagged than gaybashed. But I know what you mean.'

'I'm just tired, weary of it, watching people put both feet in their mouths, or even worse going through an absurd, spasmodic ballet as they attempt to stop themselves. But worse still, the cultivators, the I'm-your-frienders who have always got to prove it.'

Jim grunted. 'I admit I hate collectors, the ones who calculate how many of "them" brings absolution, how many is *de minimis* and has no brag-power.'

'Huh,' was all Nev could find to say. Pilot Ken wondered why the conversation stopped, switched, as he returned to the table, manfully portering four pints without spilling a drop. The Imp was dancing incensed in Frank Speke's chest and throat.

It stinks in here: Nev could smell out soap, resurgent sweat and intoxicating triumph; he nosed the undercurrents—sourness, dissatisfaction, glowering discontent.

'Cheer up y'fucker, we won! Cham-peeee-ons!' cried a voice close to the source of the bitterness.

'We had an unfair advantage. That's not winning.'

'Jealous twat.'

This sparked a flurried rematch in the back of the bus; this time with the result reversed.

179

'His dick's bigger than yours too mate,' smirked the loser who'd won.

'I can say what I want,' sulked the winner who had lost. 'The contest's over now, he's not honorary no more.'

George packed up and returned to the magic island, the place where I can never go, although parts of me—better-me, future-me—followed on his coattails. You could call it retirement, but perhaps more honestly retreat; it was the only time I saw George weary, the only time he put himself before others. The never-dead question 'Where you from?' had become 'Where *you* from?' and George had too sensitive an ear to tune out the difference. He tried to laugh it all off, but the laughter grew forced, hollow. Optimists said George had gone because his work was done, he didn't feel needed anymore, but truth is, he saw that it had all been for nothing, and he couldn't bear to start over. When the others are twitting the Pilot, they call him Saint: for his services to the tolerance of idiots, as far as I can see, but hey, he means well and that's all that matters, isn't it?

Excuse me, but I have an additional nomination—or do I mean a counter-proposal?—George Vincent Brownlee, of this parish, onceupon. I wonder how he and Ken would have got on; would they sit together, heads of the table, firm friends, joint rulers? Yes: all but for three little words. Man, how they get in the way. *Oh George*. I miss you.

As a table is so often central to our joint business, let's conjure the image of one, perhaps at a cut-above type of restaurant. You'd like to go to that table, but there's a barrier; let's make it elegant, a rope across your path but a jolly high-quality rope, neatly and delicately twined, and finished in purple velvet, suspended between neatly shining hooks. It blocks your way and with polite superiority it says *wait*. You're allowed to see who's there and what's going on, you're probably hungry too, to step forward—but—*not yet*. That rope could even have a keeper—a commissionaire, a hovering waiter, and this person is there to size you up, to say yay or nay: they could be tactful or forceful, or both as the occasion requires. Please wait to be seated. Please continue to wait, please continue... but you know the other diners have been let through with a low bow and a fawning phrase. You wait, you wait: sometimes you think it will go on forever. How long do you stand thus, supplicant, hoping? At what point do you realise that people beyond the barrier are enjoying letting you have a little looksee, to sharpen your appetite, deepen your envy? That the rope is never coming down for you, no matter how you silently plead. When do you lose your rag? The few who persist in seeking the magic words, who finally beg sufficiently entertainingly and are let through, unless they try hard to bury it, join the table with the knowledge that it is on sufferance, through an act of tolerance, they are there, and it is always on someone else's terms. Even if they finally get to sit and eat, how can they raise an appetite, having demeaned themselves so?

My cousin Katherine has a favourite t-shirt; it reads *Don't Fucking 'Tolerate' Me!* Very direct is Kath. She doesn't believe in sham rights, nor in being 'grateful', and she wouldn't hang around sheepishly waiting at that smart little barrier. If she thinks she's being patronised she says so and she's off. Gets dismissed as shoulder-chippy, 'angry'—but she's right. We have a right to seats at that table, same as anyone, but there's always some smarmy reason-why for more waiting. What's the use of lip-service equality, breached in the observance? Why should any of us be kept waiting? Why should I be made to feel I am being *tolerated*, given gracious permission, and that my case has been improved by having that wonderful thing, a white girlfriend? If you can't see this, this conflict, you don't know me well at all. And if that's the case, perhaps we shouldn't be together. I refuse to be roped-off, awaiting permission. I don't like people who *tolerate*; their friendship is conditional, it hangs by a thread.

'Did y'hear about the academic who got the sack for using a word, just one word, and a word, at that, used by the writer he was teaching about? Sacked for a word—just one word.'

'Actually, the lecturer was exonerated, and quite right too. And it was a she. But there are still some words that shouldn't be used, don't you think, Frank?' Nev grinned lopsidedly, boyishly, an expression that could be taken as apology, challenge or shy triumph. Emily threw her arms around him. Frank Speke, wordless, made his way to the bar, commencing a sustained and almighty effort to drown The Imp.

Gina's Separation

The Ways of Love

Gina and Mart were limb-tangled, overheated, fast-breathing and ecstatic. Sweat and semen lay in spots and globules on Gina's breasts; she loved the tightening sensation as Mart's come dried on her skin, it made her feel—what word?—triumphant. Mart too was feeling overwhelmed; thirteen years together and they could still do this, as vigorously, as passionately as their first night—better, because the deep, powerful excitement remained, but virgin anxieties had matured into experience and knowledge, certainty of what would please the other.

Mart caught his breath, kissed Gina lingeringly and whispered. 'I want you Gina.' He knew at once from the tensing of her body that he had blundered, broken the mood.

Why do I have to spoil things?

Why does he have to spoil things?

'You just *had* me, Mart. What's wrong with you?'

He had done it again; he had told her once too often. Gina scrambled out of bed and moments later the shower was running.

'Bird over there, the redhead with the bald guy, they're always in, they an item? They don't look it.'

'Don't think so.'

'Good, I fancy my chances.'

'With him or her?'

'D'you like hospital food?'

'She's married, lads. Husband works crazy hours, so she comes here without him, with her friends. Heard them talking about it, that lot up that table. They keep telling her to produce him, habus corpus or something the bald guy always says, to prove she hasn't killed him.'

'If she's on her own she's on her own. Available.'

183

'Since when?'

'Since I say so. Woman on her own in a pub—available.'

'Don't do it mate, you'll spoil her lunch. And the bald guy might twat you. I've heard he's a hardcase.'

'I *like* redheads.'

Gina enjoyed the come-and-go cast of characters at Pilot Ken's table, but it galled her that she could never sit alone, have a drink, read a book or the paper, do the crossword, think idly about nothing and everything in perfect peace: there was always some bloke 'offering' a drink, trotting out a well-thumbed chat-up, or the ones who were honest at least, dropping straight into blunt, libidinous crudities. She had long ago stopped trying to mention that she was married, or drawing attention to her ring.

'Married, eh? But looking for a bit of adventure huh?'

Or:

'Fuckin lesbian you mean, anyone can buy a ring.' or 'When I offer a drink, you fuckin *accept!*'

It had never paid for her to stand her ground; she never came out of such encounters feeling that the man—or men—had learned anything. There was good news, improvement, since the arrival of Evil Mand it had become possible for a woman to sit alone and remain alone, Mand saw to it. She was a pest-detector par excellence, and a chucker-out of enjoyable force and volubility. The men still didn't learn, but perhaps the message would sink in over the next geological age or two. It had always been easier to accept, with electric irritation, the protective shield of being one of Ken's table, and to let the pests' would-be amours be fended off by force of numbers.

A face more beautiful than any other; an angel in repose, Mart said, an angel in choler too, and a wild red angel when in the throes of passion. No: a china doll with absurd candyfloss hair and botox cheeks, whey-faced and spotty-dotty. Who could possibly find freckles attractive? I look like the mother of all measles. I've seen my reflection too often; in repose I look bored, pouty, arrogant, I can't help it.

In choler, all mouth and all else too-red; as for passion, I dread to think, all control, dignity abandoned. I wasn't popular at school, nor on the home street; posh, snooty, thinks she's it, but she's just shit. Don't tell me they were jealous, you're not helping.

'If one of our august number is foolish enough to fall hopelessly in love with a woman, why doesn't he go the whole hog and set his cap at someone who is hopelessly, tragically unavailable? There's no romance in hopeless-hoping and adolescent moon-facing if it's for love of someone who just *might* reciprocate, especially if her rickety romance finally disintegrates; where's the heart-rending piquancy in a soppy happy ending?'

'You just hate happiness, Frank, we've already told you. Besides, what do I know about fancying women, and I'm not listening.'

'I mean, why go for a dishwater-blonde with stress lines who can't match her sainted mother for looks or talent, when you can fix your eyes on a cold Pre-Raphaelite so clearly beyond your grasp it really, *really* hurts? At least his lovelorn gaze would rest on a paragon of beauty and not a bundle of nerves. But… I suppose the eye of the beholder is the deciding factor.'

'Luckily for you Frank, it's the ear of the hearer too, and mine have stopped working so I won't peach on you.'

'Do you know that morning and night I go and look in the bathroom mirror, and run my finger carefully over my forehead?'

'What are you talking about?'

'I'm looking for little red spots or bumps, something sharp breaking through the skin.'

'What are you—are you saying you're ill?'

'I'm not looking to frighten you, I'm not ill. It's just become a habit, looking for breakouts on my head.'

'Breakouts?'

'Something breaking out. Horns, Gina, I'm afraid of sprouting horns. I keep looking, one day they'll be there.'

'What?'

'One day you'll stop just talking about it, one day you'll just get on with it, fait accompli. The first time you ever came back from a works do hammered, that's all you talked about, broken-record.'

'I can't remember, I was pissed.'

'I can remember. I wasn't.'

'Mart, I wouldn't do that to you…'

'You threaten it; every day you seem to threaten it.'

'Not every day!'

'Regularly then, regularly, it feels like every day.'

'I wouldn't *do* anything; I just want you to agree that I can…'

'Make me a laughing-stock?'

'That's not what I want, Mart!'

'Yes. It. Is. That's all it amounts to, it's all it *can* amount to.'

'I don't want to hurt you; I'd never hurt you!'

'And yet you do, and you *will not stop*. That's the puzzle of us. Ever since we got together, I've never been able to close this subject off, every time I think things are going well, up it pops, and I feel like shit. And you know it. And you don't want to hurt me. And still, you won't stop.'

'But that's just not true!'

'It's our marriage Gina.'

'Nice to see Mart tonight eh? Must be a blue moon.'

Ken and Jim were walking home together, having stayed especially late at the Bat and Ball to hobnob with Gina's near-invisible husband. Jim, the gentle man and gentleman, was walking Ken home; he would then have to turn back and walk another twenty minutes to gain his own flat.

'Nice to see him, but I don't think he enjoyed himself so much. Tell me, Jim, why does Gina do that, behave as if he's not there? I mean, he comes along so rarely…'

186

'Perhaps she thinks they spend quite enough time together otherwise. Besides, the Bat and Ball's her territory, maybe she thought he was a sort of intruder...'

'Jim, she blanks him, I've seen her do it before. It worries me, I sometimes think there's something wrong there. Look at the way she chatted up that bloke in the beer garden... Mart was fuming, I could see it, he was trying to keep calm, but I could see the wisps of steam escaping.'

'Think they'll have a set-to when they get home?'

'Put money on it.'

'Aaargg, the ways of love. And I'm sure she does love him, absolutely sure.'

'If I'm honest, sometimes I get lonely, no one there when I get home, no light on, no nice welcome, no smell of cooking... then I see what couples put each other through, and...'

'Yep. Nite, mate.'

'Nite.'

Jim saw Pilot Ken to the door of the block, and lingered on the corner until he saw the lights come on in Ken's flat.

'Do you think you could ever share me?' They were naked on the thick rug in Mart's flat. Since a chance encounter weeks before, they had met every day for a drink after work and then, at the flat, shedding their clothes quickly, making love eagerly, passionately. They dispensed with the drink and would have dispensed with work, had that been possible. Gina's question was the first time Mart had felt the sharp bite of disconcerting doubt; it made him blather.

'I would never try to keep you from your friends. People who do that make a terrible mistake.'

Gina laughed; for the first time it was at him and had an acrid tang.

'Not that sort of sharing.'

Mart felt as if a mineshaft, a sink-hole, had opened beneath him; he was plummeting. The question he had been asked had no sure answer. To arrest his fall, he chose the briefest, most honest reply: No. Gina sighed as if to say what a shame, what a trivial point on which to end the sweetness they had known.

'You admit it's possible to love more than one person? People do.'

'Yes, true.' Mart felt as if he were chewing hot metal. 'Someone I work with is always on about their "partners"; they know about one another, they're happy.'

'There you are then.'

'Is there someone...' Mart could barely croak the words. Gina's shake of the head brought relief and confusion.

'Then what... Gina, before you say anything, such a thing may work for you, but it will never work for me. I can't do it. Not ever.'

Gina tutted; Mart felt a stubborn, selfish fool, a dinosaur, a moralising Victorian remnant; and yet... 'I mean it. If that's what you want, good luck, but it puts an end to all this.'

'But I don't want to end all this.'

'Nor do I.'

Their mouths met and there was no more talk.

'Gina, you're going to take vows tomorrow, if you don't want to, I will understand. But if that's what's in your mind, tell me now.'

'I want to marry you Mart.'

'I want to marry *you*, but I'm talking about the vows, what about the vows?'

'I understand them.'

'That's not what I'm asking. If you take them, will you mean it?'

'I understand them.'

'Perhaps we shouldn't get married, Gina.'

Emily and Gina were in close, closed conference at Ken's table, and the sight irked Frank Speke, whose hands clenched as he fidgeted, trying to follow his friends' conversation, but unable to look from the women for more than a few seconds.

'Right, I've had enough,' he decreed, 'I'm going femme-fishing. If you gentlemen haven't the guts to join me, please do not interfere.'

'We can't really do either.' Jim regarded Frank with suspicion. 'On the grounds we don't know what you're talking about.' He was waved to silence as Frank extended his arm, slid his hand into the no-man's land between Gina and Emily, and alarmed Jim and Ken by twisting his face in to a lounge-lizard rictus.

'Ladies, would you care to rejoin us?'

The quiet, urgent conversation between the two ceased, and they looked up, irritated, a little guilty. They had been discussing Emily's difficulties with Nev, his refusal to give up his own place and move in with her. Gina remained firm that Nev was wasting Emily's time and should be cut loose; Emily was equally convinced that although Nev was troubled, she was not the source of his troubles and her role was to help him.

'And what so absorbed your attention?' smirked Frank, 'Sharing recipes or household hints perhaps?'

Jim and Ken winced. Gina let loose a furious glare. Emily was more circumspect, but simmered with anger at the interruption and insult. Both knew what Frank's femme-fishing was.

'I wanted your opinion, your wisdom,' Frank played host and anchor, including all in a generous spread of his hands, 'I'm thinking of taking up a cause, it will take up a lot of my time, keep me away from here even, but I feel very committed to it.'

'And what might this cause be, Frank?' Emily spoke with brittle patience, aware that a trap was about to be sprung.

'I've decided to be like Kenny; I want to stand up for the oppressed, the put-upon, the ignored, the swept-aside. People who have decisions made over their heads and against their will and then get the blame when things go wrong.'

It was working, and he felt the surging of the impatient Imp.

'Come on, Frank.' Gina's voice dragged with weary sarcasm. 'Get it over with.'

'I've decided to form a rights group for the most downtrodden and disempowered people in our society—men.'

Gina sighed; Emily eye-rolled; Jim and Ken broiled in embarrassment.

'Misunderstood and misrepresented, accused of operating a "hegemony" by people who can't pronounce the word and a "patriarchy" by people who don't appreciate that a father is what every child needs; incidentally, isn't it time you girls stopped lolling round here boozing and started choosing baby names?'

'Frank, I'm going to write a stage show about you.'

Can you still love someone when you are so angry with them, so afraid for the future, all because of their behaviour? When we fell for one another, we realised we often had the same thing in mind at the very same time; simulthoughts, we called them, telepathy, confirmation that we belonged and were of one mind: we never believed in being of one body though, after all, two bodies was more fun. Anyway: it was Mick Evveram's party, the one he held every year at the weekend closest to the anniversary of the departure, along with all his savings, of his fiancée. It was a festival of renewal for Mick, but also an evergreen attempt to attract potential replacements.

The house was modern, much-fenestrated, light-pierced and fanatically clean, with plenty of space for a happy couple and growing family. The garden rose step-by-step from a clean-swept patio, with flat-rolled, square lawns set either side of a pink-brick path and minimalist displays of cold-looking white flowers as if to advertise that Mick and they hadn't the time to do more, they needed a helpmeet. Guests clustered on the lawns, stacked above and below as if pieces on a 3-D chessboard, chatting, laughing, threading in and out of the house to top up drinks or collect finger-food from the kitchen and the extended table, which half-blocked the open French window on to the patio, from which people and upbeat music spilled in waves.

Gina and Mart arrived at the same time as Pilot Ken, whose plus-one was not Emily, as Mick had quietly hoped, but an energetic and amicable Jim: Gina was quick to notice Mick avoided Ken and Jim except when they happened to be chatting to her and Mart. 'I think Mr Gatsby has problems,' sniffed Jim, 'but as I am eating his nosh and drinking his booze, I shall say only this: Five Star albums in his collection and suspiciously neatly folded towels in the bathroom.'

As the afternoon's heat mellowed, most of the guests remained outside. Gina and Mart, married for just over six months, were fielding occasional belated congratulations from people they half-knew as they stood in a small group centred upon a tall, slim, sporty-looking man, of an age with them but friend-of-a-friend unknown to them, as he expounded upon his recent conversion to the delights of fine wines. 'I've got a cellar—small of course, and of course no one had wine in mind when they built it—but I'm getting a good little collection together, if I do say so myself.' There was a friendly clamour for invitations to inspect the premises, but these were turned away with a smile; the newly-turned oenophile's attention was concentrated upon one figure in the group.

'I like wine, but red gives me a headache.' Gina laughed. 'I need to learn more about it, always said I'd go on a course but I never have.'

'I could teach you,' offered the sporty man with a smile that opened doors. 'I don't invite many people to sample my vintages, but in your case…' Gina smiled summer warmth, opened her eyes wide.

'You must come on your own, of course.' This was not made as an aside, there was no confidential dropping of the voice, and the man's eyes were on Mart, whose smile, already tolerance-thin, vanished.

'I'll come along.' Gina waved her glass. 'I'm eager to learn.'

'And then you flared your eyes at him again, Gina. He thought he'd got a little fish on the line, and what's more so did everyone else. They stopped treating me as a sweet newlywed and only looked at me from the corners of their eyes.'

'I would never have gone there; I was only being nice. I'm always nice to people. Besides, he was obviously gay, and I'm always especially nice to someone who's gay.'

'Gina, one of our fellow guests told me, with sadistic pleasure, that his nickname was Shag Pad, and that he was a predator who delighted in luring and screwing particularly dim married women. Especially if he could lure them from under their stupid husbands' noses.'

'I would never have gone!'

'That's not the impression our fellow guests came away with. Nor Mr Shag Pad. Nor me, Gina.'

'I was just trying to be nice to someone who was…'

'Next time you want to check who's gay and who's not, ask Jim will you?'

'I would never have…'

'I was awake all last night, Gina, wondering what would have happened had I not been there.'

'It would only have been a little adventure, people do it all the time.'

'Six months, Gina. Just six months.'

'Sometimes I feel trapped.'

'We discussed this before we got married, time and time again. We agreed.'

'You agreed.'

'What happened to simulthink, Gina?'

'What?'

'Telepathy, our telepathy, I was crying out to you in agony as you cosied up to him. You didn't hear. But I knew you didn't think he was gay.'

'You don't know what I think, you never do. Your simulthink is silly romantic rubbish.'

Jim and Mal, never the most comfortable of companions, had been sniping spikily at one another all evening, but in an indirect, coded manner of catty three-cushion shots that bounced off and around their bemused friends at Ken's table: a conversation about food led Mal to refer to 'Cottage Pie'; Jim made a remark about someone being 'a real *bec*'; Mal hit out at 'greedy boys who lick their fingers'; Jim made a crack about 'Burglars, or rather a gentleman thief'. Mal was grinning archly, which could have signified brazen triumph, but could also have been a mask for pain, whereas Jim's voice and expression never rose above apparent stoic indifference. The tension spoiled the evening until Mal took himself off to a meeting—council, club, who cared?

'Sorry everyone,' Jim flapped a deprecating hand, 'it's a queer thing.'

'*I'm* queer.'—it was Gina's voice, ringing and insistent.

'What was all that crap about being "queer" for God's sake? You confused everyone, you really embarrassed Jim, and as for me…'

'You know what I want, I want to experiment…'

'You're not "queer", that's just a silly pose. You're a bored married woman, dreaming, fantasising…'

'I'm not bored.'

'You never look it to me either—yet still this nonsense goes on. Call yourself "bi-curious", "polyamorous", whatever other self-absorbed labels you want to borrow from that smug SexLife column in that fucking middle class newspaper of yours, but don't poach "queer": that's theft, an insult to Jim, but you're too me-time to see it.'

'You're really pissing me off Mart. Ever since we got together, I've given way to you, given ground I didn't want to give, all for love of you, but I'm sick of your hangups: sick.'

'Oh come on! You're the one with the fucking hangups, I've got principles. There's a fucking difference!'

'Jesus, you're pompous when you want to be.'

'I'm old-fashioned, me and the rest of the world outside the metrosexual sophisticates of sodding SexLife. I love you and I don't need any more than that, don't want. You are a very advanced person with some very complicated thinking. For all I know, in fifty, a hundred years, everyone will be like you. But right here right now, if you put your clever theories into practice you won't be seen as some advanced sexual philosopher, people will despise you, use you and laugh at you. People will take what you offer, sure, but they will give nothing back but sneers and dirty names.'

'It doesn't matter what other people think! You always say it shouldn't!'

'But in this it does. You propose to give yourself to people who will return nothing. Your clever ideas rely on the fallacy that everyone thinks the same; they won't, they don't. Blokes, women for that matter, won't admire your liberated standpoint when they're bragging to mates about how they fucked you.'

'Don't make it sound so crude!'

'It is crude! That's the whole point, Gina! You're trying to rewrite human nature, it's just not possible. I understand what you say but I don't like it, not one bit. There's a gulf, a world, between you and other people, and in this case I am very definitely "other people". Your thinking leaves me far behind, feeling small and cold. I can't bear it. If you want to live in the way that you describe, well, I can't stop you, but I won't be there to see it, I won't stay to see the fallout.'

'What?'

'You can have your freedom—but freedom has a price. Before you start your little adventure—let me go.'

'No!'

'Then don't do it. And stop making me miserable by going on about it.'

194

'You're restricting me!'

'People do that to one another, I agree. But what you say you want, it appals me, makes me sick, I can't nod at it and turn a blind eye. Go off and take whatever it is you want, but let me get clear first.'

'That's not fair! Mart you're not listening to me!'

'Yes I am. I'm just not agreeing with you.'

'I need this, I *need* this!' Gina's hair was matted, her torso shone with sweat as she worked her hips hard on Mart; he had one hand on her back, one swishing across her buttocks as she swore and spat demands just as he liked her to. They counted three and she spun round, never losing his dick, using her thrilling Cleopatra grip; they grinned and called each other more filthy, passionate names, pet-names run wild. A few moments more of gliding hands and the slap of skin on skin, Mart came, yelling, robbed of words. Gina let herself down on to him, her breath hot; 'I love you.' Mart's lips worked, he wanted-wanted-wanted to say it back, but what would happen if he did? Gina stayed on him, grinding lightly, until she kissed him and then slipped off, heading for the bathroom. Had he ruined it again, this time by not speaking? What did 'I *need this*' mean? Was it the truth, or was she trying too hard to reassure herself? 'Useless, clumsy bastard,' whispered Mart fiercely, slapping himself on his moist brow; without thinking, he let his fingers wander for a few moments, pressing, testing.

Golf Club Interlude

'Percy here?'

'Out and about—showing some visitors the new Driving Range then round the course.'

'May be just as well. We need a word about Club business.'

'Without Percy?'

'Well, we can't discuss the celebrations in front of him, a quarter-century in the chair. He'd die of embarrassment.'

'True enough. I heard there was to be a presentation—a silver driver?'

'Not full-size of course. It's already engraved—*Percy Singer, 25 years and never bunkered!* We'll present it at the do...'

'Ooo—free bar?'

'Ah, do remember we've had to make cutbacks...'

'Sorry. I just thought we should put one something special for Perce.'

'Oh we will. But he's a modest man, as you know. D'you know, by the way, he's never groomed a successor?'

'Successor? He's not retiring yet? I'd heard he fancied another year—if the AGM agrees it of course.'

'There's a good deal of feeling that, appreciate him though we do, Percy needs to move... over. He's not well, didn't you know? Doesn't talk about it, doesn't like to worry folk. There's a good deal of feeling we shouldn't wait for the AGM.'

'But why? What's he done wrong?'

'Oh nothing, nothing at all. There's just a good deal of feeling...'

'On whose part? I've never heard anything.'

'No names, discretion is the watchword. Anyway, it's nothing against Percy, it's just that there's a...'

'Good deal of feeling...'

'...that twenty-five years is a good innings, and that the Club needs some forward momentum, something new, some changes. He and his cronies just talk about the old days.'

'Something new? We only just got the new Range.'

'But that needs to be paid for, there needs to be plans put in place, ways to get more money in, we need someone younger, more dynamic; future-facing.'

'And a modest man can't do any of that?'

'Especially when he's quite a lot to be modest about.'

'Oh come on!'

'Just saying he's an easygoing bloke, but the time for "easygoing" has run out. We need fresh blood, new energy, new ideas. Vision.'

'And who's going to provide them? You?'

'There's a good deal of talk about Charles Barclay.'

'Charlie Barclay? Fresh ideas? Energy? *Vision*? He's a chattering barfly, when he turns up to meetings at all.'

'You'd be surprised. He's got a lot of support.'

'He's going to need it; "a lot to be modest about"—indeed!'

'He does still need support—from people like you. Fresh approach, refreshed committee. We can all show our sincere gratitude to Percy, name the Driving Range after him perhaps, but after that... there will be a Special Meeting, the rules allow for it. Percy and his circle will be away at a tournament.'

'Good god.'

'It's for the good of the club, the future. You're one of our good people, one of the best. We need you to help us face that future.'

'And not a word to Percy of course.'

'We rely on you.'

'Good god.'

There Is Nothing We Can Do

The Fall of Pisa, the Folding of the Wing

There was a look about Frank Speke which made his companions ill at ease; a self-satisfaction, smugness even, something that usually indicated he had spoken truth to power, scored a victory against some fastidious politically-correct snowflake, or at the very least impishly smuggled a forbidden word or two into the conversation. Frank was holding forth in a comfortable, confident, almost fireside manner, as if recent events, the meeting at the Town Hall and the curious encounter with the Residents' Association, had imbued him with new authority, a higher profile. He was, frankly, lording it.

'An outsider may think "dreaming villages, sleepy town—dormitory, literally—nothing ever changes"; plenty of insiders fall for the same illusion, because it suits them. Their attention wanders, perhaps they too close their eyes, drift... and when they wake up—bloody hell are they surprised.'

'Did you know our glorious leaders wanted to add something to the Welcome To sign; a big metal arch bearing the words "Gateway to the Future"?' To Emily, Pilot Ken seemed to be trying hard to regain a foothold in the conversation. Ignoring him, Frank resumed his tweedily confident lecture-hall tone.

'We're trapped between the change-worshippers, these would-be futurists, the smash-it-all-and-see-what-happens merchants, and a bunch of cold-blooded balance-sheet assassins. All people want,' he swept a grand hand before him, 'is leaving alone. But no, *they* can't, can they? If it costs just a bit to improve something, make a solid, proper change, they don't like it. If it costs a fortune to twiddle-twaddle-fiddle-faddle, they bloody love it.'

'Those meetings reminded me of the consultation about "pressures for change" at Fern Hill Hospital a couple of years ago,' Ken tried again. 'Options laid out for us—A, B, C, gave us a public vote—and then they picked option D, total closure, sell the site for millions.'

'Which, of course, they'd decided long before the sham "consultation".'

'I trusted them to keep their word. We all did.' Ken was sulky, wounded.

'More fool you.' Frank pressed his advantage. 'Same with Pisa, same with the Wing. You saw what happened each time.'

Emily and Gina exchanged a glance: they were accustomed to ground-pawing in the pub, but not from such senescent stags. What was going on?

'I used to make fun of our smallness—national *and* local—but I also thought somehow it was our protection; small is not noticeable, small gets left alone,' Pilot Ken sighed into his Guinness.

'Wrong again.' Frank was without mercy. 'Small is easy, small is crushable.'

'We'll be even smaller soon. Even more crushable,' concurred Jim.

'If you ask me,' said Little Mal, who very much thought he ought to be asked, 'that committee was not properly elected.'

'How can you tell among all this bloody noise?'

'That's one of the reasons it's all wrong. Proposed-seconded-voted on the nod under a blanket of pub chatter and with unseemly haste. Either they haven't the first clue how to run an AGM or know rather too well. But I don't suppose anyone will challenge them. Nobody challenges anything these days.'

Ken was about to observe that such complaisance in the face of power usually suited Mal, but was too slow.

'That's true,' chipped in Frank Speke, 'people don't argue or protest these days, have you noticed? They're completely supine, the powers that be can do anything, walk all over them, and all the victims will come out with is a weak smile—maybe even a piped little "thank you". People these days are useless. Push em down, tread on their faces, kick em—they ask you to do it again.'

'Huh,' said Mal, which could have been assent, dissent or dull uninterest in the iconoclastic wisdom of Frank Speke. He had already turned his attention to the floor-show—what could be heard of it.

It was the Annual General Meeting of the Residents' Committee of the Ring O' Villages. Apart from its suspect election of officials, it had one special item of interest for drinkers at the Bat And Ball. First, however, for Pilot Ken and the regulars, was the surprise that an AGM, especially for people who lived some miles away, should take place at their pub.

'What happened to their Village Hall?' asked Ken.

'It was decided it was unsafe, and there were no funds to fix it,' Mal quickly explained, 'and then next thing it was in the way of a little bit of essential road-widening and got bulldozed. And of course there's no money for a replacement. They've been homeless since, flitting from pub to pub, club to club for their meetings. They asked for this one to be held at the Golf Club.'

'You refused?'

'Look at the special agenda item, just look.'

The item in question was *Proposed Closure and Sale of the Angel's Wing Pub*.

'So?' asked Jim.

'Think about it James,' Mal was impatient, 'if you want to support a failing pub where do you hold the meeting? Where do you have the drinks and chit-chat afterwards?'

'Ah,' pennydropped Jim. Mal nodded curtly, as if he deigned to forgive Jim's lapse.

'I know why they can't get the Wing tonight,' offered Ken, 'there's already a meeting being held there. In fact, two, possibly three. And it will probably all end in a fight. The new landlord specialises in abject confusion.'

Mal nodded again, either giving his endorsement or covering the fact he, like the others, hadn't known that Danny Deebee, that agent of chaos, was back in the area. 'It makes sense if that idiot's been put in.' Frank tapped his nose. 'Word is that the pubco's trying to run the place into the ground, so as it'll never recover. Sweetheart deal with the developers; moolah.' The nose-tap became a finger-rub, the expression remained self-satisfied.

Evil Mand had agreed to the meeting at The Bat and Ball. 'I'm no mug, I don't turn down trade.' But she had refused to make special arrangements such as turning away normal customers, and so the meeting took place on a lively night of buzz and chatter; through the curtain of noise the Cabinet tried to follow the evening's proceedings; Mal, with technical, forensic scorn, Ken, Jim and Emily with bemusement, Frank with contempt.

Ken's table had a small addition, a not-quite-with-you appendage like the dot under a question-mark; JC sat alone at a small round table, keeping close but showing no sign of joining, barely and rarely moving, perhaps not fully aware of his surroundings. He was as ragged as ever, his face scuffed and scarred, thin sticking-plasters strung along his boozer's conk and concave cheeks, their edges curling. His gaze, clouded as ever, and through roughly-repaired glasses that sported more tape than his face, hardly shifted from the bar. He showed no inclination to hoist himself to his feet and bargain for a pint; his Singing Pot Man act was a memory, but not one he acknowledged; drinks appeared at his elbow, small gestures of charity, and he sipped slowly at them if he recognised them at all, contrary to his customary bottoms-up relish.

A little over a week before, JC had disappeared: he failed to haunt the Bat And Ball and it became clear he was not hanging around any of the other town centre pubs. It was hard to ask after JC; how do you trace a man whose name

201

you don't know and whose address is downthegrid? Jim went so far as to drive Ken to The Angel's Wing in an attempt to scotch—or confirm—a rumour the old man had journeyed to join the shades therein.

'Best o British,' growled Frank, 'don't y need to make an offering of blood before they'll reply to you?'

Ken had an interesting discussion with Tim Carman and his mates, but in spite of their friendliness, not exactly mateyness, they were resolved never to recross to the Bat; and of JC there was still no sign until he shambled some nights later into the pub, sat stock-still and said nothing, a performance he repeated night after night, near but not with Pilot Ken and friends.

The story of his disappearance, none of it from JC, arrived in uneven, unsavoury pieces. The old man had got staggering drunk, as ever, and blundered into the night, also as ever, perhaps trusting in blottoed vagueness that one of his kindly neighbours would (as ever), intercept and guide him back to downthegrid: whomever he had encountered had not been the least kindly, and JC was found under a hedge, cold, cut, bleeding. He was in hospital a few days but, Ken decided, the old man had survived his ordeal by forgetting about it. With an answer-seeker's jealousy he wondered if anyone, police or medical, had learned JC's real name, address, date of birth? And who had attacked him? For what?

'Kids.' Frank Speke was sure. 'Hanging round looking for fun; someone to do over, to hurt. Someone helpless, for preference.'

'You don't know that, Frank,' snapped Emily.

'Kids.' Frank gave Emily his snowflake-melting look.; 'Bored cos their byoootiful TestBed has been shut down, and all their youth clubs and wherever else people like *you* would coddle them.'

'You don't know that Frank.'

'And what will our wonderful law guardians do? Nothing. I bet someone saw, but naah, they wouldn't want

202

to get involved, over the other side they passed. There'll be no justice, even if the silly old sod snaps out of it and remembers.'

'Maybe he fell. He was steaming, after all.'

'Cobblers. He was beat up.'

'No one will ever know, will they? It's all shut up in there, secret and silent,' said Ken flatly. JC turned his head, slowly and stiffly, as if aware he was the subject of discussion, but he didn't look directly at Ken, at anyone.

'They say cutback!'

'We say *fightback!*'

It had been quite a time for meetings and protests.

'They say cutback!'

'We say *fightback!*'

Some more raucous than others.

'Cut-cut-cut-back!'

'Fight-fight-fight-back!'

The leader of the protest was hanging limp between two policemen as they carried him from the Council chamber. As he was carried past the lines of council workers and members of the public, the protest leader continued to bellow his call and his followers their response as they were bundled behind. Pilot Ken was half-minded to tell the cops to take only the leader; without him, his sheep would cease to bleat. Instead, he wondered at the man being carried; he had never seen anyone attempt a curtain-call while conveyed dead-weight style down a flight of stairs to a night in a cell. He also noted the blissful smile on the face of FMC as he was carried away, a man done with talking, at last leading his revolution. Applause rang out in the chamber and down the stairs as the protesters were removed. As the grinning, twisting FMC was borne past, Frank Speke leaned low and stage-whispered, 'They're plauding the Peelers, you cloth-eared wazzock.'

The Council Chamber was impressive, if featureless white rooms were your thing. White walls, floor, ceiling, even its podium white, three-levelled as if about to hand out Gold, Silver and Bronze to exhausted athletes. The Council's logo was the only burst of colour, painted large and dark above the podium, emphasised by ceiling-to-floor deep-purple drapes on either side. The council's leader looked suitably fatigued as he struggled to restore order; a barrel-chested, bearded man with a leonine sweep of dark brown hair, he could usually make his beast-roar heard anywhere, but his demands for calm and quiet were consumed by the hubbub. As he regained control and called for the next speaker, he mopped his brow, astonished his meeting could be so rudely interrupted.

Tension simmered in the colourless space, a tension that had settled on the room as soon as the meeting was called to order. The protesters would doubtless have received a more sympathetic response had they not begun chanting before anything had been announced. The room was crowded with people who feared the loss of jobs, the closure of the town's park, increases in their taxes, cuts in their bin-days, the removal of day-care for children and the elderly, the inevitable consequences for the high street—not to mention the pubs. The fear of a slash-and-burn budget was underscored by rage that, as rumour went, the Council was to announce enormous expenditures on itself, in the form of the razing of the Town Hall and the building, at eye-watering cost, of a new Civic Centre that would scrap civic pride and replace it with civic self-delusion. Everyone awaited the news, their fate, the worst, as the pride-leader rose to his feet and called for order. He could barely shape another syllable before his big voice encountered a rival for dominance of the white-empty space:

'Item one is…'

'No ifs no buts we won't take your Tory cuts!'

'Agen…'

'No ifs no buts we won't take your Tory cuts!'

'…da item one is…'

'No ifs no buts we won't take your Tory cuts!'

'No ifs no buts we won't take your Tory cuts!'
'No ifs no buts we won't take your Tory cuts!'

It was a solo at first, stresses falling violently on each 'no', the tone stentorian, enraged. Anyone could tell this was a voice that would not tire easily, and the regulars of Ken's table, Emily, Jim, Frank and Ken, knew it well, its self-righteous, hectoring tone.

'No ifs no buts we won't take your Tory cuts!'

The lion on the podium roared for silence, and for a moment seemed to have succeeded. 'Thank you. Agenda item one is...'

'They say cutback!'
'We say *fightback!*'

Somehow the backing vocals seemed familiar too; Ken and Jim exchanged a glance.

'They say cutback!'
'We say *fightback!*'

At least this solved the mystery of another disappearance. Not long before the vanishing of the Singin Pot Man, FMC too had failed to show up as usual at the Bat And Ball: his absence drew less comment, Ken decided, as people were happy for a break from ranting, freeform allegations of class treason and false consciousness.

Now it was clear where FMC had been; developing his skills as a Pavlovian choirmaster in the PH Bar, making Scamp, Gizmo and the lugubrious Hank sing for their liquid supper. Scamp chanted as he existed; rattily, nervously, with sideways glances, scanning for predators, preparing to scurry. Gizmo was a zombie, a wraith, in face, voice and movement, doing what he had been instructed and not a scintilla more. Hank, by contrast, was a songbird, injecting a plainsong beauty in his chanting; well, after all that was how he got his name, wowing many a karaoke crowd with his golden country croon. Their CO was obviously still in prison, or hospital, or dead: had their Colonel been around, FMC would have found them far harder to control. What the hell had FMC offered—a seat on the soviet, protection from purges, a lifetime's supply of bathtub vodka?

'They say cutback!'

'We say *fightback!*'

'It's all very well for certain sectors of the community to exercise their right to free speech...' the leader made 'turn up my mike' gestures as he spoke, 'but this is a democratic space and...' At the mention of free speech, Frank's gaunt cheek twitched.

'They say cutback!'

'We say *fightback!*'

FMC modulated his voice, but he had clearly not succeeded in training his choristers to follow suit; their response to the drawn-out call was flat and terse—but loud.

'This is a democratic...'

Emily strode to the bawling group, halting them briefly with a silver scream, 'Will you *shut up?* People are wondering what's going to happen to their jobs, homes, families, their futures! You won't even let them find out, you stupid, arrogant...'

'They say cutback!'

'We say *fightback!*'

Emily was close to FMC, his bellowing overloaded her ears, yet it was his face that caught her attention; it lacked his usual myopic intensity, it was cleaner, better-shaved, his hair shorter, as if he had made himself camera-ready... there was another thing; the expression. During his pub-table tirades, that face was usually twisted with sneering, but here, choir-mastering, leading his flock, FMC was transfigured, blissful. At last, he was the leader of the masses, even if his shock-troops were a little the worse for wear.

'Notice how much he's sniffing?' Jim asked Emily on her return.

'Ah... *ah...*'

'But there is a definite niff in here—I'd call it the smell of absence. Of eminence grease.'

Looking on at the melee, stoic, sober and slit-mouthed, was a small figure almost swallowed by an improvised sandwich-board; Dennis Nugent was positioned sentry-like over the amassed councillors, watching for the moment of betrayal, the bait-and-switch that would doom the best causes, marching up-down, up-down so everyone could see his painted slogans:

WHAT ARE YOU HIDEING
FREEDOM MUST SPEKE

Nug had nodded curt acknowledgment to Ken, but otherwise maintained an unwavering vigilance, looking to Emily like a gnarled, perished mockery of the life-sized mannequin, arms akimbo, mouth smiling in brawny excess, which stood outside Grey's Butchers welcoming customers and frightening children. Nug watched the removal of FMC and his acolytes, and Ken could see that Dennis would perceive this floor-show as nothing but a deliberate distraction, conspiratorial legerdemain aimed at frustrating his relentless pursuit of Truth. His cold stare was that of the upstaged.

'It all went through, nem con no doubt?' FMC, freshly released, was lolling in a chair at the Bat and Ball, enjoying the covert whispers and finger-pointing in his direction.

'Not so much nem con.' Emily was irked by the man's ballooning self-satisfaction, 'More "nothing to be done". Like Didi and Gogo on the country road.' FMC narrowed his eyes, prickling with suspicion of middle-class mockery. Emily abandoned coy game-playing and laid in to him. 'What went through did so in a rush, nobody's quite sure what was voted for; "owing to pressure of time," they said, meaning time wasted—by you and your gang of alcoholic chimps.'

'Ahh, you all just stood there like dumb animals awaiting the fuckin knife! At least I tried to do something, stop them...'

'Always supposing you could succeed—what would you do after that?'

'It wouldn't be up to me,' FMC pronounced with righteous stiffness, 'it would be up to the people.'

'Scamp? Gizmo? Hank? The children of the revolution? Seriously?'

FMC scoffed but Emily was immune to his scorn. 'No, not them, they were just useful idiots, eh? Like you were for the lion king.' That was the last they saw of FMC for some time, although neither Emily nor Ken read the least significance into this at the time.

The leaning tower surrendered to nonexistence without the thunderous collapse and pall of dust imagined by Pomo the Clown: he heard the excited chatter at the end of the street, saw people gravitating towards the safety-barriers, packed up his gear quickly and rushed to get a good view. He stood close to the barrier, his tall frame overtopping those quicker than him to get there; in full costume and makeup, Pomo felt not the least out of place in full clowing regalia. After a long delay and a warning klaxon, the Town Hall emitted a sigh, collapsing as if it were a failed cake in a mis-set oven. There were disappointed mumblings among the crowd, whose communal exhalation echoed that of the doomed building. Pomo turned to the man standing next to him; bald head, woolly-lapelled jacket, a familiar smile. 'I wanted to see if there really were torture chambers in the basement. Or proof that Dennis Nugent was right all along.' Ken pitched his voice above the conversations around them, grinning.

'We could check the wreckage for Councillor Alexander's body,' suggested Pomo: ambitious, camera-loving and impulsive, Alexander had sworn to the local paper to 'Lie down in front of the bulldozers' and pledged to local radio he would 'die in a ditch' to stop the demolition. Curiously, he had been called away on urgent business the day before the wreckers arrived.

'You going back to work, or is there time for a pint?'

'I'd better…' Pomo indicated his box of tricks, Ken nodded.

'By the way, did you hear about Mal?' Pomo had a sudden inspiration; Ken shook his head.

'Well, they've been emptying the building for a while of course, and some folks have been "helping" the demolition from within: playing lift-shafts with crockery, throwing hat-stands like javelins, piercing the inside walls, you know, all board and plastic packing; the IT team jury-rigged a massive crossbow, so my mate says, shot a bolt clear through to the next office. Could've killed someone if it'd not been deserted. Others weren't as OTT, but they had little parties, games of cricket in the council chamber, breaking things and staging competitions to see who could kick through the inner walls.'

'And Mal?' Ken grinned in happy anticipation.

'Turned his nose up at such monkey-business in public, but gave it a sneaky go when he was lurking alone in the Leader's office; word is he kicked too hard and high, must have really put himself in to it, kung-fu style—his leg went through thigh-deep, couldn't get out. He was found the best part of a day later, when they did the last safety checks.' Ken's shoulders shuddered. 'Oh, too good to be true! If it is, call Tony the Convert—tell him there is a God!'

'You'll doubtless have noticed Mal hasn't shown up at the pub lately…'

'Ah! It's true, *it's true*! Pomo dear boy, speaking of the pub, come along, right away. And forget about your slate, you've just wiped it off. In the wall! Up to his bloody thigh! *Hah!*'

Pomo the Clown, still in his business clothes and makeup and still not feeling the least bit out of place, held his audience rapt and performed a storming gig in the clean, natural light from the huge windows of The Bat And Ball; it was a masterclass of mimic gesture, forceful comic physicality and, not least, of milking an audience; a career

209

high, compensation for the daily humiliations on the street, not to mention the Fun Day debacle of evil memory, even if there was still no money in it, not counting forgiven debts.

On the way to the pub, even when talking to Ken, Pomo had pictured and mentally developed the frozen high-kick pose now causing him some small agony, but producing strangulated guffaws from his audience; the performer always had to suffer; what about the famous men who had played through the throes of an onstage heart attack, propped up, kept alive, by the glorious high-to-low, giggle-to-blast sound range of glorious, saviour laughter. Mid-air heave-ho, grimacing, arms, shoulders working, comic desperation growing as he wriggled to escape, sweating (that was not an act), breathing hard (also not an act) maintaining his balance while twisting and turning in the relentless maw of an invisible wall, Pomo found himself so adrenaline-high that had Mal made an entrance, he could not and would not have stopped. He forgot his usual discomfited distraction in Gina's presence and could enjoy her attention as a precious rarity; to reduce the stony, unimpressible Frank Speke to tears of hilarity was an achievement beyond all but the greatest of artistes; and perhaps Emily would now consider that solo booking he had hinted at so often.

This would be one for the autobiography; *At the end of a lean period, financially if not creatively, a private, spontaneous performance helped to shape my career, the result of a confluence of events that led to a vital decision, a bedrock change to the act.* Part of his busybusy mind cried sellout, his principles protested in alarm, but Pomo allowed the moment, his unthinking, driving instincts, to transport him. Ken barked for him, called the crowd together, setting the scene with exciting, excited words, then bowing away, rejoining the audience, leaving Pomo centre-stage, a one-man show. Ken had provided a witty, well-turned introduction, a scene-setting not a scene-stealing, every word superbly chosen, and even as he worked Pomo thought rapidly—words; perhaps I shouldn't scorn them, perhaps they have a role. Keeping up

210

the one-legged frozen stance while working his upper body, squirming his hips but keeping the 'trapped' leg still was exhausting, draining play and it made Pomo's body pulse with bone-deep aches and his breath come in ragged rasps that were surely too small, too short, to support words. Still trying to break free, Pomo-as-Mal turned his head as if surveying the ruined office around him and goggled his eyes.

'Where's everything gone? It's as if Raffles had paid a visit…'

Ooooooooo! His audience hooted.

'Why aren't my friends here to get me out?' groaned Pomo-Mal, 'Why haven't I got any fr…' his voice trailed off into a pathetic poor-me squeak, and the crowd roared, a roar that swelled mightily at the last desperate squeal before Pomo executed a carefully controlled fall at the feet of his adoring audience: 'Councillor Alexander—*save me!*' Perhaps, thought Pomo, soaking up adulation and best bitter in the warmth of post-gig, there is room in the world not just for words but for a little cruel humour too. It gets results.

The Ring O' Ringers were the next item of business before the perhaps-elected Residents' Committee, but the continued buzz of business as usual meant nobody could be sure of the nature of their appeal, for funding perhaps or for help in not being defunded; all Ken could make out was the brutal interruption of their delegate's disquisition on the joys of campanology with a voluble, 'That's not relevant to this meeting.'

Emily picked out a further response, loud but flat: 'There is nothing we can do.'

The bellringers retreated to the bar, head-shaking, bemused, their bruised words adding to the hubbub. Next item of business: a couple from Mill Village, a stolid, respectable pair instantly dubbed by Emily Mr and Mrs Neighbour, presented a complaint on behalf of all the village, that heavy lorries were rat-running to the town through their narrow streets, waking children, churning tarmac, lopping wing-mirrors off parked cars. 'They think sticking the pedal to the floor is the way through a narrow gap; they even pass at 3am, shaking the windows, disturbing the whole street.' Mrs Neighbour was a measured and credible witness, Mr Neighbour nod-nodding assent by her side. 'We've kept a diary, taken photos of the damage; we've even followed them to their depot to complain—and got a right mouthful for our trouble.'

There were stirrings from the Chair, plaintive ahems that did not bode well.

'We've spoken to the police, but they say…'

'There is nothing we can do,' hissed Pilot Ken to Emily. This was also apparent from the Committee's shrugs and open palms, and the stunned, bar-bound trajectory of the Neighbours.

The arrival of three extra people in the overcrowded pub should not have been remarkable, and yet the trio—who entered just in time for the special agenda item—cut a swathe of silence across the bar and had drinkers falling back to give them room, less from politeness than superstitious awe. 'Well-well-well.' Frank Speke lowered his glass mid-gulp. 'The sexton hasn't kept a very close eye on his charges this night. What shall we call this little delegation? Trainee ghosts? The near-departed? Come on Kenny, help me out, lend me some of your stock of clever words.'

'I can't. I'm too… gobsmacked.'

'That is *not* a clever word, Kenneth. Find a better,' Frank said. There was a brief disturbance as a small white-haired woman broke the spell, pulled and slapped herself free of restraining hands and made an unsteady but determined march towards one of the group; a look of rage on her lined face. 'Tim Carman, you've got some brass neck showing your face here, I…' the confrontation was cut short as Evil Mand slipped in between Carman and his accuser, and the woman's companion caught up with her, taking her by the shoulders and turning her around, propelling her back to

212

their table. Ken and Mand exchanged a look, Ken moved to the bar, nodding to Carman and the others as he went, collecting a small glass and clacking it down before the still-protesting woman.

The Committee consulted the agenda, the Chair rose, and to his surprise, quiet—of the grave—descended on the gathering, with only the clink of glass and low-voiced requests for another at the bar in-lieu of a once untameable racket.

'Next item is of clear interest to many here. The Angel's Wing is to be…'

'*Nyerrrr yaeee-arrrr! Nyerrrr yaeee-arr! Pay yer Poll Tax, don't forget, pay yer Poll Tax, you pay it now, hear?*' JC finished the drink before him in one mighty draught, rising and walking in front of the Committee as if he were another supplicant.

'Could we have some hush here please, sir? We all wish to discuss a…' the Chair tried on JC the dismissive tone and hostile glare that had seen off the Ringers and the Neighbours.

'Pay yer fuckin Poll Tax sunshine, mind you pay it or there'll be trouble!' JC was sway-dancing, breathing *nyerrrr yaeee-arr* as he step-swayed, trot-swayed, attracting all eyes to his floorshow. 'Wossermatter wiv yu all?' JC's voice filled the room, 'Woss all the long faces fer, eh? Like a lotta orses y'are! Ere, I know a song about an orse, it goes like this…'

The Chair made a grab for JC, but the old man half twinkle-toed and half toppled out of danger; the Chair gave up the effort as he realised nobody was coming to his aid. The chatter sprang back up and those able lip-read from the Chair that the meeting was adjourned; everyone else learned this as they saw the Committee gather its papers and decamp. Oblivious, conducting the gathering with swinging arms, JC croaked a tune some found vaguely familiar beneath the wounds he inflicted on it.

'*To is orse! To is orse! E was sayin goodbye to is orse! An as e was sayin goodbye to is orse, e was sayin goodbye to is orse! To is orse! To is orse!*'

Some even joined in, 'C'mon nah, join in the singalong wiv The Singin Pot Man! *To is orse! To is orse!*'

'You realise that technically there is no end to this song?' remarked Ken to Jim, matter-of-factly.

'Let's get a beer.'

'Sound thinking.'

'*E was sayin goodbye to is orse…*'

Ken wondered again at the magnificent healing power of the old man's forgetting.

There was a look about Frank Speke that made his companions ill at ease. He had news, was relishing it far too much for it to be anything but bad.

'Mal's been talking to too many people again—some dangerously reliable witnesses. The bulldozers go in to the Wing two weeks from today. No reprieve.'

'Never mind,' Jim grinned satirically, 'Councillor Alexander will be there to lie in front of the machines, die in a ditch, etcetera-etcetera…'

'Got his urgent call-away booked already, no doubt.' Ken's smile was slot-like, mirthless.

'And they're about to pass the plans for the new Civic Centre, spite the fact that the plan's a crock, the finances dodgy and the materials wrong. Word is Gil Davis has warned the lion king and his cronies of the consequences—legal, practical, political—and they told him, "shut the fuck up." So he did. Resigned.'

'So who's left to save the Wing and stop all the other nonsense? FMC, wherever he's vanished? His piss-artist PH-pals? Dennis Nugent and his forest of placards?'

'Any volunteers?' enquired Frank Speke. 'Question is, what is the point at which any bugger will *do* something? They, you, all believe, like children, that if they appeal against unfairness, bleat, petition, seek *arbitration*, some higher power, some loving meta-parent who will come and kiss it bloody better. They are pop-eyed, so stunned, when they realise they are on their own. A perfect example of community spirit and pusillanimous helplessness.'

'Bloody hell, what feeble, useless, insignificant little creatures we are,' groaned Ken.

'And that is our resident optimist speaking.' Frank had that look on his face once more, the speaker-of-truth smugness that unnerved one and all.

Magic Whisky

Chris ordered a Magic Whisky, walked back slowly, painfully, from the bar; once she was ready to lower herself back into her seat her glass was nearly empty again. The magic—she lolled her glass back and forth—lay in the fact that if you ordered a double it came at nearer to the price of a single. Chris believed in magic. Her white hair was short but disordered, feathered as if ruffled by contrary breezes. She was a small woman, frail of build, her years showed in the cane-thinness of her limbs and her stooped, difficult bearing, but most of all in the facial lines of frowning discontent. Her eyes had once been a penetrating, nobody's-fool blue, but were less vivid and, deep within, had a look of growing doubt, infiltrating tendrils of subtle grey smoke.

Dave sat next to her, saw her tilting her glass back and forth, the last of the liquid magic waiting to thrill her lips. Dave always sat close, it was his place, especially when she was steeped in magic, shifting two for his every one. He stood his round as everyone did, but usually let Chris go to the bar to get her extras even though it cost her pain, in the fuzzy hope that pain would one day win out over magic. Dave's mates had another name for the whiskies: g'won, be a gent, they urged, nudging and grinning, get her another henpecker. He tried to laugh with them.

They were a good crowd at the Bat and Ball. It was a regulars' pub; you knew who you could find there and when you could find them. Familiar faces, voices, comforting. Some dropped out: Tim Carman had moved off to the Angel's Wing after high words with Chris, him and his stupid clique. They could stay there. Some people had simply moved away; Dennis Kitson and his missus, packed off to Sunderland to be with their grandkids; Jeff and Julie of course: Dave and Chris had said that they would go up and visit, but it was such a long way and besides, neither travelled so well, not these days. There were the lost: Crompton Corner, marked with a little brass plate screwed into the wall that bore two names, two sets of dates. They had been particular mates with Chris and Dave, a clever, bouncy woman and a taciturn but sound and decent man. Lost; missed. Danny Deebee had tried to do away with the plaque, but he thought better of his fit of new-broom-itis when his regulars had at him.

'Henpecker?' Pilot Ken lifted up Dave's empty glass, Chris's too.

'Magic,' Chris corrected him raspingly.

'Abracababra!' cried Ken, waving a wand-hand as he stepped away—when he came back everyone around the table knew he would put the new glasses down with a flourish and a 'Hey Presto!' Dave would give the showman a smile, but Chris would gnaw at her lip at the thought of the price she had just paid for that drink. She knew the regulars liked to pull her leg and that she had to bear it, feel what she may.

The windows of the Bat and Ball were more like those of a modern living-room than the old style of smoke-and-no-mirrors pub, you could see and be seen, it was a million miles from the dark doors and impenetrable frosted glass Chris remembered from girlhood, when her dad was inside, hidden from the street, though she watched for even the faintest, ghostly movement behind those whited panes.

Up-and-downer with Pilot Ken: her temper frayed, she had not forgiven him the whisky remark and it made her madder still when everyone laughed at her and said it was the magic talking, the voice of the henpecker. They couldn't resist tickling and jabbing at her thin skin; the stronger her reaction the more fun they had. It didn't matter what the fight was about, things came up and they went away again and usually they were forgotten by the end of the session, magicked away just as they had been spirited into being.

Today it was because Ken had said that it was more than ten miles to Maxford from the pub door, and Chris would not have it, waving aside Dave's advice to let it go.

'I've walked it there many a time as a lass, never took more than an hour,' she said in an irritable snarl.

'Weeee-elll, perhaps Maxford's moved a bit... after all these years,' mused the Pilot, baiting her playfully.

'You shuddup, fool!' The bait was taken, and not playfully.

'Either that or you should've been on the Olympic team.' The others were weighing in. Sniggerers, smirkers.

'She must've flown there in your plane, Kenny!'

'*Shuddup!* He's not a pilot anyway, he's a...'

Dave put his hand on Chris's shoulder and placed another glass of magic in front of her. He used the distraction to signal silently to the others enough was enough.

Everyone said Dave was a good man; a good, calm, quiet man. It was this gentle kindness that had, over all else, attracted Chris to him forty or more years before. She had always had a temper, and he had always brought her stillness, soothed her; Chris sometimes wished she was as unflappable as he, as affable, no wonder she loved him still. But nevertheless, it irked her when she found out that Frank Speke referred to Dave as 'The Acceptable Face'. Sometimes, in choler, she would wish heartily that the chair next to her was silent, empty.

This row would peter out, go away. Pilot Ken was not malicious, he was almost as kind as Dave, he would not sulk if proved wrong, nor crow if proved right. Damnit, she couldn't remember how far it was to Maxton; it may not even have been Maxton she walked to, it was too long ago. She had spoken hastily, whereas the doubts, well, they only crept in slowly as her vehemence faded. Dave had chided her many times, don't jump in, don't take the bait, but they both knew it was no good.

Dave had tried to persuade Tim Carman to come back, abandon the Angel's Wing, 'return to the land of the living'. He even spent a day at the Wing, drinking bad beer in worse company, but his persuasions came to nothing. Carman was stubborn, not worth the time. Chris had gone to the Bat and Ball that day and, with the chair next to her empty and silent, fallen out horribly with several of the regulars, once the magic's spell had become tight-woven. She found Dave's desertion hard to forgive, but at least it left her free. Dave was always the placater, peacemaker, he had an aversion to rows. Chris believed that an up-and-downer cleared the air, relieved feelings, put everything right. She didn't want his interference, his ham-fisted gallantry. Dave was weak, an appeaser, a coward. Perhaps that chair was better empty.

The lunchtime crowd dissipated, leaving behind the core, the regular-regulars. With a touch more magic, the afternoon fragmented into small advances and sharp reverses of time, patches of light, passing shades and dizzying, spinning, sharp-edged shards of forgetting and remembering: conversations stopped and started as if trip-switched, came through the air disordered, scrambled. Memory and the now, the here-present and the lost, which was which?

Dave's face as a young man; his face now. No weight in it, bones so close, thin, stretched envelope of skin; but always a smile. Red round the eyes, which had dimmed, retreated, but when? Those eyes were full of light, once.

The crash-clatter of a broken glass startled Chris; she jerked as if broken from sleep and glared at Amanda as she came reluctantly with dustpan and brush, muttering truculently under her breath.

Pilot Ken: he was no pilot, it was just his favourite jacket. No pilot. Tease-tease, tee-hee, thinks of himself as a cheekychap, lovable: think again, cleverdick. Doesn't know what he's talking about half the time either. Gentle face, gentle smile. Like Dave when he was younger.

Strangers at the bar; dark clothes, black ties. St. Arn's, or was it St Matt's, St Soddit's, was close; people would come in after, before, sometimes. Faces relaxing, relief that it's all over.

Empty glass: no good.

A small carved stone on a windswept slope, heart, teddybear; *why did you have to think of that?*

That Tim Carman will be in soon, his regular time, well he's got a mouthful waiting, and no bloody peacemaker can stop it. It'll be a short conversation. All that's needed, all it'll take. No reply required, thank-you.

More placation: another whisky appeared before her. As if by...

Pilot Ken had spoken only three words, 'I feel dizzy.' That was all. He didn't get a second chance, not like Wayne. He wouldn't have thrown away that chance, not Ken, he was too sensible.

'Take her home Dave, eh?'

'Go home y'self! No one asked you here, no one wants you, you go home, g'won eff off why don't you? G'won off to the Wing, where y'belong!'

Dave's voice; soothing, smoothing, as if calming a baby. Some of the people in here need that, yes.

To the bar, leg protesting but sod it. Just one more. One more kiss of magic.

Empty, silent chair.

Ken Day

It was only just after nine o'clock, but the July day already tasted of uncomfortable heat. Jim felt as if the world was corkscrewing inward, closer to the sun, as he arrived at the main door of the supermarket prickling with excitement, anticipation, guilt: all in a good cause, he told himself. The suit will help, the old stuffy rarely-worn formal suit.

The cool, conditioned air of the supermarket enlivened Jim for a moment, but became a jailhouse chill as he walked with studied who-me deliberation to the metal hoppers of newspapers. He was distracted by the loud, silly chatter of tabloid leads, regaining control enough to stoop over the broadsheets. Crisis headlines; it didn't matter today. Jim picked up the paper, examined it soberly, folded and tucked it under his arm. Composing himself; calm, respectable, besuited, unimpeachable, he paced himself, not too quick, not too slow, to the side door, stepping aside for oncoming shoppers then swerving round their rearguard and making his way to the concrete steps. He waited for alarms, cries of outrage, pursuing footsteps, but nothing came.

'What did you do *that* for you fairy dimwit?' demanded Frank Speke later.

'Authenticity,' said Jim.

Frank Speke had announced that he would say 'a few carefully-selected words' and had recoiled from the reactions like a man who'd touched a live wire.

'No!' Emily, sharply

'No, Frank!' Jim, wearily.

'I beg your pardon?' Frank's gorge rose, 'Since when did you piss-the-beds get to decide who gets to speak?'

'Frank...' Jim's tone dipped into exhaustion.

'So... who gets to do it?' asked Frank sulkily as he realised this was not a coup, but something sanctioned.

Jim moved to the lectern, having stopped at the coffin to place the folded copy of the day's paper on it; this gesture elicited a low, warm '*ahhh*' from the first few rows. At the lectern, he could see suspended above the crem's artistically rendered cross, a mass of lines, blurring movement, a symbol of a hundred paths to redemption or a portrait of an exploding star. Jim had seen it at other funerals; today its midair curtain was drawn, only Jim could see.

Before Jim could speak, JC's voice burst out from somewhere near the back, 'Whassis? Whurr's Kenny?' followed by the sound of frantic shushing.

If he goes off on his Poll Tax kick, I'll get the giggles, how would that look? Shaking slightly, mouth dry, Jim prepared to say his piece: he couldn't help the sweep of his gaze across the packed room, seeking familiar faces. There was an array of pub landlords from the town and the Ring, Danny Deebee among them (wow, he didn't get the wrong day, didn't promise to be several elsewheres), people who would have starved had they relied on Ken for their bread, but it was gratifying to see them. In the middle of the gathering he recognised the carnivorous-scarecrow features of Tony the Convert: well, sunbeam, you're too late to gather up Ken for your cause, but thank you for coming. Tony was dressed up, Sunday best, as was the youngish unknown man seated next to him, whose short-cropped head was slightly bowed; he appeared to be praying fervently. Face scrape-shaven, besuited, tie perfect length, immaculately knotted, he remained unknown, unrecognised apart perhaps from some intensity in the eyes and a furrow of the brow. Pomo, was it Pomo, had Tony got his joyless claws into—no, Pomo was over there, two rows behind Mand. No more time for guessing games. Jim cleared his throat.

'Ken left instructions. We rather thought he would. Fortunately, they are not in the form of a puzzle.' This elicited a gentle laugh, but Jim felt a wave of cold, an inrush of awkwardness; too late, press on. 'No flowers; keep them in the ground. Keep it short. Tell the truth. Everyone back

222

to the pub, quick as you like. If you have stories, tell them there. We will be pleased to comply.' That bit went better; emboldened, Jim continued. 'That so many people have come along is proof of how well-regarded Ken is… was. Anyone who has ever walked down the High Street with him knew it too; it could take half an hour, all the hellos, how-are-yous and handshakes. All of them genuine, warm, the smiles too. You could never rush anywhere with Ken by your side.

'He took genuine pleasure in company, had many friends, and that is what he saw them as—friends. Not people to measure himself against and outpoint, not useful idiots or cannon-fodder for arguments he knew he could win. He did argue, and he had his foot in his mouth and his points defeated as often as any of us. He didn't mind. He'd call an idiot an idiot, but he cared about everyone. If he took a close interest in you, you felt doubly blessed. Now, please, let's do as he asked and go back to The Bat And Ball to share our stories and memories. One special request—if any of his old girlfriends are here, we'd *really* love to hear from you.'

Before he stepped from the podium, Jim saw a mid-room figure stir; with mentions of stories, he had caught the interest of Rob The Writer. Could this be an unexpected silver lining, the revival of a lost talent to faithfully record everything, every tale, immortalise Ken and his world, recover a reputation thrown away thirty years before? Or had Rob merely come half-awake from a sub-alcoholic semi-coma to check if it was all over and he could go to the pub?

Frank Speke stood near the bar, the part nearest to the door. He played with his cufflinks, pinching them, twiddling, as if to make sure they were still in place: it was no affectation, Frank did not know he was doing it. He was alert for the swing of the door, and as another figure entered, he stepped over carefully to usher the young man to the free drinks table. It took Frank a long moment to place the short-haired youngster with the shy expression and oversized glasses who hesitated, diffidently dithering over what to choose.

'Ah, Funnybones,' said Frank, 'went as well as it could, eh? 'S'matter, you not comfortable in civvies?' Pomo was pushing his finger into his collar, turning his head like a reluctant child, but he could not make the curious, restrictive cricked feeling go away. 'Loosen your tie and top button,' advised fatherly Frank, 'the rest of us have.' Pomo squinted towards the table. 'You'll know everyone, of course,' prompted host-Frank. The first figures to swim into Pomo's view were Evil Mand, Jim and Emily, engaged in earnest conversation. 'Three widows.' Frank's tone was more as-usual abrasive. 'Make that four,' he added, as a bemused Little Mal wandered by. Pomo turned to ask a question, but the host was back at the door, directing arrivals to the drinks table.

The Bat And Ball was full, the crowd spilling into the beer garden where bright sunlight played cheerfully over dark suits, gloomy faces; forced smiles that became less forced as the drink flowed. The garden was now rather less porous than previously, its fences restored, higher, gapless; it was no longer possible to wander into the pub from the sports field, nor filter out that way at closing time, to save the extra walk. There were no fields to walk through any longer; no more football, cricket or athletics, no more access to the pub from the side door of the supermarket. Beyond the fence of the Bat And Ball now stood tall, square steel-mesh screens clamped together into an impenetrable wall, and beyond that was either long-grassed and neglected or bald, scored, marked out in uniform plots resembling a series of crime scenes.

'Ken wouldn't like that,' observed Jim gloomily.

'Lucky he's dead then, isn't it?' countered a saturnine voice.

'Frank!' scolded a snowflake chorus.

It's now or never, decided Emily. I will talk to this man. Make my peace in our shared grief. After all, we will never have anything else in common, bar antipathy. At first, she thought he was cutting her, Mal's stare was intense behind bottle-glass, but instead of its customary unwavering focus, mainly on his ambitions, it was aimless, a wandering thing, as if Mal could not take anything in.

'Mal, I...'

He could do little apart from lift a glass and gulp, lift and gulp. It wasn't clear that Mal had registered her presence. Rafael came to help him out, but even then, Mal could not comprehend what she was saying, that she was even there before him. Emily was gripped by a vengeful revelation, a temptation: *he's helpless, defenceless: why not say your piece, your other piece, your real piece and not the forced words of reconciliation you were about to mangle in your mouth?*

'Mal, I...'

Go on: *'I hold you responsible for my mother's death. I know it was done indirectly and with perfect deniability, but let's cut out the twists and turns, you know and so do I. I've wondered often how to exact my revenge, should I choose the path of devious manipulation, slow violence through creeps and cronies—or just bash your sodding head in? I hear your pious mouthings and off-the-peg praise: a pillar of the arts, a leading light, an innovator, an inspiration; but you killed her. Or let's say that without you, she would still be alive? You never forgave her for outmanoeuvring you: the closing down campaign—stirred people, made them realise what they were about to lose, even those who never set foot in the theatre—you weren't expecting that, were you? You thought your propaganda worked. It's an elitist luxury, a self-indulgence, cut it, close it, no one will notice or care. From the shadows and cobwebs, you plotted to get back at her, you fed titbits to the press, wasteful Waveway and its commie-coddling theatre; I think you leaked to the likes of Tony the Convert or other offence-taking monomaniacs whenever there was a controversial production. I think you wound up FMC whenever there was bourgeois sentiment to hate. Letter-writers, rumour-mongers, whisperers, you controlled them all. Mum knew that one false step would cost her, cost the theatre; it played on her mind, unrelenting, she wouldn't give way but worried the whole time.*

'We were backstage, men in makeup, the sights and smells of every season of every past year; she was on her way to watch the first act from the Producer's Chair, but she never got through the door. It wasn't much of a stage death, "I feel dizzy"; not an act—exit. You allowed her daughter to take over, to inherit, it was beyond your power to stop, but still the hiss-hiss echoed, "She's not the woman her mother was, she's only got it because they're sorry for her." I was less talented, less resourceful, less popular; softer, more easily diminished and humiliated; more removable. You did it, Mal Stokeley, you killed her.'

'Mal, I…'

But there was no point; he was distracted, distraught. For the loss of Ken, or as Frank claimed because of rumours that dodgy dealings were about to be exposed, about the housing that was to swallow the sports ground, of developers given special favours and let-off affordability quotas, or 'no-prole housing' as Frank put it.

'Mal, I…' With a nod to Rafael, Emily turned away, in the grip of a novel and uncomfortable emotion: pity for Little Mal.

'We saw that.' Gina stroked Emily's arm as she returned to the main group, 'Poor Mal, he looks devastated, the worst out of us all.'

'Ah yessss,' Frank Speke eased his shoulders as if attempting to beat invisible wings, 'mourning his great pal. But of course, his distracted state could be just a little to do with all of that.' Frank gestured with his glass at the measured-out former sports fields. 'That and the grubby deal regarding the spanking-new Civic Centre; Mal has always avoided leaving fingerprints, but this time his grimy dabs are everywhere and someone's going to notice, someone he can't twist. Not to mention the hoo-hah at the Golf Club, of course.

'Mal loved Ken because Ken was safe: Mal didn't want anything from Ken. You can't say the same for his other old mucker, poor ol' Pitch And Putt Percy; betrayed without a flicker, as would Ken have been, had it proved necessary. But even that little side-project isn't going too well; Mal's little client-king is causing him headaches, having proved as idle and useless as everyone said, he's more an absence than a presence at the dear old club, and Mal is finding you can't manipulate a puppet who's not at the end of the strings. But of course, he *could* just be missing Ken.'

Frank Speke was ushering the PH Bar mob from the free drinks, simultaneously waving their expectant gazes away from the free food, which was still covered as people continued to arrive. They had hovered in the doorway of the crem, unable to find seats in a full house and lingering like bad smells, clearly expecting to be expelled, and they were much the same at The Bat And Ball: their CO still in prison, or dead, they were aimless, their malice blunted. Scamp attempted a 'here by rights' stance, Gizmo looked haunted and hungry, Hank had the expression of a man pondering defection from the bloc, drifting from his pals but returning slowly as if reeled in. When Scamp and Gizmo locked eyes with Evil Mand, seated with Jim at Ken's table, it was hard to say which man's nerve broke first. They didn't fall over one another as if auditioning for Pomo, but became hollow-faced, hollow-eyed, frightened, and without discussion they drank up and drew slowly to the door. Mand was of the opinion that had anyone so much as said hello to Hank, the poor man would have remained, his chains broken: but, still hovering, havering, unacknowledged, he drained away to the door and slithered, sad-faced, in the wake of his comrades. 'Not my job to rescue people,' Mand told Jim, 'especially today. He can work out his own fate. Unlike the other two if he comes back, he won't be hurled out with broken kneecaps.'

'Very decent of you to attend, Tony,' rumbled Jim after the Convert and his companion were ushered to him, via the free drinks table, by the helpful Frank Speke.

'Decency is my business,' replied Tony mildly.

227

'And your friend?'

'Oh, a recent addition to my small community. His name is Phillip. I don't believe any of you know that, because you never asked. You do know him, truth be told, but not as he is. He scrubs up well, does he not?'

'Sorry my friend, I don't think I… FMC?'

'Phillip,' insisted Tony quietly, 'I told you.'

'Cat got your tongue, son?' Frank Speke was back on hand, plainly alarmed at the meek silence of his fellow fiery libertarian. He spun on Tony the Convert; 'Jesus Christ, what have you done?'

'*Please.*' The holyman winced. 'He has always been a seeker after truth, now he has found it.'

Seated at Ken's table, FMC in the custody of a disbelieving Mand, Tony was now confident and expansive, 'Had you ever taken a proper interest in him, you would have known that Phillip has been on something of a personal journey—I know Ken would tell me not to use game-show patter, but he is no longer here to correct us, is he? Phillip began on the hard right of politics; would you believe it? Buzzcut, bigotry, bad breath: he skipped quickly into being a respectable, if anti-immigrant, pale-blue, winked out of existence and reappeared as a virtue-signalling tree-hugger, morphing in short order into the Stakhanovite mouth on legs you all knew but didn't. The cause of all of these tectonic shifts is something else about which you never enquired, never even speculated, which is most unusual for your little group, I should say. It was a colour-code which you might say was blonde-ginger-brunette-blonde. His passion for each cause was a perfect match for his more earthy lusts. Perfect.'

'The last of that list being one of your flock. Oh, naughty Tony—have you been encouraging a little flirty fishing by any chance?'

'That is a reprehensible suggestion!'

'Accurate though, I suspect.'

'I always thought he was aiming to bag one of us,' remarked Gina on hearing the tale. 'He's got his boyscout badge at last, and as Wayne once said, he can add "er" to his name.'

'Tony-er?' goggled Jim.

'Idiot.' Gina handflapped him, 'I don't think he got his prime target, but…'

'In fact, he got the most worthless,' observed Frank Speke stonily.

'Now there's a phrase to chew over,' mused Gina. 'Ken would have loved to parse that one.'

The Imp surveyed the scene with dissatisfaction. Frank was flagging, worn out, weary. His tongue was less sharp, his wit too. The chances of a new host-home were slim; Wayne was dead, FMC hollowed out, a complaisant shell, his rage sublimated into shameful sheepishness. It was necessary to remain with Frank for the time being. Perhaps his increasing weakness would allow The Imp some leeway to take over; like Richard Francis, the construct that was Frank Speke could be eased aside, replaced. There was so much to be said to this middling, mediocre world, *someone* had to say it: imagine what would happen without, a world of mindless agreement, calm discussion, pussycat disputes resolved by *arbitration*. Anyone with self-respect would rather be dead.

Freed from bar duty, Julie running the show—cheerfully resistant to supervision or advice—Evil Mand was engaged in intense conversation with Gina and Mart. The scene looked odd as Mand was gazing at Gina's hand, as if she wished to kiss it, then screwing her eyes and peering at a ring; silver, with three small emeralds held in silver-thread cages. As she peered closer, Mand resembled a pawn broker rather than a lover.

'It was Mart's idea.' Gina's smile was bejewelled also. Mart smiled and shifted his shoulders diffidently.

'I've never had an eternity ring,' Mand said, almost to herself. Gina and Mart, sensitive and sensible, did not

229

attempt to capitalise on the revelation. Mand and Gina changed the subject by mutual consent, and Nev Batham lowered himself into the seat next to Mart.

'Hail, fellow outlier.' Mart shook his hand.

'Nice stones,' Nev nodded towards Gina.

'You any nearer a ring of any sort?' Mart grinned.

'Phhhh—complicated. Still. No doubt Gina will be disappointed.'

'Don't let Gina chart the course of true love for you, or "complicated" won't be the half of it.' Nev did his best to contain surprise and curiosity at Mart's, well, 'complicated' tone. He did not know Mart well enough and scolded himself for being unable to resist devising ways of teasing out more details.

'Are you more likely to come here often now?' asked Mart, seeking to put Nev off his plan.

'No. nothing has changed from that point of view. I admit there's a barrier, but he was never it. You've got a barrier too, yes?'

'Yes. But not Ken. And, at a wild guess, not the same as yours, either.'

There was a long pause: two men without much to say to one another.

'D'you think they'll always call this Ken's table?'

'Why not… mind you I already heard someone refer to it as Jim's. Face like thunder.'

'Jim?'

'Frank. He seems to think he's in line to inherit.'

'That's complicated too. The will wasn't. The other thing…'

'I heard about that. Did you mind?'

'No. The letter was no surprise, not to Emily, not to me. And it was honest. He'd lived with those feelings for years; he didn't try anything. He didn't go mad. You've got to give him credit for that. Poor bastard. That a man could be so in love he'll live on crumbs.'

Jim's stop-now alarm was buzzing in his head, but its warning was in danger of being drowned by the occasion; the red wine too. He forced himself to change the subject and put away the little piece of paper in its clear plastic bag that he kept waving about like a manic policeman with his killer evidence. He pulled it out of his pocket again, minded to pass it to Mand for safekeeping, before realising Mand was as wobbly as him. Lodging the paper with Julie, reliable Julie, Jim told her what it was for, but his words dried up.

Julie knew, he had already told her—twice. But it was important; had to be done, everyone agreed. It would stand out from the ownerless, unloved Godzillacorp non-art on the pub's walls, at just below eye level close to the big window that let the day's light on the big round table in the corner: Ken's table. Jim fancied a square walnut frame: from a distance it would look like a newspaper cutting, a photo perhaps, but up close it was a panel of black and white blocks, some of the white spaces had letters but some remained blank as if abandoned by a lunchtime drinker who couldn't be bothered to waste any more time on the gratuitously sadistic clues. The piece of paper didn't quite fill the frame; jagged edges where the crossword had been torn from the page, the fragile greyish paper stained in one corner, looking as if one breath of air would render it dust. No one would move it, not some future clever-dick manager with a fabulous idea for a refurb, not the grandest panjandrum from GodzillaCorp, not while the regulars were alive.

'*Oh my god, Ken!*' Jim had never heard Mand shriek like that. Ken had knocked his glass over; Guinness spilled on the paper, soaking through quickly to stain, but not ruin, the crossword. He was stuck on five down. '*Oh my god, Ken!*' Jim and Mand stayed with Ken, but the work of the ambulance people was futile, no matter how urgently performed. Nothing to be done. Ken on the floor. Mand's voice. The stained crossword. '*Oh my god, Ken!*' Every year, on July the

Ninth, we will come here, as many as can, and remember, we'll tell those stories, just as per written instructions, and it won't matter that those stories are five, ten, twenty, however many years old, we will repeat them anyway on Ken Day. I will be here every time, pledged Jim silently, and tell those tales even if it has to be to strangers, even to the bloody wall, to the crossword in its frame. After I'm gone, it's over, fair enough. Only JC will be left, if Ken's theory is right, and he isn't fit to carry on the—'Jim, Jim! Hey Jimmy!'

'Yes, JC?'

'Whurr's Kenny? He'd like this; free food, bitta free booze.'

'JC, why do you think we're here?'

'Free food, Jimmy, free booze, thasswhy! Whurr's Kenny?'

'Never mind, JC. Good health.'

'Down the atch.'

Jim couldn't bring himself to watch anything go down that atch, but he was called back sharply.

'Jim, Jim! Eh, Jimmy!'

'Yeah?'

'Pay yer fuckin Poll Tax eh? Mind yer pay it!'

'Okay, JC. I will. I will.'

Once again, the old man had forgotten.